Gandhi's Sorrows (A Lady Marmalade Mystery)

by

Jason Blacker

PUBLISHED BY:
Lemon Tree Publishing
Copyright © 2013
Jason Blacker

Visit www.JasonBlacker.com on the web to stay up to date

Editing: Andrea Anesi

ISBN: 9781927623459

For the Great Soul who taught us so much

Table of Contents

One

Eric was in the dining room having breakfast when Frances came down to join him. Breakfast had not been served yet. Ginny was busy cooking it in the kitchen. It was a beautiful spring day. Monday, May the 24th, 1930. On the front page of the The Guardian was the ongoing saga of the Salt March.

Eric subscribed to both The Guardian, which was more inline with his left of center views, as well as The Times which was unabashedly right of center, but it kept him honest and aware of the broad spectrum of political thought within the country. He looked up as Frances walked into the dining room.

"You look absolutely ravishing, my darling," he said to her.

She smiled broadly at him and came over and gave him a kiss on the mouth. And she did look marvelous. She was not a woman to wear a lot of makeup but what she did use highlighted her natural beauty. She was forty-eight, though many would put her in her late thirties. Eric was a trim and handsome fifty-two.

His piercing blue eyes watched her as she took a seat next to him where her place had already been set. Eric folded the paper and put it down to his right side. Frances was on his left as he sat at the head of the table. It was eight in the morning and he was dressed impeccably in a light gray suit with a pale blue shirt and his dark blue Queen's College tie from Oxford. He was not wearing a waistcoat which was unusual.

Frances was dressed in a light yellow dress with a matching cardigan. Her hair was full of brunette curls which augmented her milky complexion. Eric grinned at her.

"What?" she said to him smiling.

"I never tire of seeing you every morning, my love. Last month we celebrated our twenty-seventh anniversary. I can't believe I've had such happiness for so many years."

"Oh stop," she said blushing and slapping him gently on the shoulder.

"Alright I will," and he made a motion of zipping his mouth closed.

"I was only joking," she said, winking at him. "Twenty-seven years, my darling, and I still love you as much as I did on our wedding day."

Eric leaned in and kissed her on the lips. As they broke their intimacy, Ginny and Alfred came in with Alfred carrying a tray of food for breakfast. He put the tray down on Frances' left and Ginny served Frances a plate of food. On it was one fried egg and two sausages. Ginny also put a toast rack with four slices of white toast in the middle of the table and a butter dish and a bowl of strawberry jam next to it.

Alfred picked up the tray and went around to Eric's right where he lay it down again. Ginny served him a plate consisting of two fried eggs and four rashers of bacon.

"Thank you, Ginny, looks wonderful and smells great," he said.

"You're welcome, my Lord."

Lastly, Ginny put a pot of tea on the table with cream and sugar as well as a plate with a few lemon wedges. Generally, but by no means a rule, Lady Marmalade preferred lemon with her tea in the mornings and cream and sugar in the afternoon and evenings.

Ginny picked up the now empty tray and took it back into the kitchen while Alfred positioned himself behind and on Eric's left by the wall.

"Thank you, Alfred," said Frances and she smiled at him.

"Not at all, my Lady. I had the easy part, carrying the tray."

Lady Marmalade took a piece of warm toast from the rack and placed it on her side plate where she buttered its face. She took salt and pepper that were already on the table and liberally sprinkled each on her eggs and sausages. Eric did the same when she was done. Frances took a bite of her sausage.

"They spoil us, darling," she said to him.

Eric cut up his fried eggs then he cut up a piece of the bacon and took a forkful of egg and bacon and put it in his mouth.

"Too right," he said. "It's a small miracle we stay so slim, my love."

He smiled at her.

"Are you meeting Declan at work this morning."

"Yes."

"I wish the two of you were closer."

Frances looked down at her plate and took a bite of egg.

"I know you do. And you also know I love my children."

Frances nodded and then looked up at him. She put her knife down and patted his hand.

"It's just that you seem so much more comfortable with Amelia."

Eric looked at her for a moment.

"Look, I'm trying my best. I just don't understand him that well. Honestly, Fran, I just don't understand why he's a homosexual."

There was a slight tone of frustration in his voice that Frances picked up on.

"I don't want you to get upset, darling, but I don't think it's something he chose."

11

"So you say. Then is it my fault? Was I too lenient with him? Not strict enough."

Eric shook his head and released his hand from Frances' grip. He put more food in his mouth.

"No, darling, I don't think that's it all. I think that's just the way God made him. I don't think he chose it, the same way I don't think he chose the color of his eyes."

Eric shook his head.

"I can't accept that. It doesn't seem natural. Why would God make somebody unnatural?"

Frances knew she wasn't going to get anywhere this way, and she didn't want to upset Eric before he went off to work.

"I don't have all the answers, darling. But I know that he loves you very much. He used to worship you when he was a boy, and he's a good boy, he's grown into a fine young man. You have to admit that."

Eric nodded his head and put another forkful of food in his mouth.

"Yes, that he is."

"Just try and be kind to him, and compassionate. Perhaps try and understand how difficult it might be for him. To be the way he is in a world like ours."

Eric looked at her steadily for a moment.

"I'm good to him, aren't I? Are you saying I'm not?"

Frances shook her head vigorously.

"No, not at all. I know you're doing your best and Declan knows you're trying. I'm just asking you to keep doing that. You just seem a bit stand offish from him sometimes, that's all."

Eric ate more food, chewed it as he thought about what Frances was saying.

"I'll try. But it's difficult for me too you know."

"I know."

And Frances decided that she had said her piece and now was the time to move onto other topics. She looked over at the newspaper on Eric's right. She could read the headline. "Gandhi Arrested, Protesters Beaten by Police." Frances took a bite of her toast.

"What are we doing with these poor people?" she asked.

Eric looked up at her from his plate of food.

"Which poor people?"

Frances jabbed at the newspaper with her knife.

"Those poor Indians. Is it not bad enough we've practically confiscated their country and taxed them to death. Now we're beating peaceful protesters."

Eric looked over at the newspaper and nodded at it.

"It's a damn shame," he said. "I think Great Britain has lost her way. First they arrest Gandhi, which I can understand."

"Why is it understandable?" asked Frances, taking a piece of sausage onto her fork and eating it.

"I'm not saying it's right, I'm just saying it's understandable. We've put ourselves in this pickle and that was probably the only course left to us. He is after all breaking the law."

"I see," said Frances a bit curtly.

"I know you don't agree with me..."

"No, I don't. The poor man is just trying to lead his people on a peaceful quest for justice and we go and lock him up. What sort of civilized country does a thing like that?"

"I agree with your sentiment, my love. But he was breaking the laws and he did it flagrantly. But this beating of innocent protesters is just too much. That I cannot condone and mark my words, this is the beginning of the fall of the British Empire."

Frances looked up at Alfred.

"What do you think Alfred?"

"About what, my Lady?"

"About the arrest of Gandhi and the treatment of these protesters?"

Alfred smiled thinly and cleared his throat.

"I fear you've put me in a pickle now, my Lady," he said smiling.

"Go on, Alfred, you know you're always welcome to an opinion in this house," said Eric.

"Yes, my Lord. Well, to be honest then, I agree with your Lordship that Gandhi was breaking the law so I can understand why he was arrested. However, I sympathize, my Lady, in that he is indeed only trying to seek justice for his people."

"Well said, Alfred," said Frances, smiling as she took a bite of toast.

"As for the terrible treatment of those protesters, I just can't excuse that. I find no rhyme nor reason for such despicable treatment. I thought that we as civilized men and women were beyond such brutality. Alas, I was wrong."

"Indeed, Alfred, we should be beyond such brutality. We are no longer Roman barbarians. It astonishes me that England would treat her subjects so dismally. I've written to the Viceroy, Lord Irwin, but I fear that he is deaf to any reasoning."

"How so?" asked Frances.

"Last I heard he felt no sympathy for the Indian cause nor was he particularly concerned with the Salt March. He felt it wouldn't have much of an effect."

"Imbecile," said Frances. "How do they continue to put these people into positions of authority?"

Eric laughed out loud.

"Yes, I quite agree. Not sure about imbecile though. He is quite an intelligent man on the occasions that I've had to meet him, but he is rather blunted to anything other than the British cause. You could call him a true patriot if you wanted to be kind and that is perhaps exactly why he was chosen for the role. To safeguard Britain's interests in that area."

"Yes I suppose so," said Frances, turning to her food and putting a forkful of sausage in her mouth.

"But they're being bloody stupid about the whole thing if you ask me. I think now is the time to open the conversation about independence. It's obvious that is where this is going."

"Too right, darling. And if we don't start now we might cause irreparable damage to our future friendship with the Indians. Might as well start while there exists goodwill between the two."

Eric nodded and put the last bite of bacon and egg into his mouth.

"I think the tea is strong enough. Don't you?"

Frances nodded with a mouthful of food.

"May I pour you some, my love."

Frances nodded again and Eric began to pour her a cup of tea.

"Sadly though, I think this government is not likely to see things that clearly. Prime Minister MacDonald, I fear, doesn't have the courage to do the right thing. And this being his second go at it."

"I suppose he does feel as if he's under a lot of pressure. They're saying that unemployment might double by the end of the year. I think he thinks the Salt Tax is an important income generator for the empire."

"That's likely got something to do with it," said Eric, "though I think he's generally incompetent and not setting a good example for Labour in the future. He's not taking any advice."

Frances nodded and squeezed a wedge of lemon into her tea and took a sip. It was perfect.

"This Mahatma Gandhi though, he does seem to be gaining momentum, darling, doesn't he?"

Eric nodded and squeezed lemon into his own tea. He pushed his plate to the side and Alfred picked it up and then Frances' and took them out into the kitchen. Eric put a slice of toast on his side plate and spread a thick covering of butter over it and then spread a dollop of jam on top.

"I think Gandhi is brilliant. He's dedicated to non-violence which is a brilliant strategic approach."

"But I get the sense that it's more than just strategy for him," said Frances.

"Agreed. He's a believer in this satyagraha as he calls it. However, it's still brilliant from a strategic point of view. When have we ever had to fight against unarmed, non-violent opponents? I can't remember if that's ever happened."

Frances nodded her head and took the last bite of her toast. She took a moment to enjoy it and then followed it with a sip of tea.

"Yes, I don't believe we've ever had to deal with such a strategy. And what happens? These chaps over there get infuriated and start bashing in skulls of peaceful people. It will only make it worse for us on the international stage."

Alfred came back in and stood by the wall in his usual position.

"What do you think of this satyagraha approach, Alfred?" asked Eric.

"I don't know much about it to be honest, but it sounds very clever. I think it can only warm people to his cause. Especially if we lose our equanimity as it appears we have in this instance."

Eric nodded his head and took a sip of tea.

"That's exactly what I'm saying. You can't go around bashing people if they won't fight. It just makes you look like a bully. Mark my words, this is just the beginning of the end for us."

"In what way, E?"

"The sun is setting on the British Empire as I said before. We have terrible problems of our own at the moment, what with unemployment and the depression. Add to this our lack of control of the situation abroad in India and the writing is on the wall. We'll have handed over rule of India to the Indians before the decade is out," said Eric.

Eric took another big bite of toast and sipped on his lemony tea. He would be dead before the decade was out and he'd be wrong about India's independence from Great Britain. It wouldn't be until 1947 that India gained autonomy, but he was right about the eventuality of it.

"Lord, I hope you're right," said Frances, "but that still seems so far away. Another nine years or so seems like an eternity."

Eric looked at her.

"I know, love, but these things take time. It might happen sooner than that. Only time will tell. One mustn't forget that we've been in India since the beginning of the seventeenth century. Many would consider India part of Great Britain in many ways. How many of us have immigrated there for the weather or even taken holidays?"

"Quite a few I suppose. I must confess I have greatly enjoyed our time there. The weather is so wonderful."

"Sometimes too hot for me," said Eric.

"Yes, sometimes. But when the gloomy English winter comes, India is a sunny, warm and cheery relief."

Frances smiled at Eric. They had spent many occasions there and all of them were filled with wonderful memories.

Two

They had marched a long time to get to the seashore of Dandi. It had taken them just over three weeks. But that seemed like a lifetime ago. Mahatma Gandhi had set up an ashram at Dandi where he and his followers continued to encourage the faithful to disregard the boycott and to boil their own salt.

Gandhi had considered it a great success. But for many, the satyagraha had only just begun. They knew that the British were stubborn and would hold firm even with a knife at their throats. But perhaps without violent means, the hope and prayer for an independent India would come more swiftly.

The ashram at Dandi had been a hive of activity and an anchor of successful campaigns, including the recent boycotting of liquor stores and foreign cloths, mostly around Bombay. There had been bonfires built to burn up all foreign cloth as Gandhi had suggested. It had made for great news and Gandhi had earned his international reputation honestly. His next major action was coming up.

Gandhi had written to Viceroy Lord Irwin about his upcoming plans on the raid scheduled for the Dharasana Salt Works in Gujarat on May 21st. Gandhi sat with the group who would lead the demonstrators to the salt factory on May 21st. It was late at night and they gathered in a mango grove by the light of a fire.

The weather was warm and sticky and sweet smelling like mango juice and the woody fire burned brightly.

"We have much preparations to do over the next several days," said Gandhi. "It is a long trip and we might need to be fortified for the journey. But do not worry yourself, satyagraha is on our side. The force of truth will guide our footfalls."

"What is the purpose of our walk to the salt factory?" asked Abbas Tyabji.

"We will with patience and non-violence take the salt which is rightly ours and we will distribute it to the poor and those who need it more than we do."

"And what if they do not allow us to take it? You have written to Lord Irwin and he is a stubborn man who will not allow us through. This I am sure of," said Sarojini Naidu.

Gandhi looked at her and smiled.

"Yes, I fear that you might well be right. We will stay and we will sleep out under the stars at the salt works until we are heard or until we are forcibly removed."

"I fear that we will be forcibly removed," said Maulana Abul Kalam Azad, "or, worse yet, that we will be beaten. They have not shown mercy to us before."

There was a general murmur of agreement amongst those gathered round. Gandhi nodded and smiled and put up his hand to bring quiet to the group.

"You are right. We might be met with blows and angry voices. I ask none of you to join us who are not willing. And I must fervently request that none of you join us who are not willing to adhere to the principles of non-violence and satyagraha."

The group fell silent as the fire crackled and coughed and spat. They had made great strides in just these past few months but yet so much work remained, and the British were as immovable as granite mountains. Worse than that, they had pillaged India of her jewels and gems and they had abused her people for centuries. And still they were unrepentant. Gandhi knew this and it needed no voice. It was only justice and equanimity that he sought, by peaceful means.

But the British had so far not been moved by peaceful means, and he feared that the poor and the disenfranchised would be moved to violence if their voices would not be heard. He stared into the fire and watched it curl its fingers as he had seen a belly dancer do once.

"We need to get our rest," he said at last. "We have many days ahead of us of satyagraha. The journey has just begun my friends. We have a long way to travel yet before Indian independence is attained."

Gandhi looked around at the group of leaders who sat around the fire. He leaned in and kissed Kasturba on the forehead.

"Good night husband, sleep well."

She smiled at him as he stood up.

"Good night Gandhiji," said Sarojini Naidu.

Gandhi walked over to his bed which was not much more than some blankets folded up at the foot of a mango tree. He lay down upon them in his dhoti under the dark blue sky with its twinkling stars. The warm, moist air comforting like a puppy's breath. With peace in his heart and non-violence in his soul he was soon asleep.

Gandhi awoke to loud, abrasive noises. He sat up and saw the glaring lights from several police cars lighting up the ashram. He went to investigate further and noticed that dozens of policemen were kicking and shouting to awake those still asleep on their beds. Women and men were equally abused.

Those who by now were awake were lined up against one side as the police worked vigorously to rouse the heavier sleepers. Gandhi noticed the one man in charge of them all. He walked up to him and introduced himself.

"I am Mohandas Gandhi."

The man looked him up and down.

"Good. You're the one we are looking for. You are under arrest for engaging in unlawful activities. Hey, that's enough, we have him," the man shouted to two Indian officers. The police stopped what they were doing and came over to see Gandhi. Several of them stayed back to control the crowd. Though there was no need. The crowd was peaceful and quiet.

Kasturba was awake by this time and came over to his side.

"What do they want?" she asked him.

"They are arresting me for unlawful activities."

Kasturba turned to the man in charge.

"But we aren't doing anything unlawful, we are sleeping."

The man turned to Gandhi.

"I am the District Magistrate of Surat," he said with a posh accent. His lily white skin freckled from too much Indian sun. "Did you not write to Lord Irwin recently about your upcoming march on the Dharasana Salt Works?"

Gandhi nodded.

"Then you are guilty under regulation 1827 and you will have to come with me."

"I will."

Gandhi turned to his wife.

"You must carry on without me. You and Abbas Tyabji must lead the march."

Kasturba nodded and leaned in to kiss him, but he was already being manhandled by one of the policeman and being taken to the car. Kasturba watched after him, as did the others. And when the rest of the policemen and the cars had gone, they had not tired of their cause and the more difficult work that had been put upon them by the arrest of their Mahatma.

Three

The march was going as planned. The day was warm and the spirit of the crowd was hopeful. They were five miles outside of Gujarat and the Dharasana Salt Works. It was Wednesday, May 21st, 1930 and this was their Dharasana Satyagraha, but without their Mahatma. He was still in jail in Poona having been held all the while without a trial.

Kasturba walked at the front with Abbas Tyabji at her side. Behind them a thick throng of hundreds of Indians walked along the dusty road to Dharasana. As they crested the hill in the middle of the afternoon Kasturba pointed at the horizon. A clot of buildings including the salt works could be seen.

Abbas smiled and turned towards those behind him.

"The Dharasana Salt Works is within site. It will not be long until we have the salt pouring through our hands."

A roar of enthusiasm erupted from the crowd and subdued as if carried upon an ebbing wave. The faces were smiling and there was plenty of murmuring amongst those in the group.

It was a mixed group of men and women, though the men outnumbered the women by a great margin. Most of those drawn into the ranks of those marching on the salt works were the poor and the disenfranchised. The very same that the Salt Tax harmed most severely.

"We must continue on through the barricades and the gates until we have taken control of the salt pens where we will dole it out to those who are here with us," said Kasturba.

Abbas nodded.

"If we get that far," he said.

He was pointing to the horizon. In the distance came several vehicles billowing dust in great clouds behind them. There was only one reason those vehicles were coming and it wasn't to help them get to the salt works any quicker.

"Just as I feared," said Kasturba.

Abbas grunted in agreement. Kasturba turned to a woman and man walking at her side.

"If they arrest me and Abbas, the two of you must continue onward towards the salt works.

"We will," said Sarojini Naidu.

"I will make certain," said Maulana Abul Kalam Azad, "we will not fail Ghandiji, not with all the work that Ravi has helped us with."

Kasturba smiled at him and nodded.

"I know we won't."

They continued their slow march towards the buildings as the vehicles continued to race towards them. It wasn't long before the first car, a police car, had stopped about one hundred feet where the crowd was. Other vehicles came up and stopped by the first. Policemen stepped out of the vehicles carrying steel tipped lathis.

Kasturba and Abbas continued their walk, slowly until the front of the group was only feet away from the line of police. A man who was clearly in charge in both deportment and lacking a lathi stepped up to Abbas and Kasturba and put his hand out to halt them. He had a walking stick tucked under his left arm, and he was taller than all the other policemen around him. Kasturba, Abbas, Maulana and Sarojini stopped.

"I am Sergeant Ryan Webb, you are ordered to halt."

Kasturba looked at the young man. He had a boyish face and was probably not much older than in his early thirties. He had taken the post in India as a way to prove himself. It was almost a guaranteed path to speedy promotion.

"Who are you?" he asked, looking at Abbas.

Abbas looked into the boy's blue eyes. He was pale faced with a pink glow, likely from too much Indian sun. He stood over six feet and looked down at Abbas, and his uniform was crisp and clean.

"I am Abbas Tyabji," he said, his voice clear and calm.

Webb nodded curtly and looked at Kasturba as the crowd gathered up behind her.

"I am Kasturba Gandhi," she said, smiling at him with genuine benevolence.

Webb turned around and nodded to two of his constables. The stepped forward quickly and eagerly.

"Arrest these two."

One of them took Kasturba and the other took Abbas. Kasturba turned towards Sarojini.

"Carry on with the satyagraha."

"Not a good idea," said Webb as the crowd started to move towards him.

He got back into his car and ordered his men to get back to their posts. The police vehicles backed up and turned around and headed towards the salt works more quickly than they had come. The last car carrying Kasturba and Abbas veered off from the pack heading towards Gujarat.

The hundreds of white dhotis moved towards the salt works like a frothy white river. They were of one mind and one body. With determined but peaceful hearts they marched on. Though their bodies were weary from the twenty five mile march, their spirits sang of triumph and hope.

The Dharasana Salt Works were about a mile away and they marched on behind the billowing dust clouds of the police vehicles. And after awhile it seemed as though the world stood still as the dust settled and slowly dissipated like morning fog.

They got within a hundred feet of the salt works when Sarojini turned and spoke to the crowd.

"You must not use any violence under any circumstances. You might be beaten, but you must not resist. Do not even raise a hand to ward of the blows. If you cannot do this, you should turn around now."

She waited a moment with Maulana at her side, but nobody moved or turned around. So Sarojini did. She turned and faced the barbed wire barricade and marched onwards, the throng of men and women behind her offering great strength and comfort.

"Do not come any closer," said Webb through a megaphone.

A line of dozens of smartly dressed policemen stood behind the barbed wire barricade that was between them and the marchers. Behind the police were the salt pens. Sergeant Webb was under strict orders not to allow a single soul to get past the barricade, and he had been instructed to use any means necessary to secure those ends.

His men had been told and forewarned. They had been advised to use the minimal amount of violence necessary. They were after all confronting a pacifistic group of peaceful demonstrators.

"Steady boys," said Webb as he looked to each side at his men. They all held their lathis diagonally across their bodies. It was brutish and barbaric stick encrusted with steel at its end. The sticks were six feet long and almost as thick as a woman's wrist. Some of the policemen were slapping the sticks against their open palms.

The crowd continued onwards towards the barricade.

"I order you to stop! Turn back now!" yelled Webb into this megaphone.

But the crowd was unmoved and kept on towards the salt works as Sarojini kept on. There were journalists milling around, watching the event from the far corner of the salt works at a safe distance away. Some were already taking photographs. The crowd was now twenty feet from the barricade.

"This is your last warning! Turn away now!"

Sergeant Webb was getting nervous. He had hoped it wouldn't come to this that he would be able to convince them just through a show of force and British determination that they were taking the wrong course. Surely with their leader, Mahatma Gandhi in custody and now with Gandhi's wife and one of his trusted men also in custody, the crowd would see the futility of their cause.

But such was not the case. Webb watched in awe with butterflies in his belly as the crowd continued marching towards him and his men. The first line of the protesters reached for the barbed wire barricade and started to pull on it.

"Stop it! Get back! Get back! Stop it!" he yelled into the Megaphone, but he might as well have been speaking upon deaf ears.

It wouldn't take them long to dislodge the barbed wire and then they'd have a hell of a time keeping the throng from the salt works. Webb knew he had to make a quick decision. He looked up and down the ranks of his men. They were well trained, they knew what to do. He looked out over the crowd which was now five and six men deep. He had to make a decision and he had to make it now.

"Beat them back! Beat them back!" he yelled to his men without the use of the megaphone.

No sooner had the first words leapt from his lips than the lathis had lashed out at the clutching hands and the bare heads of those within reach. Sarojini was hit smartly across the temple and she fell like a shot to the ground, a trickle of blood at her temple.

Other men fell about her left and right as if the policemen were using scythes to harvest wheat. Coming in and out of consciousness she could hear pandemonium erupt about her. Men were groaning and screaming as the blows pelted down upon them like hailstones.

Nobody in the crowd put up so much as a finger to ward of the brutal blows. They sat down if they had not been knocked down and waited for the blows to come. The policemen were incensed by the pacifity of the group and it only enraged them further. They leapt into the crowd kicking and swatting at them as if caught in the midst of a swarm of mosquitoes.

Webb was horrified at what he saw. His men were becoming undisciplined, they were losing their composure and this would not help at all. He started yelling at them to stop, but just like the crowd before them, his words now fell upon the deaf ears of his men.

Sarojini looked up and off in the distance she saw the dropped jaws of several of the journalists. They were scribbling like mad and others were taking photographs as quickly as they could. She smiled. She knew that through this violence the tide had now turned in India's favor.

Webb was reaching out for his men, trying to grab them one at a time to stop the violence.

"Why won't these bloody Indians just bugger off," said Trafford Leak, kicking at an Indian's groin as the man sat and then toppled over squealing in pain.

"They just don't bloody well get it. You have to knock some sense into this bloody people," said the much taller Kian Hudnall.

He was throwing his lathi around as if here trying to harvest wheat. Great swathes of men toppled from his blows. He and

Trafford were new to India. They had come right after having sworn their oaths as constables. They had come for the warm weather and the opportunity for easy promotions.

What they had found was instead an oppressive heat, a smell that could make you cry and a land that was filthy and full of beggars. They hated it here. At their earliest opportunity, both of them would be heading back to the isle just as quick as they could. The other thing they couldn't understand and nor could they tolerate, was the cowardice of these satyagrahis.

As far as they were concerned, a man who wanted to change something was a man who would fight for it, not sit down like a pin to be bowled over.

Webb was trying his best to bring his men under control. He had glanced at the journalists and he wasn't happy with the looks on their faces or the vigorous movement of the pencils in their hands. Slowly, one by one he was corralling his men, but it was a laborious task made all the more dangerous by having to dodge the backswings of lathis.

A slim Indian man fell to the ground having been bashed on the head with the steel end of a lathi. He was out cold before he toppled over. Medics had been called and were trying to haul away the injured as fast as they could, but the police were injuring more than they could keep up with.

"Dev," cried a man as he writhed in pain clutching at his groin. He was calling on his friend who lay unconscious in front of him, blood already matting his thick black hair like thick oil.

"Shh, shh," said a woman as she lay next to Dev Jani, holding him and protecting him from anymore injuries. It was a kind but unnecessary effort. The police had already moved on as their ranks were being thinned by Webb physically bringing them back to order.

"Why did Ghandiji put us to this task?" cried Govind Mitra. "For what, Amita? So that we might be bludgeoned to death for nothing."

"Quiet, Govind, you'll just encourage them to come back and beat you more. Gandhi is trying to bring us independence. You know that. Do not question his leadership," said Amita Nagy her voice a hoarse whisper, hard to hear over the groans of the others.

Govind squeezed tears from his eyes as he sucked in his breath and tried to wait out the pain as it slowly started to ebb.

"I'm finished I tell you, finished with this nonsense and Gandhi's satyagraha," said Govind.

"We'll talk tomorrow when you are not in so much pain," said Amita.

Stretcher bearers came by and put Dev Jani on a stretcher, his eyes fluttered, he was starting to gain consciousness. Another couple of stretcher bearers came to help Amita Nagy onto a stretcher. She clutched at one of their arms and told him she was okay.

"Take Govind," she said, taking her arm from the stretcher bearer's and placing it on Govind's shoulder.

As if on cue, Govind started to moan all the louder, pleading and crying. The tears flowed freely and easily. For although the pain had been severe at first, it was the memory of it now that he milked for all its human kindness' worth.

"I'll see you soon, Govind, stay strong," said Amita, but this just encouraged Govind to cry all the louder.

They placed him on a stretcher and carried him off to the medical tents that were quickly being put up to help all the wounded. The police were finally coming to their senses and regaining their composure. But it was too little and too late. Practically anyone who could have been knocked over with lathis had been.

Men and the few women in the crowd had been equally assaulted. Some of the Indians, like Amita, had been smart about it and pretended to have been knocked unconscious. These few slowly started to get up, and limped, doubled over to the medical tents, even though there was nothing wrong with them.

Webb looked over at all the carnage, he was horrified and sickened by it. But he gritted his teeth and patted his men on the back to help them keep their sense about them. But he knew that heads would roll. Perhaps his own, and if so, he would take several of the others down with him, including Leak and Hudnall. He had watched them, especially aware of their almost sick enjoyment of the spectacle.

Webb glanced at the journalists, they were still writing hurriedly. Many of them were making their way now over to the medical tents to bear witness to the numerous injuries, the hundreds of injured Indians.

Sergeant Webb looked on, stationed like a statue behind the barricade as his men started to repair it. He couldn't count the number of injured but it was easily the vast majority of the protesters. Hundreds of them, perhaps hundreds upon hundreds. He looked around at those still lying in front of him and the bulk of those who had now been carted off to the medical tents far off on his left side.

He hoped that there were none killed today, but he was sadly mistaken. Two men had been murdered by the police, they were amongst the older men in the crowd. Ajit Pai was sixty-three and his lifelong friend, Chetan Panchal, was sixty-four. They had both left wives and children behind.

Four

The summer of '31 was winding down. It had been a warm and drier than normal summer for the United Kingdom. Something that Frances was thankful for. Though the warm welcome weather was no comfort for the economy which had only worsened. Some had put the number of unemployed at over 3 million. Whatever it was, it wasn't a welcome change.

Not to say that Britain had it worse than America. It had started there and that was where the brunt of it was located. Their masses of unemployed were not to be envied.

Frances walked into the living room where Eric was already seated at the dinner table and he had a glass of red wine in front of him. It was September the 6th and the grandfather chimed six times as she sat down opposite Eric. Sunday evening dinner was always something that they tried to enjoy together. And tonight the four of them would all be eating at this table.

Declan came into the living room carrying his glass of red wine in his hand, accompanied by Everard. They were smiling and talking together. Behind them, Amelia and Alfie walked into the living room. Alfie was drinking a gin and tonic and Amelia was enjoying a glass of white wine.

Declan sat next to his mother on her right side and Everard sat opposite him on Frances' left. Amelia sat next to Everard being on her father's right and Alfie was opposite her, sitting next to Declan. Amelia leaned in and kissed her father on the cheek. Eric beamed at her.

He raised his glass to those at the table and each of them raised what they were drinking. Frances had not had a drink yet, so she and Everard raise their glasses of water.

"To family," said Eric looking at his wife and then at his daughter and lastly at his son. "And to friends," looking at Alfie and then at Everard. "May the hearth fire always burn warmly."

They clinked their glasses. And each said "cheers" together.

"My Lord," said Alfie, looking at Eric.

"Yes, Alfie."

Alfie coughed and cleared his throat.

"I would like to take this moment to ask you something personal if you don't mind. I throw myself at your mercy."

Amelia giggled quietly to herself. Eric looked at Alfie and frowned in curiosity.

"I will try and be merciful," he said smiling, then he looked at Amelia. "Do you know what this is about."

Amelia nodded, her cheeks were flushed.

"Then go ahead young man," said Eric looking intently at Alfie Nash.

Alfie looked nervously at Amelia and then at Frances. She smiled at him and he stole courage from that. Everard and Declan were both looking at him, curious as to what all this was about.

"My Lord," said Alfie, and he cleared his throat again. "I humbly ask for your permission and blessing to marry your very beautiful daughter and my soul mate."

Alfie swallowed and his face burned. He was redder and more flushed than Amelia at that moment. Eric didn't say anything for a moment. He looked sternly at Alfie and raised an eyebrow. He looked at Amelia and gave her just as stern a look as he had offered Alfie.

Amelia had her hands to her mouth and her eyes were wet with hope and love. Eric looked back at Alfie. Alfie felt himself wilting like a fragile flower under the glare of a sunlamp.

"My Lord," he said, and his voice cracked.

Time passed as slowly as a camel marching across the Sahara. Alfie looked down and wondered if this had been a mistake. Amelia wanted to marry him, he was sure of that. They had spoken about it and he had told her he was going to ask for Eric's permission on this very night. She thought it was a marvelous idea.

Certainly they were young, but they were in love and had known each other since her first year at University of London. She had caught his eye in the library. It was 1925 and times were good. He was just finishing up his medical degree as she was just starting down that road.

He was a commoner. In fact he had been orphaned and raised by a kindly cobbler and his wife. Alfie had worked hard all his life trying to save money to pay for university. Alfie wondered now if he'd been stupid to think that he could marry a peer's daughter. He sat with his eyes cast down waiting for Eric to laugh at his stupid request.

It was over now, he could never show his face again in polite society once he had been spurned. And the love of his life was lost forever. His heart sank into the pit of his stomach and he wondered how he might carry on. Perhaps he'd head to Australia as Amelia and he had planned to do in the near future. He'd take his heavy baggage and try to start a new life.

The silence in the room was as loud as drums thumping right up against his ears. Alfie wished he could turn into a mouse and just scurry away. Even the butler was standing there, still as a statue, ready to be witness to this amusement. He couldn't stand it any longer. And the ring that was in his jacket pocket, it now felt like a lump of lead. He'd saved for three years to buy it.

It wasn't fancy. Nothing near to the rock that Lady Marmalade had on her ring.

But still it was something, and he'd sacrificed new clothes and even medical equipment to buy it. Now he'd maybe be lucky to get half of the two hundred pounds he'd spent on it. Alfie swallowed hard and thought he might even cry. How had he been so blind to put himself at the mercy of a marquess in front of so many. He'd be leaving right away, he was sure of it.

"Eric. Stop it!" said Frances.

She looked at Alfie and then at Eric, her voice was soft and mischievous.

"Can't you see the poor boy is beside himself with anxiety."

Alfie looked up at her and smiled thinly, thankful for the small mercy. Next to him, at the head of the table, Eric laughed heartily.

"I'm sorry, my dear boy, I couldn't help myself. Of course you have permission to marry my daughter. There's no one I'd be prouder to call my son-in-law."

"Oh, Daddy," said Amelia, and she burst into tears of joy and slapped her father across the shoulder tenderly.

Declan patted Alfie on the back and then shook his hand. Declan picked up his wine and raised it to the others.

"We have admitted to our ranks one of the finest gentleman around. A real gem amongst the rabble."

There was more clinking of glasses. Alfie stood up as did Eric. He shook Eric's hand.

"Thank you so much, my Lord," he said, almost breathless.

Eric put his arms around him and hugged his soon to be son-in-law.

"You must call me Eric or Dad from now on."

Eric held him out at arm's length and grinned.

"Well, what are you waiting for?"

Alfie walked around to Amelia and got down on one knee. He pulled out the small box which held three years of his savings, hopes and dreams.

"Please don't let me down now, my love," he said to her. His eyes were wet with tears. "My dearest and kindest Amelia. Will you marry me so that I might become complete and promise to make you the happiest woman for all of eternity?"

He opened the box and showed her the modest engagement ring with its solitary diamond. Amelia nodded and threw her arms around his neck.

"I will," she said, sobbing happily.

There was a round of applause. Alfred was clapping enthusiastically as was everyone at the table. Alfie put the ring on her finger and slowly got up and took his seat back at the table.

"Well, that was quite the shocker," said Eric, grinning as if he'd won a prize.

"Did you know about this?" asked Declan, looking at his sister.

She nodded.

"I did, but I wasn't certain he was going to do it tonight."

Amelia was admiring her ring as it twinkled and sparkled under the dining room's lights.

"I'm so happy for you, my dear sister," said Declan, raising his glass up and winking at her.

Amelia grabbed her glass and reached over the table and clinked with him. They each sipped on their drinks.

"Jolly good show, Alfie," said Declan. "I bet that took plenty of courage."

Alfie looked over at his soon to be brother-in-law.

"It did. I almost wet myself when your father didn't say anything. I thought I might be leaving without even dinner, with my tail between my legs."

Alfie laughed aloud, relieved, the pressure over now and his hopes solidified. Eric slapped him on the shoulder.

"I couldn't help myself, Alfie," said Eric. "You know I love you just like a son. I really am delighted and I couldn't be happier to have anyone taking Amelia's hand than you."

"Thanks, Dad," said Alfie, the word thick and awkward in his mouth like a gobstopper. Though he liked the feeling of it. Eric grinned widely.

"You are such a tease, darling," said Frances looking at her husband. Then she turned to look at Alfie and raise her glass of water to him. "I couldn't be happier, and I couldn't be happier for the two of you. You will take good care of my daughter won't you, Alfie?"

"I promise on my life, my Lady," he said.

"Frances or Mum will do," she said.

Frances sipped her water and Alfie beamed. He felt light and full of joy. He looked over at Amelia and she beamed at him. He winked at her.

"I think I'll take a drink now," said Frances. Alfred stepped up towards her, "I think I'll join my daughter in some of that white wine."

"Yes, my Lady." Alfred turned to Everard. "Anything else for you sir?"

"Yes, I should think so. Tonight calls for a celebration. Perhaps a glass of tonic water please, Alfred."

Alfred nodded and walked over to the bar at the one end of the room. Eric sipped on his red wine and looked around at his family. A family that was growing. He would soon have grandchildren to spoil and the thought brought him immense joy. Alfred came back with the drinks and handed Lady Marmalade her glass of white wine and then offered Everard his tonic water.

"May I serve dinner, my Lord?" asked Alfred, returning to Eric's side.

Eric nodded. Alfred left for the kitchen. Eric turned and looked over at Everard.

"So you've always been a teetotaler, Everard?" asked Eric.

"Yes, that's correct."

Declan looked over at him and smiled.

"Can you tell me again why you do not drink?" asked Eric.

Declan raised his eyebrows at Everard, which Everard caught. He looked back at Eric.

"Not at all, Eric," he said. "I was raised a Quaker and part of the teachings is the abstinence of alcohol."

Eric nodded.

"Yes, I remember that now, but you are no longer a Quaker from what I understand."

"That's right. I was raised that way, but I've lost my faith in Christianity in general and Quakerism specifically. I consider myself agnostic."

Alfred returned with Ginny and she put a tray containing plates of Waldorf salad down on a side table. She served everyone up and then took the tray away back into the kitchen.

Everyone started digging in. The Waldorf salad had lately become a favorite around the Marmalade house.

"Such a tasty, sweet and tangy salad," said Everard to Frances. "I do thank you for having me over for dinner."

Frances smiled at him.

"Not at all. I know you are as close to Declan as Alfie is to Amelia. You're always welcome here, you know that."

Everard smiled and went back to eating his salad.

"Thanks, Mum," said Declan looking up at her.

Eric shot Frances a quick glare and then looked over at Everard.

"You're a vegetarian too, if I recall?"

Everard looked up at him and nodded.

"I am. I try and avoid dairy and eggs when I can too."

"Why is that?"

Eric's tone was not malevolent but it was a little more abrupt than it needed to be.

"Well, it's simply that I don't believe it is necessary for a healthy life to eat animal flesh. And if it isn't necessary then depriving an animal of its life just for palate pleasure seems to me, to be unnecessarily cruel."

Eric took a bite of salad and chewed for a moment.

"You can't argue with that," said Alfie, "though I'm not sure I could do it."

"Yes, but the bible says that we have dominion over animals. We can eat them if we choose."

Everard nodded.

"Quite true, and that is one of the reasons for why I have lost faith. There are several problems with the bible that I see. One of which is that it was only written a century or more after this man, Jesus Christ, walked the earth. Secondly, you can find arguments for both sides of pretty much everything in the bible. Genesis chapter one verse twenty nine for examples speaks only of plant foods as being food. But you are right, later, in Genesis chapter nine verse three it mentions that every living thing is ours for food."

"Father, do we have to get into this again?" asked Declan.

"I'm just curious," said Eric, putting another forkful of salad into his mouth.

"And then again," continued Everard, "Proverbs chapter six verses sixteen and seventeen talk about what God hates, one of them being the spilling of innocent blood and I'd argue that animals are innocent. But the problem is, as I said before, that you can argue any side of an argument with the bible."

"Except homosexuality," said Eric, loud enough for everyone to hear.

"Dammit, Father, are we really going to get into this again?" said Declan.

"Eric, can we please have an enjoyable meal together without arguing about this again?" said Frances.

"That's alright, I'll answer. You're right, Eric, there is much that has been interpreted in the bible about homosexuality being condemned, yet we might find in the decades to come that perhaps the meaning was not clearly understood. Sodom and Gomorrah are seen as the quintessential argument against homosexuality but some scholars have argued that the sin was not one of homosexuality but rather a lack of charity and the attempted rape of angels."

Eric looked up at Everard and couldn't help but admire the young man for his equanimity. He was practically attacking him and yet he suffered these slings and arrows with poise.

"Regardless, at the end of the day, I'll not follow a religion that condemns me for being a homosexual. A homosexual, I might add who was born his way, dare I say, made this way by the very God that apparently finds my sexuality an outrage."

"Hear, hear," said Declan lifting his glass of wine towards Everard, "and that is why I love you."

Everard picked up his tonic water and clinked with Declan and winked at him.

"I'll drink to that," said Frances. "The world could use more love."

Eric looked over at Declan and then at Everard and then at Frances who gave him a stern nod. He picked up his glass half heartedly and raised it with much effort. He took a sip of the red wine and finished his salad.

"I love you too," said Amelia, clinking glass with her brother and Everard.

"I can't argue with love," said Alfie, "however you find it."

Eric didn't say anything but pushed his plate off to the side. Everyone was finishing up their salads and Alfred walked around collecting the dishes and he put them on the side table. He went into the kitchen and came out with Ginny who was carrying a tray and they took the plates away. Eric sipped his wine and then looked over at Everard. For some reason he found it easier to talk to Everard about his sexuality than his own son.

"Aren't you worried about the law and homophobia and what other people might think?"

Everard looked up and across the table at Declan. He took a sip of tonic water and Declan sighed heavily. Everard turned to Eric.

"No, no, no. I don't particularly worry myself about any of that. I mean really, unless the government puts spies in my bedroom how would they know what Declan and I do in our private moments..."

Eric winced, that wasn't something he wanted to think about. Not his son with another man.

"As for homophobia and what other people might think, I don't worry about it and I don't think Declan does either. I mean you wouldn't know that I was homosexual if your son hadn't come out as it were now would you?"

Eric nodded.

"No, I suppose I wouldn't have known. You don't seem queer to me."

Declan shot his father a look and rolled his eyes at him.

"That's a very condescending word, Father. You might as well be calling women wenches."

Eric looked up at his son.

"I didn't mean it like that. I meant that Everard nor you for that matter seem homosexual."

"Not all homosexuals are effeminate if that's what you mean," said Everard.

"I understand that now. And the two of you probably don't remember this, but one of our greatest playwrights, Oscar Wilde, was sentenced to hard labor just for being homosexual."

"That's not entirely true," said Everard. "I've read up on Oscar's case and as much as I disagree with the punishment he was very outspoken about his homosexuality and will no doubt go down in the history books as one of our great martyrs and perhaps eventually even as one of our earliest emancipators. But in some ways he brought the difficulties upon himself..."

"What would you have done?" asked Declan. "I mean the poor man was accused in public of having committed a crime. Surely you would have defended yourself?"

"I'm afraid, my dear Declan," said Everard, looking at him with a smile, "that I do not have the courage that Mr. Wilde had. In fact, I'd likely have gone to France or even perhaps Southern Italy where homosexual sex is not illegal."

Eric furrowed his brow, it was obvious this was a difficult topic for him to listen to. Frances looked at him steadily, admiring what was, for Eric, great fortitude and patience. Indeed, if Frances could wave a magic wand, she would have had Declan born heterosexual. But one does not have the gift of magic nor of creation other than to be the vessel through whom life travels on part of its journey.

Yet she had watched Declan grow into a fine young man. An erudite, kind and even tempered young man. He was a shrewd businessman, perhaps even more so than Eric, and even as a boy he had never treated his younger sister unkindly. They were close, closer than Frances could have imagined.

And Everard could easily have been another son to her. He was patient and kind and stood upon high moral ground and was never swayed from his beliefs by inconvenience or expediency.

45

And if Frances turned a blind eye to the fact that he was her son's lover she found the love they shared to be as deep and committed as that between Amelia and Alfie. And wasn't that all that a mother could ask? That her children grow up kind and healthy and successful with a life overflowing with love?

That was what she had received and what she felt was her greatest gift. She just wished that Eric might see things in that light. But he struggled with Declan's homosexuality. He found it difficult to look past it and through to the relationship itself.

"I didn't know that about Oscar Wilde," said Eric, looking up at Everard.

"Because you've never been interested in my life in that much detail," said Declan.

Eric looked at his son, and tried to understand. He remembered the small boy who looked up at him through those blue eyes filled with love, not the flinty anger he saw in them now.

"I find it hard to understand," said Eric. "I've never known how to interact with you. I'm sorry."

At that moment Alfred and Ginny came back into the dining room carrying a tray full of plates of food. Alfred put the tray on the side table and started dishing up the fried fish and chips that was for dinner. It was one of Declan's favorites and had been prepared just for that very reason.

"Oh my," said Ginny, as she served a plate to Amelia, "that is a very fine ring you have there my Lady Amelia. Please let me wish you congratulations and may God bless your marriage all your days."

"Thank you," said Amelia, "that's very kind."

"Good on you, sir, you've done well for yourself," she said as she served up Alfie.

"Thank you, Ginny. I think I've caught the catch of the century."

Everyone chuckled along with him at his pun. Ginny served up Everard. He had before him a plate of chips with carrots and peas as well as a good serving of broccoli with cheese sauce.

"I hope this will do?" she asked him. "I can rustle you up something else if you prefer."

"This looks simply marvelous, Ginny, thank you," said Everard. "You always spoil me."

Ginny grinned widely from ear to ear and then served up Declan last. She then put a bottle of vinegar on the table as well as ketchup and mayonnaise. Ginny then took the tray from Alfred and headed back to the kitchen.

"Will that be enough for you?" asked Frances, looking at Everard. "It makes me nervous not seeing some fish on your plate."

"This is wonderful, Fran, thank you so much. It will be plenty."

Frances nodded and asked for some vinegar which Declan passed to her. He then took it and drowned his chips in it. The fish had a wedge of lemon on it which he squeezed all over it. Everard took the ketchup and dribbled it over his chips and then added a dash of vinegar for good measure. Amelia took the vinegar from him and drowned her chips in it just like her brother had done.

The smell of vinegar was sharp and pungent on the nostrils. Alfie took the bottle of mayonnaise and scooped out a generous helping of it with his fish knife which he then scraped off onto the side of his plate. He dunked a chip into it and bit it.

"You like it European style?" asked Eric, looking at Alfie.

"I do. Depends on the day though, and today feels like a mayonnaise kind of day."

"I don't know how you do it," said Amelia, taking a chip from her plate and dipping it into Alfie's mayonnaise and then biting the mayonnaise end. She pulled a face, and Alfie laughed. It even elicited a grin from her brother which was her goal. She wanted to lighten the mood.

"Yuck, still don't like it," she said.

Eric took the salt and pepper grinder and salted his fish and chips and ground pepper all over it.

"To get back to your earlier question, Eric," said Everard. "I would never let anything happen to Declan, I'd go to the gallows first."

He looked up at Eric and his face was sincere and his eyes pleading for understanding. Eric looked up at him and nodded.

"I suppose that's all I could ask for."

Eric had a begrudging respect for Everard. The young man was committed to his ideals and although not belligerent about them, he wouldn't be dissuaded otherwise. In fact, whenever Eric would prod and probe about his sexuality Everard was always patient and slow to anger, in fact he had not seen the young man moved to anger yet.

He respected that, and in a way, it was only through Everard's thoughtful and patient responses that he was beginning to understand in some small way, his son's homosexuality. One thing that Eric found harder to appreciate was Everard's insistence upon equality. Not so much his insistence for homosexuals being given equality, that was something that Eric could agree with, but rather he had the suspicion that Everard would never have addressed him as 'Lord' even if he had insisted upon it, which in any event he hadn't.

"Your mother wanted Ginny to cook you one of your favorite meals for tonight. She knows how much you love your fish and chips. Always have since you were a young boy. Isn't that right," said Eric, looking up at Frances.

Frances nodded.

"I thought you might like it. We haven't had it in quite sometime, and now that you've moved out into your own flat I wanted to help you reconsider."

She laughed, knowing full well that Declan was happily immersed in his own life and living on his own. Declan laughed, looking at his mother.

"So you're trying gastronomic blackmail. It might actually work. It is nice to have some fish and chips again, just the way that Ginny makes them. Those chaps in Kensington are no match, even though I keep going back trying."

"I'll say," said Everard, grinning at Declan, "whenever we're having lunch together it's always at one of those blasted fish and chips shops. All I get to eat is chips."

"So Alfie," said Eric, "when are you going to make good on your promise to marry Amelia?"

Alfie finished his mouthful of fish and looked up at Eric.

"Amelia and I were hoping for September of next year. In fact, we've chosen September the 11th as the day we'd like."

Eric nodded.

"That gives me time to save," he said laughing.

"We should have it at Avalon at Ambleside," said Frances, looking at her daughter. "If that's something you'd consider?"

Amelia looked at her mother and smiled.

"Yes of course, Mum, Alfie and I were hoping we could have it there. It would just make it perfect to be out in the country and not to have to worry about anything."

"I see," said Eric, "so you're hoping to invite the whole of England, and maybe Scotland and Wales too? What about the Irish?"

Eric winked at his daughter and she frowned at him.

"Well, Daddy, if I remember from what mother told me, your wedding to her was quite the national event."

"I have no recollection of that, I think I might have been drunk the whole weekend."

"Nonsense," said Frances, "he was stone cold sober and putting on a brave face. But I could tell that he was a little nervous. In any event, you are welcome to as big a wedding as you'd like."

"Thanks, Mum, though to be honest, Alfie and I are just hoping for something small and manageable. Just family and maybe a few close friends."

"Whatever you like darling," said Frances.

Amelia nodded.

"Yes, that's what I'd like and Alfie too. Just something small, no more than about one hundred people."

"What about your best man?" asked Declan, turning to look at Alfie. "Have you chosen him yet?"

"Yes, I have. You probably haven't met him, but he's a dear friend from varsity. Actually we go back quite a few years before that. But to be honest, I was hoping that I might impose upon you to be a groomsman?"

Declan smiled at him.

"That would be a great honor, I would be delighted."

"Thank you," said Alfie, beaming a smile. "I was hoping I could impose on you too, Everard. If it's not too much to ask."

He looked at Alfie and grinned, nodding his head.

"Yes, of course. It would be my pleasure too."

"Thank you. You've both been so good to me and I wanted to acknowledge that and let you know how important the two of you are to me. Like older brothers I never had."

"Anyone who's important to my sister, is important to me," said Declan and he raised his glass to Amelia and they clinked again.

Frances smiled, feeling wonderfully warm inside as she took in her wonderful, loving and kind family. She had been blessed beyond measure. Beyond all merit that she had even hoped to deserve.

Alfred came around and cleared the plates away and put them on the tray and took it out to Ginny in the kitchen. Declan turned to his mother.

"Everard and I wanted to invite you to an event," he said.

Frances looked at him.

"What event is that dear?"

"Well as you probably know, the second Round Table Conference is opening up tomorrow and Mahatma Gandhi will be here. In fact, from what we've been told, he arrived this past Friday. Anyway, Gandhi is giving a speech about his philosophy of satyagraha with a view to positive action through vegetarianism. We'd like you to come along. You and Dad."

Declan looked over at his father.

"What time is it?" asked Eric.

Declan looked over at Everard.

"It starts at six thirty and there will be a large buffet of Indian vegetarian food."

"That sounds absolutely wonderful," said Frances. "We haven't had Indian food in quite some time have we, dear?"

She looked over at Eric and he nodded.

"I'd be interested in hearing what he has to say about his Round Table Conference which seems to me more posturing than real negotiating on the part of Ramsay MacDonald's government."

"Yes, well I'm not sure he'll be speaking much about the negotiations. This is strictly about how vegetarianism fits in with his satyagraha."

"Where is it being held?" asked Eric.

"At Alcott House in Surrey. Which incidentally was where one of the very first vegetarian groups ever gathered," said Everard.

"But isn't it an orphanage now?" asked Frances.

Everard nodded.

"Yes it is, but it is still run with the philosophy of vegetarianism as the basis of the diet for the children. There's a separate building or hall where the lecture will take place away from the main house where the children live. All funds being raised are going to be donated to the orphanage."

"How nice," said Frances.

"Yes, the Vegetarian Society is putting it on and Gandhi has kindly donated his time for this cause. He's an honorary member of the society if you didn't know."

"I didn't and rightly so I imagine."

Everard nodded.

"I think we'd love to go, wouldn't we Eric?" said Frances, giving him a look that made it clear they were both going. Eric smiled.

"Sounds interesting."

"What about me?" asked Amelia. "Can Alfie and I come too. We'd enjoy it wouldn't we, darling," she said, looking at her fiancé."

Alfie nodded.

"I'd be very interested in hearing what Gandhi has to say. He's an exceptionally good speaker from what I've heard."

Alfie looked around from Declan to Everard.

"We'd love to invite you along Amelia," said Declan, "but the event's been sold out for weeks. I'm sorry, I didn't think you'd be interested."

Amelia pulled a long face.

"Oh rubbish," said Everard, "don't listen to him, he's just teasing you. We got four extra tickets just in case. Though as Declan says, the event has been sold out for some time."

"How much were the tickets?" asked Amelia.

"Free to you," said Declan, "but they cost us five pounds each."

"That's not cheap," said Eric.

"No, but you're getting a once in a lifetime opportunity to hear the Mahatma speak. He doesn't do these sorts of lectures very often and all the proceeds go to the orphanage in any case and heaven knows they could make good use of the money."

"Well, I look forward to it," said Frances, "but I insist that you allow us to pay you for the tickets."

"Absolutely not, Fran, I can't allow it. This is our gift to the four of you," said Everard.

And before she could object, Alfred and Ginny came in carrying the silver tray which had upon it six plates with date and walnut pudding on them with a jug of steaming hot custard on the side.

Five

Bijay Panchal had prepared his father for antyesti. It had been hard, his eyes had dropped hundreds of tears like spilled jewels over Chetan's body as Bijay had bathed him the night before, keeping his feet facing south so that he might join the dead.

Bijay was the eldest son and this was his responsibility and his privilege, but it was still hard. Never had he thought it would come so soon. His father was a peaceful man, well liked by all members of the community, and yet he had been savagely beaten to death just for wanting to bring independence to his beloved country.

Bijay had dressed his father in plain white clothes, the same color that he now wore. He had looked down at him as he lay there, dead. But he looked peaceful and the injury on the side of his temple and the back of his skull from the lathi were hard to notice now. His mother Kanti had been proud of how well Bijay had prepared his father.

On the morning after his murder she came in to see if Bijay was ready. He was, and they hugged each other and Kanti held back her tears, the mourning would start soon enough. Bijay's eyes had dried like hot stones in the summer heat as he had burned through his first wave of anger and sadness the night before.

"Did you remember the holy water from the Ganges?" she asked Bijay, looking deeply into his brown eyes.

"I did mother, he will be liberated today," said Bijay.

He reminded her so much of his father. He was as lean and as handsome as the young Chetan had been. Even though Bijay was already a grown man, he had a boyish face cropped by thick black hair.

He had visited the Ganges many years ago during one of his pilgrims and he had brought back a small bottle of the holy water. It had been blessed by a brahmin for a small fee, and it was this water he had used to ensure that his father's soul would attain liberation. He had placed a few drops in his father's mouth just after he had bathed him and clothed him.

Kanti looked down at her dead husband as he lay on the stretcher, ready to be taken out to the funeral pyre. He looked so peaceful lying there with his hands clasped together. Kanti noticed the basil on the stretcher by his right side. Just as it should be. Her eldest son, Bijay had taken his task very seriously and she was very proud of him.

Upon Chetan's forehead was a dab of sandalwood paste. Kanti couldn't smell it as she looked down at him, his body was adorned with flowers and they offered the strongest smell that she could discern. Chetan was also adorned with jewels. He had around his wrists a gold chain, one with a ruby that dangled on the outside of his wrist and the other with an emerald.

"Is Chetan ready to make the journey to the Shmashana?" asked Kanti.

Bijay nodded.

"He is ready."

"Good," said Kanti, smiling at her son. "I will get Indra."

Kanti left and returned shortly with her youngest son. Indra and Bijay picked up the stretcher and brought Chetan's body outside. There were dozens of family members and friends waiting by the cart where Bijay and Indra placed their father's body.

The cart was simple and wooden with low sides. They took a large white cloth and covered Chetan with it and tucked it up under the stretcher. It wasn't windy but it was warm. The sun had only recently bobbed up from the horizon. A single ox who was leaner than he might have liked was attached to the front of the cart.

The journey to Shmashana, which was located by the Surya river, was nine miles away. It would take them the better part of the day to walk there. Bijay took the thin whip out of the back of the cart and as he walked up to the head of the ox he gave it a light tap on the hindquarters and the ox started off slowly. Bijay grabbed a length of rope that was attached to the yolk and held it in his right hand.

The rope looped slack like a sickle from the ox's yoke to his hand, as he walked alongside the ox on it's left. Indra walked on the opposite side of the ox and across from his brother. Kanti was behind her eldest son as they all walked along the dusty road in unison, heads cast down.

The rest of the group of mourners straggled along behind the cart. They headed east while Chetan's feet pointed south. Bijay's mind was racing with unpleasant thoughts. There was only one person he blamed for this and that was Mohandas Gandhi. He always managed to stay out of trouble, conveniently it seemed to him.

The group of thirty to forty people wound their way out of the outskirts of Dandi and trudged along the mostly flat and barren land towards the Surya river. As they walked along, the sun started its rise up into the sky and burned hotly above them. Bijay's brown face started to glow and soon it blistered in little droplets of sweat. He took a cloth from one of his pockets and he wiped at this face.

A bit of wind would be a welcome relief but the wind would not blow, it seemed to have run out of breath, much like Bijay's soul had been emptied of happiness. The funeral procession was quiet for the whole journey. For almost seven hours not much was said, for now was not the time for speaking or the time for noise. It was a time of quiet and of reflection.

Watching them walk their way slowly towards the river it was hard to grasp the despair and the feeling of loss that Bijay endured. His head was cast down as most others were, but there was no sign telling of the depth of despair that he was feeling in the pit of his stomach or the ache in his head.

Bijay carried on in quiet resolution, the funeral rites or antyesti would guide him through the process and after the thirteen days of mourning he would have a clearer mind and a better idea of what was needed for him to honor his father's death and perhaps to seek restitution.

But that would come in time. In less than a fortnight he would come to see things clearly, and during these next days he would pray to Lord Vishnu for guidance and understanding about what to do.

They had stopped a few times on their way at some of the smaller villages to drink and replenish their strength. The ox needing it perhaps more than the men. On more than one occasion, Bijay had encouraged his mother to ride in the back of the cart with her husband, but she would not hear of it. She was determined to walk the whole way to the Shmashana and she was finding it surprisingly easy to do so.

The walk, as long as it was, and as tiring as it was also therapeutic. Kanti found as the body tired during the journey, the mind was able to find moments of peace and solitude. Her thoughts turned to the forty years she had spent with Chetan. The happiest times of her life.

She remembered him as a young man courting her and bringing flowers, sandalwood, incense and saffron. He had been so shy in those first few days but had grown into a proud and confident husband and father. They might not have been the richest Indians, but they had riches of a different kind. The love and happiness of a happy family. Why he had to be taken from her so early she was at a loss to explain. He was a healthy man with no ailments.

He had believed in Gandhi's satyagraha and independence movement, and his conviction in the rightfulness of non-violence was strong. He was sure it was the safest and surest approach to an independent India.

But he had been wrong and she looked at him as he rode in the back of the cart for the last part of this journey. He looked so peaceful lying there that perhaps his sacrifice had not been in vain. But for her and her sons it was too much to ask.

Bijay guided the ox through the last pass and below them the fertile valley of the Surya river opened it up. And it was lush and green and there was more activity upon its banks than they had seen for many hours since they had left Dandi.

They trod on, not particularly buoyed by the end in sight. This was not a pilgrimage, it was rather, a beginning of loss and mourning and an acknowledgement of that fact. Bijay looked down at the settlements by the river and chose a spot on the outskirts which was flat and level, the vegetation light. This was where he would build the funeral pyre for his father.

He goaded the ox on further. The animal was more stubborn than he had ever known it to be. Perhaps it was aware that it was bringing its master to his final burial spot and it wasn't happy about it.

Bijay pulled on the yoke and slapped at the animals hindquarters with both his hand and his whip. He did not wish to hit the animal hard. His father had always encouraged kindness and the gentle treatment of animals and he found that his wrist would not flick faster or harder than his father had instructed him when he was a boy.

The ox lumbered on, slowly and with great difficulty, clearly stuck between two minds about it.

"Come on Abhi, we must get father to the bank of the river. Please, my friend," Bijay whispered into the ox's ear.

It didn't seem to help so he gave up and walked on ahead of the animal. The last thing he needed was a stubborn ox what with everything else he needed to complete within the next couple of hours.

He turned around and the ox looked at him strangely. Bijay slapped his hands on his thighs.

"Come on Abhi, come on."

He was trying to use his softest and most tender voice as he slapped the tops of his thighs again and tried to encourage the ox to move towards him. At the side of the ox, Bijay's younger brother, Indra, doubled over and started laughing hysterically.

"Bijay, you are so funny. That is not the way to call an ox."

"You think so, do you? Well then why don't you come and show me how it's done."

"I will," said Indra as he trotted up to his brother, still laughing.

"You need to use a firm voice. You must show Abhi that you mean business. Just like father did."

Indra turned and looked at the ox. He put his hand up and straight out and then as he spoke he pulled his arm downwards vigorously until his finger was pointing at the ground by his feet.

"Abhi, come here! Now!" said Indra in what was supposed to be his sternest voice but didn't seem all that stern. The ox looked at him as if he had lost his mind. Now it was Bijay's turn to start laughing. He slapped his brother on the back.

"Aha, I see you have the gift, my brother."

And he laughed and laughed as the ox stood still and watched them blankly.

"But it worked for father," said Indra.

And then he burst into tears and threw his arms around his brother's neck and cried. Bijay held him tightly to him. His own eyes burned with the acid of tears as they welled up. He squeezed them out, but he would not allow any more. He needed to be the strong one. He was the eldest. And as he held his shaking and sobbing younger brother, the ox started towards them on its own accord.

Bijay patted his younger brother's head and he patted him on his back.

"It is okay, Indra, we have each other and we will always have each other. Look, Abhi comes. He does not want to see you sad."

And Indra looked up from his brother's embrace and saw the ox walking towards him. He smiled sadly at Bijay.

"See, I told you. You just have to be firm."

Bijay grabbed his brother's shoulder and gave it a gentle squeeze.

"You did, my brother, you did."

And they both walked alongside the ox, each on opposite sides as they led the group of mourners down towards the river bank. The sun was at its zenith and it felt to Bijay as if it were trying to burn a hole through his head. He turned to everyone and suggested that a bath in the river might be the first order of business before they start building the pyre.

There was much relief at hearing this and they all took a quick dip into the cool Surya river and cleaned up as best they could. When they were done, Bijay walked over to one of the vendors who had set up a business of selling firewood for those who came to this part of the river for antyesti.

"You have chosen well. Lord Vishnu has blessed this place. Your family member will never be a ghost, but will see a speedy departure."

Bijay smiled at him.

"I need enough wood for the pyre, do you have enough?"

"I have plenty. Come round back and I'll show you."

They walked around back of the wood merchant's stall and in a fenced area was enough wood for three or four funeral pyres. Bijay smiled at the old man again.

"How much?" he asked.

"Fifty rupees," the old man said as if he were asking for a few pence.

Bijay swallowed. That was a lot more money than he had expected, but family and friends had helped pitch in and he had over fifty rupees in his purse, but there would be other expenses to come. He clenched his jaw and paid the man.

"This is the best wood. The cleanest burning wood you will find in the whole of India. The gods will be happy."

Bijay went back to the crowd who were by the ox and were now drying themselves in the sun.

"We have the wood, and we can take as much as we want."

The men went with Bijay and Indra and started hauling wood out of the pen behind the old man's shed. It was good wood. It was clean and dry and it would burn well, but whether it was the best wood in the whole of India remained a question that Bijay didn't have an answer to. But he was happy with it, and he wanted this funeral to be a highlight for years to come and something that those in Dandi would speak well of and make him feel proud that he did right by this father.

It was important for him to do right on this occasion. It was the first time he had been called upon to conduct antyesti. The first time he had been called upon to be the man of the household. It was a role he had both looked forward to and feared. He had hoped it wouldn't have come by way of his father's funeral. But such was the careless pendulum of life as it swung back and forth, knocking some to their deaths and birthing others.

Moving the wood was heavy, laborious work. The men hauled it out and laid it in piles according to size. The women, led by the elder women in the group, Bijay's grandmother amongst them, started to build the pyre.

By the time most of the wood had been brought out, the scaffolding of the pyre was solid and the younger men, including Bijay and Indra, helped the women build the pyre into something that would burn for hours. The act of building the pyre was perhaps more important than many other aspects of the funeral rites, but it was the least celebrated.

A real shame, thought Kanti, considering that without a long and thorough burning time, the body would not be burned sufficiently. But that was how it was with women's work, and it didn't seem like it would change anytime soon.

It was after three in the afternoon when Bijay and Indra and their mother took Chetan out of the back of the cart and placed him on top of the funeral pyre, removing the cloth that had covered him. His feet pointed south and his body lay parallel to the fast flowing river.

Bijay took a moment and looked at the current, and he wished that its speed was suggestive of the speed with which his father would find peace on the other side. Everyone stood silently around the body of Chetan as Bijay went up to it and looked over it thoroughly. He adjusted the holy basil, tucking the sprig under his father's elbow as it bloomed outwards on his right side.

Chetan's hands were still clasped together over his abdomen, though it was hard to see through all the petals and flowers that lay thick upon his body like a carpet. The body was vibrant and bright with oranges, yellows, whites, reds and pinks of the flowers placed upon it. Roses and marigolds and jasmine made up the bulk of them.

Bijay carefully took off the jewelry and gems around his father's wrists and handed them back to his mother. Kanti was not crying, she was measured and focused on the upcoming cremation. Bijay bowed his head and silently thought a prayer that he offered up to Lord Vishnu.

He then went to the back of the cart and pulled out a small silver vessel within which was water. He went back and stood at the head of the pyre. He slowly started to walk around the body in an anti-clockwise fashion, keeping his father always on this left.

As he did so he dipped his hand into the small vessel and sprinkled water as he walked slowly around. He did this three times. When he was finished, he put the vessel back into the cart and brought some kindling back with him.

He opened his father's mouth and put the kindling inside with some ghee. Indra passed him a small twig which he lit from a torch that was burning brightly. Bijay lit the kindling in his father's mouth. Indra offered him the burning torch which he took from his younger brother.

There were tears welling up in Indra's eyes as he passed the torch to his older brother. Bijay took it and bowed at him. He walked around the pyre, anti-clockwise and touched the torch to its foundation as he did so. The wood took to the flame eagerly and quickly. The pyre was engulfed within moments and soon his father disappeared behind the licking orange flames.

Behind him Kanti fell to her knees and started wailing and crying. Other women joined her, for now was the official start of the mourning period which would last for thirteen days from Chetan's death.

Bijay turned to his brother who was crying freely and he hugged him. Bijay's tears flowed freely now like the stream that flowed next to him.

"Baba will be with Vishnu now," he said to is brother, though needing to hear it as much as him.

"We must not let his death be in vain," said Indra.

Bijay nodded. There must be payment made for this. His father did not deserve to die in the manner he did. Bijay had not read the papers, but he would. And they would tell of a callous disregard to civility and justice and honor on behalf of the British that Bijay had never before seen.

All of the mourners, the extended family and friends, held vigil well into the night, keeping the funeral pyre burning. As the day turned to night the orange flames continued to lick and tickle the sky and heaven. The smoke burned thick and gray taking Chetan's remains with it.

After nine in the evening, it appeared that their was nothing left of the body but its ash and the ash of the wood. It was time to let the fire die out. As it did so, everyone took another bath in the river.

In the morning, the pyre was still hot. It would be at least another day before Bijay could collect his father's ashes as was his duty.

"I will stay with you, my brother," offered Indra.

"No, Indra," said Bijay, "this is my duty and I must do it alone. Go home and take care of Mama, she needs you know. I will be back within three days."

Bijay watched them leave, Indra walking on the left side of the ox and Kanti sitting in the back with three other older women. They didn't look back at him and he watched them until he lost them from view. He sat and stewed for the next two days.

Six

The night before, Amir and his younger brother Fadi had washed their father according to Islamic tradition. It had been hard on both of them. Their tears could not be held back and they had cried, each separately, during the washing and preparation for burial.

Their father had been a kind and devout man. He had raised them up as good Muslims in the faith and taught them chastity and compassion and a love for Allah. Ajit had embraced Gandhi's satyagraha as a Muslim because Gandhi had embraced all the faiths, and Ajit believed as Gandhi had believed, that a peaceful, vibrant and independent India could only be achieved if Indians of all faiths were included in the dialogue.

It had not been easy. Not everyone in the Muslim community had felt the same way or condoned Gandhi's methods, but some had. Like Ajit and like Maulana. But Ajit's senseless death at the hands of British authorities had only created a deeper hatred in Amir and Fadi for all British.

As they prepared their father for burial during the morning of May 22nd, they had spoken of vengeance and their anger towards the British. And even at Gandhi, who Fadi thought was most responsible for his father's death.

"There will be lots of time, my brother, for us to discuss the repercussions of our father's death. But for now, let us not fill our hearts with anger," said Amir, "but let us focus on ensuring that our father is buried properly according to our custom."

Fadi nodded, as they wrapped their father in three pieces of plain white cloth. When they were satisfied with the kafan they went out into the main room where family and friends had gathered and they all started the funeral prayer. The Janazah prayer was spoken with earnestness and hope as they prayed for the forgiveness of any sin that Ajit might have committed.

Amir was not sure that his father had committed any sin in his whole life. He was a man of such kindness and truth that he had become a much respected and beloved elder in the Muslim community and one whose wisdom was often sought. As such, the room was full to bursting with those who had come to pay their farewell.

After the funeral prayer had been said, Amir and Fadi along with Ajit's two brothers carried Ajit's body out of the house and towards the local cemetery. It wasn't a long walk. It took them no longer than fifteen minutes. The rest of the mourners followed the four men who carried Ajit's body.

The sun had just risen over the horizon as they got to the cemetery, as if to preside over the burial and ensure it was conducted in an appropriate manner. Amir, being the eldest son, oversaw the digging of the grave. With the help of his two uncles he made sure it was perpendicular to Mecca.

When it was sufficiently deep he took the responsibility of laying three balls of dirt in the grave. As Fadi and their uncles lowered Ajit into the grave, Amir adjusted the three balls of dirt so that they lay appropriately. One under his father's head, one under the chin and the third under the shoulder.

They lay Ajit down on his right side, facing Mecca and as they did so they prayed. When Amir was satisfied that his father had been placed in his place of rest properly, those present threw in three handfuls of dirt, reciting the appropriate prayers each time. Then Amir oversaw the filling of the soil and ensuring that it was stamped down firmly enough.

Then he placed the small headstone on top of the grave. Then they stood around, silently as each said their goodbyes silently. Ghadda, Ajit's wife, cried openly but dignified. There was no wailing and gnashing of teeth. Islam did not condone such exaggerated grief and Ghadda was a good and pious Muslim woman.

Amir and Fadi embraced their mother and they made their way slowly back towards their home as the other mourners dispersed to leave them to their mourning privately.

"I will ensure that father's death does not go unanswered," said Amir.

"And I will answer Amir's call for restitution, mama," said Fadi.

Though what that would be, Amir had no answer. For starters, he did not know who to blame. Surely it was the British for they had killed his father. His anger at them burned hot like a glowing coal in the pit of his stomach. But his mind kept turning to Gandhi. If Gandhi had not sent his father on this ridiculous march to the salt works then his father would be alive still.

And where was this Gandhi, this great soul, when things got difficult? How come he conveniently got arrested and never suffered the blows and stings like the others did? These were questions that Amir would seek answers to during his next three days of mourning and he would dwell upon them until he had all the answers and his path forward was clearly marked.

But in the meantime he would sit and watch over his father's pyre until he collected the ashes and took him to his final place of rest.

Seven

Declan and Everard were especially excited to be seeing Gandhi on this evening. There had been only a small article written up about it in the back pages of the paper. What had taken up most of the front pages was the usual political pandering about the Round Table Conference and how successful MacDonald and his government felt it would be.

Everyone was dressed smartly. The men in their suits and the women in long dresses and blouses. Frances was looking forward to hearing what Gandhi had to say. She was open minded about vegetarianism but not convinced of its benefits which Everard had often expressed. Frances was more interested in hearing about how that lifestyle was important in Gandhi's overarching philosophy of satyagraha.

They all waited patiently by the front door for Eric to make his way downstairs from the bedroom. There was nervous chatter with Everard explaining happily how thrilled he was that everyone was going to the lecture.

Eric came down the stairs slowly, wincing a bit as he did so.

"Are you alright, darling?" asked Frances.

He nodded.

"I put out my back trying to get my shoes on," he said. "That's what was holding me up. But I think I'll be alright."

"Are you sure? Perhaps you should stay home?" asked Frances.

"Nonsense," he said, "It'll do me good to get out and walk about."

There was no convincing him otherwise so they left Marmalade Park and made their way towards Abbot House in Surrey in two cars. Eric leading in the Rolls Royce and Alfie and Amelia following in Alfie's Austin Seven Swallow Saloon. Abbot House was about an hour and fifteen minutes from Marmalade Park and the drive was leisurely and pleasant once they'd gotten out of London.

By the time they got there just after six, Abbot House was already lively with throngs of people. Being out in the country there was plenty of parking. Some of the young children looked at them from the orphanage and smiled and waved as the visitors passed by towards the larger building which held the lecture hall.

Frances and Amelia smiled at the young boys and girls as they passed.

"Aren't they sweet?" said Frances.

"They certainly are," agreed Amelia.

Alfie looked down at his wife and grinned at her.

"We'll have some just like that one day," he said.

Amelia nodded her head and tucked her hand into his elbow. They followed Everard and Declan and Eric and Frances towards the lecture hall. Everard offered the tickets at the entrance and a young man nodded and punched holes in them.

"Enjoy the show," he said.

"We will," said Everard.

They walked inside. The hall was quite plain with a raised platform upon which plays and other shows might be offered. There was a red curtain that was draped in the first third of it, closing off the rest of the stage from the viewers. The seats were simple but cushioned and sloped downwards towards the front of the stage. Everard turned around and looked at Eric.

"Where would you like to sit?"

"Towards the front, I think," he said.

Everard gestured with his hand, and Eric lead the way. They found a row of seats close to the stage but not so close that you had to strain your head to look up at the lectern. Eric led them with Frances following and then Amelia and Alfie, and finally Everard and Declan.

It was busy as more and more people came in and took their seats.

"You said it was sold out right?" asked Amelia, looking over at Everard.

"That's what I heard."

And just before six thirty there wasn't an empty seat in that hall at Abbot House. The hall was abuzz with the noise of anticipation and voices speaking quietly to one another, wondering what Gandhi might speak of.

A tall, thin Caucasian man stepped out from the wings of the stage and walked up to the podium. He looked out towards the crowd and smiled at them for a while, taking his time to look over all the faces.

He took his time as his gaze took in the whole room. He had dirty blonde hair that was a mess, but he wore a clean and crisp suit. The auditorium was small and intimate, but it likely held at least two hundred people. Perhaps more.

"I wonder where the food is?" asked Declan, looking at Everard.

Everard leaned in to answer, in a soft voice.

"I think I overheard someone saying that they would be putting out the buffet in the garden under some tents during the talk."

Declan nodded.

"Good evening, ladies and gentleman," said the young man at the podium. "It is a great honor to have you here tonight and we have a very special guest for you. But first, let me introduce myself. I am Giles Hume and I am the president of the Vegetarian Society."

Giles smiled out towards the crowd. He had a very infectious and warm disposition that put people at ease. He paused for a moment before continuing.

"Some of you might be wondering where our delicious buffet is. Do not be dismayed, we have the finest Indian chefs preparing it as I speak. It will be your reward for listening to the esteemed Mohandas Karamchand Gandhi."

Laughter and clapping erupted from the group. Giles smiled down at them from the podium. He rested his hands lightly on the lectern. He was relaxed as if this was something he did every day.

"For those of you who are interested in the vegetarian lifestyle and philosophy, you will find brochures on all the tables when you leave the lecture hall to enjoy your buffet. I, as well as other members of the Vegetarian Society will be milling around if you'd like to speak to us personally. With that aside, let me introduce you to tonight's speaker..."

Declan looked over at Everard.

"I might like to pick up one of those brochures," he said.

Everard smiled at him.

"I think you should. It's healthier for you, you know." he said, smiling at his partner.

"Mohandas Karamchand Gandhi comes from a small village in India called Porbandar in the Indian state of Gujarat. His father was Chief Minister of Porbandar State. Mr. Gandhi is affectionately and reverently known as Mahatma Gandhi, Mahatma meaning 'great soul'. It was a title bestowed upon him in 1914 by the people of India whom he serves. It is similar to our word saint, and used to honor a person who has given much to his community."

Frances looked over at Eric.

"If only our Lords were as humble?"

She smiled at him and he looked back at her and smiled back.

"If only they were, perhaps we wouldn't be in the depression we find ourselves in."

"Mahatma Gandhi, as many of you are aware," continued Giles, "has taken up satyagraha, which means the 'adherence to truth'. Gandhi is on a mission to free the Indian people from British control, by non-violent means. He is here as part of the Round Table Conference, and I am both honored and delighted that he has seen fit to grace us with his presence for tonight's talk titled 'Vegetarianism, Satyagraha and the Road to Peace'. I am also pleased to call the great Mahatma both a friend and fellow vegetarian. Ladies and gentleman, without further ado, will you please warmly welcome the great Mahatma, Mohandas Karamchand Gandhi."

Giles stretched out his left hand towards the end of the stage and behind the wings a small and thin Indian man walked out, wearing a simple and plain gray suit. He was balding and the hair that was left on his head was cut very short. He wore an English style mustache and round rimmed glasses. He shook hands warmly with Giles who stood a foot taller than him.

He walked up to the lectern and took a moment to take in all of the audience. He smiled at them and his eyes twinkled. He cleared his throat.

"Thank you all for coming to hear me speak tonight. I hope that it may prove to be a good use of your time. He turned to his left where Giles had just recently left the stage.

"Thank you to Mr. Giles Hume for that very warm introduction."

Gandhi's humility was sincere and infectious. You couldn't help but to warm to the small man who stood up there with his emotions and truth naked for all to see. And to think that such a small man was such a giant on the world's stage was a profound dichotomy but testament to his lion heart.

Gandhi started speaking and he carried on, clearly and with erudite logic and compassion for almost an hour. It was a thrilling and enraptured talk which held everyone on the edge of their seats.

If there had been many who had not understood Gandhi or his focus on truth and non-violence, there were none left in the audience at the end of his talk. And those who had come to hear him but had not come in support of his cause had their opinions mostly changed.

"I will be happy to visit with any of you who would like to discuss what I have said in greater detail. I will be available in the garden where I understand they are serving a wonderful Indian buffet. Thank you all for listening to an old man speak of his hopes and dreams of peace amongst our two nations."

Gandhi bowed and the audience erupted in loud applause and stood as he walked off the stage. Giles returned and waited patiently until the audience settled down and took their seats again. Giles turned to his left.

"Thank you, Mahatma, for that wonderful and inspiring talk."

Giles turned back to face the crowd.

"I am sure that many of you can smell the wonderful curries and food that our chefs have prepared. I have been informed that it is ready for you now all to enjoy. If you'd like to partake in the wonderful meal, please depart out to your left and into the garden where tents, tables and chairs have been set up. Mahatma Gandhi will be out shortly to visit with any of you who wish to speak with him in greater detail about the topic of tonight's speech. Please remember that there are many who might have questions and if you can conduct yourselves with that understanding, we'd all be terribly grateful. For those of you who won't be joining us for any dinner, you are welcome to depart to your right, the same way you came in. Thank you, ladies and gentleman, and goodnight."

"We are staying for dinner aren't we?" asked Declan looking over at his parents.

Frances nodded.

"Most certainly, I gave Ginny the night off, so it's either this or we'll starve."

Declan smiled.

"Good, because I'm absolutely starving and it all smells so delicious."

"I agree," said Amelia.

And they all stood up from their chairs and walked out of the hall to their left and into the garden. It was still light out as the sun started its slow descent into the bottom of the earth. Looking around, Frances was amazed at how many people from the audience were so eager for the dinner buffet. She would guess that possibly half of the audience was staying for dinner.

They made their way to the end of the long line of hungry people. It moved rather quickly for such a long line, and as they made it to the front and picked up their plates and cutlery, empty pans were being taken away and fresh ones were being put in their place.

Frances had some saffron rice and pakoras as well as some dahl which she poured over her rice. Eric and the boys heaped their plates high with an assortment of vegetable and bean curries as well as pakoras and samosas. Amelia took a chickpea curry and a samosa and poured the curry over a bed of rice.

They found a table large enough for the six of them and placed their plates down upon it. Everard didn't sit.

"Can I get anyone some water while I'm up?" he asked.

Everyone nodded, so Declan got up with him to help. They came back with six glasses of water and put them in the middle of the table where everyone helped themselves. They started to eat quickly and quietly. The food was both warm and spicy but not overpowering for their palates. They were quite accustomed to Indian food, though they all had to agree that this was some of the best they had ever tasted.

When they were about halfway through their meal, they noticed a group of people crowding around by the exit of the hall. Declan noticed that they had gathered around Gandhi. As more and more people noticed, the crowd around the small Indian grew larger and larger.

"Looks like it might be difficult to get a word in with Gandhi," said Everard looking over at the crowd.

Declan nodded.

"All things come to those who are patient," said Eric. "I'm sure we'll get a chance if we wait. We aren't in any rush, are we?"

"I don't think so," said Declan, looking over at his sister.

"We're not. We've got all night to spend with the family," she said.

"What are you hoping to ask him?" asked Declan.

"I want to ask him how sincere he feels the British government is with these Round Table discussions."

"That's a loaded question," said Frances, looking up at her husband and smiling at him.

"Well, I suppose it is, and we'll see how he answers it."

"Probably not as openly as you might like. I'm sure he's going to say the political things, like the government is making the right sort of gestures and so on and so forth," said Declan.

Eric nodded.

"I agree, but I want to hear it from the horse's mouth so to speak."

They ate the rest of their meal while occasionally looking up at the throng of eager citizens trying to have a word with Gandhi. The crowd around him didn't seem to be thinning and Frances noticed that there were a couple of other Indian men with Gandhi. They were clearly associates of his. Perhaps there to protect him from the pressing crowd. They looked particularly nervous, but perhaps that was because the crowd was thick and close around them.

The crowd was mostly made up of British Caucasians though there were a few Indians amongst them and a couple of Africans, most likely students studying in London.

After some time, servers came by and cleared their plates. The group of diners had started to thin, but the crowd around Gandhi ebbed and flowed. Eric watched for a while as he drained the remainder of water from his glass. It didn't look like the crowd was going to dissipate soon, so Eric stood up.

"I think I'm going to go and join the throng and see if I can't get a question in," he said.

"I'll join you," said Frances. "Not sure how much longer we'll have to wait and those two over there look like they might not wish to trouble Gandhi with this crowd much longer."

Frances was looking over at the two men who seemed most concerned with the crowd around Gandhi. Frances stood up with her husband.

"Anyone else interested in speaking to the Mahatma?" asked Eric.

Declan shook his head.

"I wouldn't know what to ask him," said Amelia.

"Me neither," confirmed Alfie.

"I think I'll come along too," said Everard. "I might like to ask him about his thoughts on dairy foods and if he thinks they're any good."

Everard stood up and the three of them started off towards the crowd.

"We'll wait here for you three," shouted Declan after them.

Where they had sat was only about fifty feet from where the crowd had gathered around Gandhi. They started up towards them, by the main exit of the hall when they froze. A sound like thunder and lightning splitting the sky erupted from within the crowd. And then again.

The crowd quickly dispersed and there was pandemonium. Frances saw men running every which way, but she didn't see anyone with a gun. Though she knew there must have been a gun amongst them. But in the chaos she couldn't see any. Two of the Indians ran off together, through the exit where Frances lost sight of them. The third Indian ran off the opposite way, around the hall's length before disappearing behind it.

The two Africans ran off away from Frances and around the closer side of the hall to her, where they too disappeared out of view. A couple of canes and walking sticks were flailing about as the group dispersed.

Frances looked at Gandhi, he was kneeling down by one of his colleagues. Frances started up towards them, with Eric and Everard right behind her.

"I don't think this is a good idea," said Eric after her.

She turned to look at him briefly.

"But we must help. Everard, go to the main house and see if you can't get hold of the police. Tell them that a murder has just been committed."

Everard nodded and took off like a jackrabbit through the hall and up towards the house. Frances continued at a brisk pace towards Gandhi, Eric caught up with her and walked with her. They reached Gandhi and Frances knelt down. She could see that Gandhi's colleague was bleeding from the stomach.

Eight

"What happened?" she asked, looking at Gandhi.

Gandhi had his hands on his colleague's stomach. His gray suit was wet and dark with his burgundy blood. Frances looked at the man, and he was gasping for breath. He seemed to be choking too.

"I heard two loud bangs and then Ravi fell down into me. I looked at him, wondering what had happened and then I saw him clutching his stomach."

"My son has called for the police," Frances said to him.

Gandhi nodded and smiled. Frances looked down at the injured man.

"Did you see who did this?" she asked him.

He nodded and tried to speak. Both Gandhi and Frances kneeled down towards him to listen more carefully.

"The...the Indian..."

Ravi looked up at them, his eyes were wide and scared and he coughed and choked and tried to breathe.

"Indian...p...p..."

That was all he could say before he died.

Frances stood up and looked at the other Indian whom she had seen with Gandhi and his now dead colleague.

"Did you see who did this?" she asked.

He shook his head sadly.

"I was looking over in this direction," he said, pointing to his right. "I heard the bangs coming from my left side."

"What is the young man's name who has been shot?" she asked.

"Ravi Meda," he said.

"And what is your name," she asked the young man.

"I am Sujay Patel," he said.

Looking at him and then at his fallen comrade, Frances noticed a remarkable resemblance. They might have been brothers, they looked so similar, though the man she spoke with had a thin, wispy mustache and the man lying dead, Ravi, was clean shaven. But they both had black, shiny hair and delicate features and their brown skin had the similar hue of gently roasted coffee beans.

"May I ask what your role is here?" asked France.

Gandhi stood up, and Frances noticed just how small he was. Sujay stood eye to eye with Eric, and even though Frances was very petite, Gandhi didn't stand much taller than her.

"Sujay and Ravi are my dear friends. They are here to keep me on schedule and to provide any help if I should need it," said Gandhi.

"They are here to protect you then too?" asked Frances.

Gandhi looked down, his hands clasped together, still slippery with Ravi's blood.

"Yes, that would be one way of looking at it," he said.

"Clearly," said Frances. "I am Frances Marmalade, and this is my husband Eric."

Eric went to offer his hand but noticed that Gandhi's were blood stained.

"Terrible business this," he said.

Gandhi looked up at them and nodded.

"Ravi was a kind and generous friend," he said.

"Why would anyone want to do this to him?" asked Frances.

"Perhaps it was not him the bullets were for," said Gandhi.

Frances nodded.

"I suspected the same. Have you had other attempts on your life before, Mr. Gandhi?" asked Frances.

"Please call me Mohandas," he said.

Frances nodded, and Gandhi shook his head.

"No, I have not had any attempts on my life. Though I hear about it all the time. It seems that I cannot please all of the people. The British do not care for me and they find the very idea of non-violence troubling."

"How so?"

"They do not know how to react to it, and then they overreact."

Frances nodded. Declan, Amelia and Alfie came up.

"Are you okay, Mum?" asked Declan.

Frances nodded.

"This is my son Declan, my daughter Amelia, and her fiancé Alfie."

Gandhi smiled at all of them in turn. Declan offered his hand to shake. Gandhi opened his, palms facing up and Declan saw the blood.

"Sorry," he said and put his hands in his pocket.

"You were saying, Mohandas, that you have received threats on your life," said Frances.

"Yes, that is quite true. The Muslims do not appreciate my non-violence nor do they particularly want to associate with Hindus much. The Sikhs think that I am too passive in my approach and then within the Hindu community, where I belong, there are factions on both sides who do not agree with what I am trying to accomplish."

"What are they unhappy about?" asked Frances.

"Some are unhappy that I am not more forceful in protesting the injustice that the British are causing. They think we should be more active. Others think that there is no need to fight for an independent India at all, that we will naturally get our independence in due time when we come to embrace the British as equal partners."

"I see, and yet you continue with your fight for an independent India," said Frances.

"Of course, it is our country and we should be the ones to govern it."

"Can't argue with that," said Eric.

Gandhi looked up at him and smiled. Frances looked at Gandhi and then at Sujay.

"Did you recognize anyone at all in the crowd who might have had a threatening demeanor or gesture?"

Sujay shook his head and looked at Gandhi.

"I did not notice anyone. They were all new faces to me. But you must understand, Frances, that I am meeting lots of people each day, sometimes hundreds, like today. Nobody in the crowd stood out to me."

A smaller crowd than had previously been hanging around Gandhi to ask questions, now gathered to gawk. Declan and Everard had decided to take up crowd control and were doing a good job of keeping the smaller crowd back.

A cameraman had arrived on the scene with a camera and large parabolic flash. Declan stood in his way as he tried to snap some pictures, unsuccessfully, thanks to Declan.

Gandhi noticed and took off his jacket and lay it over Ravi's chest and face to offer him some dignity in death. He moved closer to his dead friend's body, as did Sujay. Lady Marmalade stepped up as a third and made it very difficult for anyone from the crowd to see Ravi very easily.

Frances looked down at the ground and tried to determine if she could find any casings. There were none that she could locate. She turned around, facing outwards from Ravi's body and scanned the area. She couldn't see any from that vantage point either. She turned to her husband.

"Darling, could you see if you can't scour the area for any bullet casings. I think there should be two."

Eric nodded and bent down as low to the ground as he could. It was almost eight and dusk had fallen and the sky was losing any residual light that would help make his job easier. A small, stingy light that barely dribbled light out into the garden was glowing from the side of the hall, but it did not much improve his view.

"Can you remember where you were standing when the gun went off?" asked Frances.

Sujay stepped forward and towards the hall a couple of steps. Gandhi stepped up next to him.

"I was standing here," he said, "and looking over there."

He pointed with his right hand away from the hall.

"I heard the bangs come from somewhere here on my left."

With his left arm he made a circle in front and to the left of him. Gandhi nodded.

"I was talking to someone here," said Gandhi, facing Lady Marmalade who was slightly off to his right. "I heard the gunshots from that area too."

With his left hand, Gandhi waved in a circular motion in the general vicinity that Sujay had. It was off to his left, just slightly, and ahead of him. Eric came over and bent down looking for spent shell casings. He still couldn't find any, and the light was quickly disappearing like mercury in his hand.

Behind them, a flashbulb went off. Frances turned around to see who it was. It was the reporter.

"Have you no shame," said Everard, and he took the man by the elbow and walked him away from the crowd.

Declan looked back and saw his mother.

"I don't think he got anything," he said. "We've been blocking him every chance he has."

Frances smiled. In the distance, walking towards the crowd, she saw a familiar face. He waved at her and she waved back. At least now they might start getting somewhere.

Nine

The two police officers stepped up towards the crowd and maneuvered between them until they were within the inner circle where Frances, Gandhi and Sujay were. Two constables came up after them and took over crowd control and started to march the crowd much further away from the crime scene.

"Lady Marmalade," said Inspector Cameron Davison, "this is Sergeant Devlin Pearce."

Frances smiled at him and shook his offered hand.

"We've met before, Inspector," she said.

"Yes, right, I wasn't sure if you remembered."

"It's the well groomed mustache and smart deportment. I think he'll be going places, Inspector."

Inspector Davison nodded his head and grumbled his agreement. Davison was a stocky man of average height with a thin and wispy pencil mustache that rode the crest of his upper lip. He had short black hair with a high forehead and droopy small eyes that seemed to look past you.

"So what do we have here?" he said, not really asking it as a question of anyone.

Pearce had his notebook out and he was taking notes of the scene.

"Mr. Gandhi, eh?" said Davison, looking over at the small Indian. Gandhi smiled at him. "What brings you here?"

"I came to give a lecture on satyagraha and vegetarianism."

"I see, the Round Table not keeping you busy enough?"

Gandhi didn't say anything, but the smile on his lips was unmoved.

"Inspector," said Frances. "I think that there was an attempt on Mr. Gandhi's life this evening."

Davison looked at her and then down at Ravi's dead body.

"Looks to be they weren't very accurate then, were they? Who's this chap they shot?"

"He is a dear friend of mine, Ravi Meda."

Davison nodded. A third constable had now joined them and was standing with a flashlight in his hand, using it to survey the scene.

"Put it over here," said Davison as he leaned down and took Gandhi's jacket off of Ravi, exposing the gunshot wounds on his stomach. The constable steadied the flashlight on the body for Inspector Davison to take a good look.

"Two bullets to the stomach," said Davison as he stood up and looked around. "Looks to me like they got the man they wanted."

"I must strenuously disagree," said Lady Marmalade, "I believe they were meant for Mr. Gandhi."

Davison looked down his nose at her, clasping his hands behind his back and rocking back and forth on his feet. Eric had some time ago given up on looking for the shell casings. The night had become too dark.

"Is that what you believe, Mr. Gandhi?" asked Davison.

Gandhi kept the small smile on his lips as he answered.

"It is possible, though it is also possible that perhaps whoever shot Ravi was trying to shoot Ravi and not me."

Davison nodded.

"We'll investigate this thoroughly. Tell me, Lady Marmalade, why you think the bullets were meant for Gandhi?"

"Mr. Gandhi is a well known person who is trying to agitate for a free India. I imagine that there are many who are unhappy with his philosophy, and indeed, he has told me that there are many who disagree with his approach."

"Is that so?" asked Davison, looking over at Gandhi.

Gandhi nodded.

"I have received some threats on my life."

"Yes, well that is to be expected for someone whose political leanings are public. Doesn't necessarily mean that they'll follow up on those threats. Do you know how many death threats are actually acted upon?"

Davison had shifted his gaze to Frances. Frances shook her head.

"Not many. I'd likely suggest that less than one in a hundred are carried out."

"Still, Inspector," said Pearce, "we should investigate all possible motives."

Davison still had his hands behind his back and he turned his head to look at the taller, younger and more handsome sergeant.

"Yes we shall, sergeant, thank you. Mr. Gandhi, tell me if you would, have you received any death threats leading up to your trip to England?"

Gandhi looked over at Sujay. Sujay shook his head.

"Sujay here, takes care of my mail on a day to day basis. He usually keeps me informed. I have not had any death threats since...the Dharasana Satyagraha protest."

Gandhi looked back over at Sujay for confirmation. Sujay nodded his head.

"That was the last one you have received," said Sujay, looking at Gandhi.

"And what was that?" asked Davison.

"That was a march my colleagues conducted on the salt works factory in Dharasana. Hundreds of satyagrahis marched upon the salt works and were beaten savagely for their peaceful protests. Two satyagrahis, or protestors died from their injuries sustained by the British police."

"That is most unfortunate. And who was the last death threat from, related to this event?"

Davison was looking at Gandhi, looking through him so it seemed. Gandhi looked over at Sujay and nodded his head. Davison followed with his eyes and looked at Sujay.

"We don't know for certain, as death threats are usually not signed, but it must have been from one of the family members of one of the two men who were killed."

"Why is this chap, Sujay, is it?" Sujay nodded, "always speaking for you?"

"Because he has a better memory for these things than I do. I do not wish to pay very much attention on these matters of negativity," said Gandhi.

"Very well," said Davison. "Then tell me, Sujay, what makes you think that this last letter had something to do with the family of one of the two dead?"

"Because it spoke about how Mahatma must pay for the death of their father."

"I see," said Davison.

He cast his eyes down and stared at Ravi's body for a while before speaking.

"And this fellow here," said Davison, looking down at Ravi's body. "Was he involved in anyway with this Dharasana business?"

Gandhi looked down at his dead friend and nodded. His smile was gone now.

"Yes, Ravi was instrumental in setting up the whole event actually. He suffered beatings at the hands of the British police, but he didn't have it as badly as some of the others."

"Did he know those who were killed at Dharasana?"

"I can't say for certain, but we can find out for you," said Gandhi.

"Yes, please do."

"Inspector," said Frances interjecting. Davison looked up at her.

"I believe that Ravi identified his killer," said Frances.

"Is that so. Did he tell you?"

"He tried to. I got here right after the two shots. In fact, the three of us were on our way here to ask Mohandas..."

"Who?" asked Davison.

"Mr. Mohandas Gandhi," said Frances.

"I thought your name was Mahatma Gandhi," said Davison to Gandhi.

Gandhi smiled again and shook his head slowly.

"No, my first name is Mohandas. Mahatma is a title, much like Lord or Lady, but much more informal."

"Actually, it is a title that means 'Great Soul'," said Frances.

"I see."

"As I was saying, Inspector..."

"Yes, please go on."

Inspector Davison's mustache twitched as his upper lip twitched involuntarily. He was finding this whole thing about Indian names and titles both tiresome and confusing.

"Eric and Everard and I were walking up here to ask Mr. Gandhi a question when we heard the shot. So we were the first here other than Mr. Gandhi and Mr. Sujay Patel."

Davison looked over at Gandhi and Sujay and then down at Ravi.

"As soon as I got here, I saw Mohandas bent down over his friend Ravi. I immediately saw that Ravi had two gunshot wounds to the stomach. I leaned down and asked him if he knew who had shot him and he nodded."

Frances looked at Gandhi and Gandhi nodded his head.

"That is so, Ravi gave the impression that he knew who had shot him."

Gandhi looked back at Frances and she looked at Davison.

"I asked Ravi to tell me who it was, and he said 'Indian p'. I didn't quite hear him at first, so I leaned in, we both did, Gandhi and I and he said it again. 'Indian' then a pause for breath and 'p'. We waited to see if he would tell us more. I think he wanted to. I think he was trying but he couldn't get it out. He expired then."

"So what does it mean do you suppose?" asked Davison.

"Perhaps Ravi was trying to say the name of who it was, or maybe he was just simply letting us know that it was an Indian person."

Davison looked at Gandhi and he shrugged a little.

"I think Lady Marmalade is correct. He might have been trying to give us the name of the shooter or he might have been telling us that it was someone generic like an Indian person."

Davison nodded and took his right thumb and index finger and spread them out across his thin mustache, he was deep in thought.

"How many Indians do you know with a name that starts with 'p'?" asked Davison.

"Well, there is Sujay Patel whose surname starts with a 'p'. Though of course he didn't do it as he was right next to me and I would have known."

Gandhi looked at his friend and winked at him quickly to reassure him he was only teasing.

"There is also Anil Puri, but he is not here in England so far as I know."

"What about chaps with a first name starting with the letter 'p'," said Davison, getting a little impatient.

"I know a Pradeep and a Prem. Pradeep Sharaf and Prem Wason. There are likely others though I can't recall at the moment. But I am also fairly certain that Pradeep Sharaf and Prem Wason are not here in England either."

"We'll be sure to investigate that," said Davison. He looked over at Pearce. "Are you taking good notes, Sergeant?"

"I am, Inspector," said the young Pearce.

"I'm just thinking," said Davison, "that if Ravi knew who killed him, then why would the shooter have been trying to shoot Gandhi and not Ravi?"

"As I said before, Inspector," said Frances, "Ravi was involved with the Dharasana satyagraha more intimately than Mr. Gandhi, that might be the only reason why he knows who killed him. Still doesn't mean that the bullets were meant for him."

"Lady Marmalade makes a good point, Inspector," said Gandhi. "I had planned on leading the march to Dharasana Salt Works, but very shortly after I had written to Lord Irwin I was arrested in the middle of the night about two weeks before it was planned. I was in jail at the time of the march. Ravi helped plan it. He was really the driving force behind it, along with Abbas Tyabji and my wife Kasturba. They were both arrested and so it fell on the shoulders of Ravi, and Sarojini Naidu who led them to the salt works."

Two men in medical coats carrying a stretcher came down the grassy knoll from the far side of the hall. They walked up to Inspector Davison.

"We're with the coroner's office, Inspector. Can we take the body away?"

Davison nodded and the men put the stretcher down on the ground next to Ravi. They picked him up carefully and placed him upon the stretcher. Then they covered him with a cloth and picked him up.

"Let the coroner know I want to hear from him at his first opportunity."

One of the men grunted his understanding and the walked off, carrying Ravi's body the very same way they had come. Davison looked around at the darkening night. All three constables now had their flash lights out to shine some light onto the scene.

"I think that's about all we can do tonight," said Davison. "The light is no longer good. I'll post constables to watch over the crime scene tonight and we'll come back tomorrow with fresh eyes and a bright day to look for any clues."

"Speaking of clues," said Frances. "We haven't managed to find the two shell casings from the bullets."

Davison nodded.

"I'm sure they'll show up in the cold light of day," he said, with the smallest smirk on his mouth that was almost imperceptible.

"You'll also take a look at the ticket sales, won't you? To see if we can't uncover who actually came to the lecture tonight. I'm sure that will be very helpful to the investigation, Inspector," said Lady Marmalade.

"Yes, Lady Marmalade, it will be very helpful, and I am very aware of my responsibilities and duties when it comes to investigating crimes."

Frances smiled and nodded.

"Of course, Inspector, I didn't mean to suggest otherwise. I just do want justice to be served."

Davison grunted under his breath.

"Well, I think that will be all then. You'll excuse us while I talk to my men," Davison said to Frances.

"Certainly," Frances turned to walk away, when she noticed Eric come up to Davison. Eric placed his hand on Davison's shoulder.

"I would consider it a personal favor if you would accept my wife's offer of assistance."

Eric looked at him steadily, his eyes were hard and determined. He was not asking Davison as much as he was telling him.

"Yes, my Lord. We would be happy for your wife's help."

Eric smiled and nodded his head.

"Good," he said and turned and took Frances' hand and they started to walk away.

The last thing that Frances heard was Inspector Davison asking Gandhi where he was staying. He replied that he was staying with friends in Ealing, West London.

Ten

Eric was reading the paper again when Frances came down to breakfast. He looked up from it and smiled at her. He folded the paper and sat it down next to him. His plate was clean except for the telltale signs of grease and yolk that suggested he had already finished.

The grandfather clock chimed nine times shortly after Lady Marmalade sat down for breakfast. Ginny came in from the kitchen and asked what she'd like for breakfast.

"One fried egg and one sausage, please Ginny, and one slice of toast."

Ginny bowed herself out of the living room and Eric looked at Frances.

"Quite the evening last night, wasn't it?" he said.

Frances smiled and nodded her head.

"Frankly, quite an awful business this murder business. Can't say I like it. Can't say I like you being involved in it."

"Well, if it's any consolation darling, I don't like it either, but someone has to be sure that justice gets served."

"Yes, but does that someone have to be you? Can't you let the police handle these things?"

"They do, Eric, they do. I hardly ever get involved in only the smallest fraction of murders. But when one happens in front of you, you ought to do something. Besides, you already encouraged Inspector Davison to take up my offer of help."

Eric sighed and grinned at her.

"Yes, I suppose I did, and I'm already regretting it."

"Do you remember our neighbor from a couple of doors down. Ms. Hummingham, poor dear. I went for some sugar and instead found her dead."

Eric nodded.

"I do remember it well."

"Her soul would never have found rest if we'd left it up to the police. I worked tirelessly on that case to ensure that the real murderer was found, didn't I?"

Eric nodded again.

"And we finally got the bugger, didn't we?"

More nodding of his head.

"I can't help it, Eric, you know I'm a stickler for justice and I can't let it go."

"No you can't, you're very much like a bulldog once you've gotten hold of something."

"And I have a natural ability for it, so it seems."

Eric smiled and nodded.

"You do, I'll grant you that. I just despair of you having to witness these gruesome acts of violence. I more than had my fill of it in the Boer War."

Lady Marmalade remembered that well. It had taken Eric some time to find himself after he had returned from that dreadful war. She had been quite worried about him for some time following.

"Anyway," he said. "Who do you think did it?"

"That's hard to say. I think I first have to convince Davison that it was someone who was after Gandhi. From there we have to determine who it might have been from those who were around him, or in the vicinity."

"What do you mean about being in the vicinity?" asked Eric.

"Well, I've been thinking, and I wonder if it had to have been someone in the crowd. You know, from where Sujay and Mohandas say the gunshots came from, someone might have been hiding behind the buffet tables. That would give them line of sight."

"Now that will open up a whole can of worms, won't it?"

"I suppose so. But this is so early in the case, Eric, that one hardly knows where to being. The puzzle pieces have been scattered all about. You have to pick up each piece and see where they might fit. If you narrow yourself down too much at the very beginning then you might be focusing in on the wrong area. I learned that very quickly in Ms. Hummingham's case."

Eric nodded, and looked at the paper lying next to him.

"Speaking of Gandhi, do you think he'll carry on with the conference under these circumstances?"

"I don't think why he wouldn't, he is after all seeking independence for India. I would be surprised if he didn't, frankly."

"The paper is saying all the right things about it. How it got off to a good start and all. That both sides are looking forward to 'honest and committed dialogue', which really means nothing."

Ginny came into the room carrying a tray with Lady Marmalade's food on it. She placed it down on Lady Marmalade's left side and served her a plate with the egg and sausage. She put the tray of toast down in front of her, butter and jam were already on the table, and lastly she put a small pot of tea in front of Frances with a teacup and saucer.

"There are two slices of toast, my Lady, in case you wanted a second," said Ginny.

"Thank you, Ginny, looks absolutely marvelous."

"Anything else?" asked Ginny, looking from Frances to Eric.

Frances shook her head as did Eric.

"No thank you," he said.

Ginny left again and Eric and Frances were alone in the living room. Alfred wasn't present either.

"You're not hopeful then, my darling, about this conference," said Frances as she started cutting into her egg.

"No, I'm afraid not, love. I think Gandhi will be disappointed. I can't see why the government would want to give up India when we're in such a bad spot with the economy. India gives us cheap labor and cheaper materials. Strategically it would be a terrible move to give that up at this time."

Frances looked up at her husband and nodded at him as she ate some egg, and rested her fork and knife on her plate.

"Now, that doesn't mean that I agree with it, I think that Indians should be allowed to govern themselves. I've been against all this appropriating of foreign lands since after the Boer War. I went because I thought I was doing the right thing for England, what I realized was that both of us, the Boers and the British, were fighting over a land that wasn't really ours in the first place."

"So do you think we English shouldn't be living anywhere else but on our own little island?"

Frances knew the answer but she wanted to give Eric a chance to elucidate it himself. She didn't want him worrying about her murder investigation. He smiled at her.

"I'm not going to fall for it," he said. "You know exactly how I feel. Of course I don't believe that. I believe we're all part of one community, the human community. We should really all be allowed to live where we wish so long as we're happy to abide by local customs and laws. No, what I am saying is that we should not be trying to take over other lands through force as we have been wont to do for some time."

Frances took a bite of sausage and chewed for a while.

"Then clearly we should start the process of turning over India to the Indians."

"Quite right," said Eric, "but it's not going to happen right away."

"Well, if it did, at least Gandhi wouldn't have to worry about death threats anymore."

"I'm not sure it's that simple, my love, he's a very popular public figure, but that doesn't mean he speaks for all Indians. As you heard him suggest yesterday, there are those within his very own community who are not happy with his approach or goals. Some will likely think that he does not speak for them or their cause."

"But perhaps that's partly due to the propaganda that the British government has been using to try and indoctrinate some of them."

"Perhaps, it could also be social and religious differences. There are at least six major religions present in India, that I'm aware of. Hinduism, Islam, Christianity, Sikhism, Buddhism, and Jainism in that order of popularity. Hindus are by far, the largest group with over eighty percent of Indians. So you have five other religions with minority representation who might get agitated if they don't feel their interests are being acknowledged."

"I'm sure Gandhi is quite aware of all this. He might be a peaceful and non-violent man, but I get the feeling he is quite politically astute."

Eric nodded as the clock chimed on the half hour. He looked at his watch and it was indeed nine thirty. He needed to get off to work.

"What are you up to today, my love?" he asked.

Frances looked up after spearing a piece of sausage in her fork.

"I thought I'd have Alfred take me back to the scene of the crime after breakfast and see if I can't help them find some evidence and make any inquiries about how the case is progressing. I'll also want to speak with Gandhi later and his man, Sujay. Perhaps we can get some passport photos of the Indians who were at the event and see if Gandhi or Sujay recognize any of them."

Frances put the piece of sausage in her mouth and Eric nodded.

"Sounds like you have a good handle on everything. If you don't mind darling, I'll be off. I have a meeting with one of my building managers at ten."

"Not at all, I'll be quite alright."

Eric got up from his side of the table and picked up the newspaper. He placed it down next to Frances and leaned and kissed her.

"I'll see you for dinner then?"

Frances nodded.

"Have a good day, my darling," she said after him as he left the living room.

Just as Frances was finishing up the sausage and egg and buttering her toast, Alfred came into the living room.

"Sorry to intrude, my Lady," he said.

"Not at all, you're not intruding."

"Lord Marmalade suggested that you might like to go for a drive later?"

"Yes, Alfred, I was thinking of heading out to Abbot House. There was a terrible crime their last night."

"I heard, my Lady. Lord Declan and Lord Marmalade were talking about it this morning over tea. I'll go and get the Rolls ready."

"Yes, thank you, Alfred."

Alfred left to do exactly what he had said he would do which was to get the car ready for the trip. Frances started on her toast and poured herself a cup of tea. The start to her day would have to wait until she had her first cup of tea.

Eleven

Alfred was waiting for Lady Marmalade by the foyer. He helped her into a light jacket and she tied a colorful scar around her head. It was red and orange. Alfred closed the door after them and helped her into the car. He got into the driver's side and made their way slowly and leisurely towards Abbot House.

"I feel for this poor chap, Gandhi," said Alfred.

"How so?" asked Frances.

"Losing a friend like that, right in front of you. Can't be easy. As I understand it, he's had more than his fair share of difficulties."

"I imagine that any one hoping to free their country has a significant uphill climb."

Alfred nodded, looking out the front window, trailing a couple of cars length behind a dark blue Mercedes Benz 770 cabriolet, with the roof down. There was a young couple in the back seat, she was holding onto her cream colored hat and laughing at something her companion said.

"Why would anyone want to murder a pacifist like Mr. Gandhi? Lord Declan mentioned that you suspected the shooter was actually trying for him."

"I do, and Gandhi, regardless of his popularity and pacifism is still someone working for change and not everyone is going to agree with that change."

"So who do you think it might have been?"

Alfred snatched a quick look over towards Frances.

"Too early to say Alfred. I'm starting to wonder if the shooter was even in the crowd. He might have been kneeling in behind the buffet table. I suppose the evidence will say."

"To do something like that right out in the open. I can't imagine what they must have been thinking."

"That's an interesting idea, it might have been two of them. Though I'm inclined to think that it was more likely just one person."

"Lord Marmalade said that there were a few Indians and a couple of Africans in the crowd. Why would one of them do it, I wonder?" said Alfred.

"Because they don't agree with the position Mr. Gandhi is taking I suppose. Though we don't know for certain that it was one of the Indians or Africans who did it, but from what we've heard, I wouldn't be surprised if it was one of the Indians."

"I overheard Lord Declan mentioning that the chap who had been shot dead had mentioned something to you about it being an Indian."

"Yes, that's quite true. Ravi was his name, and he said 'Indian p'. That was it. I'm thinking someone with a name with the letter P or, as was mentioned last night, he might just have been trying to say that it was an Indian person."

Alfred shook his head slowly.

"I don't know how you do it," he said. "This is quite the puzzle. I wouldn't even know where to start to be honest."

"You've started off quite well actually, Alfred. You start investigating any crime with the evidence at hand and then by asking questions based upon that evidence."

"But what if you don't have any evidence. I understand that there are no shell casings that you were able to find."

"You'd make a good detective I think, Alfred. You have a curious mind. The thing is though, we do have evidence. We have

Ravi's dead body, and within it are two bullets which will provide clues."

Alfred nodded.

"Yes, I see it now. Hadn't quite thought of it like that before."

"And don't forget all the witnesses, this wasn't exactly a murder in broad daylight, it was after all dusk, but it was a murder right out in public, with many who were present. I'm sure that we'll start to put this together slowly but surely, by asking the right questions of the witnesses."

Alfred nodded and they drove the rest of the way to Abbot House in silence. Just the soft whirring of the tires on the road and the gentle whistling of the wind as the zipped along at a leisurely pace.

It was just after ten thirty when they made it to the house and a number of children were playing in the large garden between the house and the hall. A number of caregivers were keeping them away from the crime scene even though the children's curiosity was trying to get the better of them.

There were a couple of police cars parked by the hall and Alfred drove up and parked next to them. It was a bright and sunny day with pure white cotton ball clouds dotting the blue sky.

Alfred got out and went around to Frances' side where he opened the door for her and they started off towards the crime scene. A young and fresh faced looking constable stopped them at the far end of the hall.

"I can't let you any further. This is a crime scene, mum," he said with some authority.

"I know that," said Frances, "I was here last night when it happened. Please inform Inspector Davison that Lady Marmalade is here."

Frances spoke with patience and kindness.

"Yes, my Lady," he said and he trotted off to a clump of policemen that included Davison and Pearce at the other end of the hall where the shooting had taken place.

Frances watched as Davison gave the young man a stern warning. Though it wasn't his fault, Davison should have warned him that a middle aged woman would be coming who was entitled to help out at the crime scene. The young man trotted back towards them and in the distance Frances saw Davison raise his hand and wave them in. She and Alfred started towards him.

"Terribly sorry about the misunderstanding, my Lady," said the somewhat flushed young constable as he passed them, heading back to his post.

"Not at all," said Frances, and she offered him a genuine smile in return.

"Good day, my Lady," said Davison as she and Alfred joined the group. Pearce looked up from his notes and nodded at her, as did another constable she hadn't met before.

"Please, Inspector, call me Frances."

Davison nodded and looked back at Pearce, then he turned to Frances.

"We haven't found much to go on at this stage," he said, looking glum-faced. Pearce twirled his mustache with the hand that held his pencil and almost caught his eye. He readjusted.

"I wanted to speak to you about that," said Frances. "What if the shooter was behind the buffet table over here."

Frances walked off towards the hall, diagonally, to where the buffet tables still stood. The men joined her.

"There is a chance that the shooter might have hid behind here, at the corner of the table. Have you looked for any shell casings here?" she asked.

Davison shook his head.

"My men have been scouring the area where the group had been gathered."

Davison looked over at the constable and nodded at him vigorously. Frances stepped aside as the young man got on bended knee and started looking for shell casings.

"I've had my men scour around the area where some of the crowd who were gathered around Gandhi dispersed to. But we haven't come up with anything yet."

Frances nodded, and kept her eyes on the ground where the young constable was still fumbling around. This area was in the shade which, although still bright, wasn't in direct sun, which meant any shell casings wouldn't glint.

"I had them pay particular attention to where the three Indians ran off to."

"Right," said Frances. "I saw them go once I heard the shots fired. Two of them ran right through here," she said, pointing to the exit just off to her right where she had exited the hall last night for the buffet. "The third took off down the length of the hall before disappearing behind it."

She opined off to her left at the far end of the hall where she had just come from. Davison nodded.

"Quite right, that's what we've gathered from the witnesses we've spoken with so far."

"And anything there?" asked Frances.

Davison shook his head.

"Nothing. We looked all the way through the hall and up towards the house but we didn't find anything of importance. The same around the side of the hall. We also looked around the near side of the hall," said Davison looking over his shoulder, "and nothing again."

"That's the direction that the two Africans went, if I remember correctly," said Frances.

"That's right."

"Have you found anything at all, Inspector?"

"We have found a number of tickets for the night's lecture. As you can imagine, in the pandemonium, lots of people panicked and tickets flew everywhere."

"And these tickets are numbered, so that will help identify who they belonged to," said Frances.

"That's correct," said Davison, "I've requested the logs from the Vegetarian Society for all tickets sold. I'll be picking that up later today."

"How many tickets have you found?"

"We found six tickets around the general area where Mr. Gandhi was fielding questions."

"That's a jolly good start," said Frances.

She looked down at the constable still scurrying around on the ground. He hadn't found anything yet.

"What's going on down there, Button," said Davison looking at his constable. Cst. Button looked up with an unhappy face.

"I can't find anything Inspector," he said. "There are no shell casings down here."

Frances got down on her bended knees and hands and scurried around under the table and then back towards the hall and up towards the far end for several feet then back to the end of the buffet table. She got back up and dusted her hands off on the front of her dress.

"He's quite right," she said. "I can't find any shell casings at all, and there should be two. Don't you find that strange, Inspector?"

Davison shook his broad shoulders.

"Not particularly, it just means to me that he didn't use a pistol but probably a revolver."

"Yes, I suppose that does make sense," said Frances. "It just sounded to me, more of a muffled sound than what you would expect from a revolver."

"Yes, well, sometimes we get these things wrong."

Davison walked off back to the area where Ravi had been shot. Frances and Alfred and Pearce and the constable joined him. The grass was clearly stained with Ravi's blood. It was a large amount considering that he had been shot in the front. Frances suspected that the bullets had caught arteries. The blood was dark, almost a black red against the green grass which was no longer damp from the morning dew.

"I'm waiting for my photographer and then I'll be off to the Vegetarian Society," said Davison.

"Perhaps we can meet up together later," said Frances.

"If you wish," said Davison, staring down at the blood in thought.

"What is it?" she asked him.

He looked up at her and rested his chin on his thumb and index finger.

"What if it really was this Ravi chap they had wanted to shoot, and not Gandhi?"

"Then you should proceed with that as your focus," said Frances, still not convinced that was who the target was.

Davison nodded absentmindedly.

"And what are you doing this afternoon?" he asked.

"I'd like to visit Mr. Gandhi, if you have an address for him," she said.

Davison looked up at her.

"He'll be at the conference today," he said.

"Yes, I know, but perhaps Sujay will be home."

"Very well," said Davison. He looked at Pearce and nodded. Pearce flipped back a few pages in his notebook. He found what he was looking for.

"101 Cuckoo Dene," said Pearce. "Residence is home to Amar and Gita Bhandari."

"Thank you Sergeant," said Frances.

"What are you hoping to find with them?" asked Davison, looking at her with a raised eyebrow.

"Not quite sure, but I'm sure I'll think of something. I'll keep you informed if I uncover anything helpful."

"Good," said Davison.

"Well, I'll be off then. Thank you for your help, Inspector."

Davison nodded and went back to speaking with Pearce and the other constable as Alfred and Frances left.

"Good day, my Lady," said the young constable who was still keeping the riffraff from the crime scene, although the only riffraff he had stopped had been Lady Marmalade and her loyal butler. Frances smiled at him as she passed.

"Not much evidence at the scene, my Lady," said Alfred as they climbed the slight embankment towards the car.

"Not much, no, but despite what Inspector Davison thinks, I find it odd that there were no shell casings, and it certainly didn't sound much like a revolver."

"I'll take your word for it, my Lady."

"I'd like to find out what kind of bullet the coroner is able to extract. That might explain something about the type of gun used."

"Sounds reasonable."

"But the tickets, Alfred, the tickets are quite valuable."

"How so?"

"It proves that we know at least six from the audience were actually there, mostly gathered around Mr. Gandhi. They cannot argue that they bought the tickets but elected not to attend."

"I suppose a guilty person might do that."

"I suppose they would. In any event, it would be hard for anyone to suggest they bought a ticket and weren't there. Everard said it had been sold out for some time, and when we arrived I couldn't see an empty chair for the life of me. But at least now we know who some of the crowd were who had gathered around Mr. Gandhi to ask him questions."

Alfred nodded and walked up to the passenger door and opened it for Lady Marmalade. Frances stopped for a moment and looked down. Something silver had sparkled in the sun and caught her eye. She leaned down and dug her fingers into the gravel and dirt to pull it out.

"What is that, my Lady?" asked Alfred.

Frances held it out and showed him. It was a police whistle, a little tarnished and dirty from the ground but otherwise in good shape.

"I wonder if one of Inspector Davison's men lost that?"

Frances shook her head.

"I don't think so. This looks like it has been trampled over and been here at least a day or so. Would you mind taking it back over to Davison and tell him we found it here by the car. Ask him if he would find out who it belonged to. It's got the constable's number on it."

Alfred took it from her and jogged off down the hill and around the hall where he disappeared from view. He returned shortly to find Lady Marmalade already in the car with the door closed. He got in and looked at her.

"To Ealing then?"

Frances nodded.

Twelve

It was shortly after noon when Alfred pulled up the Rolls Royce in front of 101 Cuckoo Dene. Cuckoo Dene was a quiet neighborhood of row homes in the Tudor style. It was the sort of place where you could raise a family not far from the hustle and bustle of central London.

The area of Ealing was dotted with green space and parks. It was the kind of place where neighbors were nosy but hid it well. Where gossip ran up and down the streets like children kicking a soccer ball around.

A Rolls Royce brought stares from behind glass windows as old and young women alike stood next to curtains to gawk at who might be the lucky one to have a visitor pop by in an expensive car.

It was no surprise then, to the neighbors, when Alfred and Frances walked up the short path and stairs that led to Mr. and Mrs. Amar Bhandari's home. They were after all hosting Mr. Gandhi, and everybody wanted to know what Mr. Gandhi was up to.

Alfred knocked on the white front door in the style of half French door with the windows on the upper half. It wasn't long before an older Indian woman in a saffron colored sari came to the door. She had in the middle of her forehead a red bindi representing her third or spiritual eye. She opened the door a quarter of the way.

"May I help you," she said, and her accent was British as if she had been born and raised.

"Good afternoon," said Frances. "I'm Lady Marmalade, and this is my butler Alfred. I was hoping to speak with Mr. Gandhi or Mr. Patel if either one of them is available. It is regarding the unfortunate business from last night involving Mr. Meda."

Frances beamed at her as innocent and as doe eyed as she might have looked on her wedding day. The Indian woman nodded.

"Please come in, my Lady. My name is Gita Bhandari."

Gita opened the door fully and stretched out her left arm towards the back of the house. Frances and Alfred stepped inside the house.

"Please call me Frances."

"Please come this way," said Gita as she led them into the living room which was down the hall and on the right hand side.

The living room was busy. There were a few Indian men in the living room and one young Indian woman. Frances remembered Sujay Patel from the night before, and she assumed the older Indian man to be Amar Bhandari. She did not know who the other young Indian man or the young woman were.

"Amar," said Gita, "this is Frances Marmalade and her butler, Alfred, they want to speak with Sujay about last night."

"Please come in and sit down," said Amar as he stood up and offered Frances his hand. He had no discernible accent either. Sujay and the other young man had stood up. Gita readied two more settings at the table. Frances took a seat next to Amar on his right as he sat at the head of the table. Alfred took a seat on Amar's left.

"You know Sujay, obviously," said the slim Amar with a twinkle in his eye. "This is my son Ajeet and my daughter Chandra."

114

Frances shook hands with both of them before she sat down, as did Alfred. Chandra was sitting across from her, next to Alfred, and Ajeet was seated next to Frances.

"I hope you will join us for lunch," said Amar, "we have just started."

And you could see it was so by their plates. The food was piled high but not much had been eaten.

"We are vegetarian, so I hope you won't mind."

"Not at all," said Frances, smiling, "my son's friend is vegetarian too. That is how we ended up at Mr. Gandhi's lecture last night. A very inspiring and informative lecture too, if I might add."

Amar smiled. He seemed happy and relaxed in front of his family and the feeling of warmth and caring immediately put Frances and Alfred at ease.

Amar was wearing a white dhoti, which stood in stark contrast to his son and daughter, who were both wearing European style clothing. The son in a white shirt and gray pants, and the daughter looking lovely in a patterned yellow summer dress.

"All the food is on the table," said Amar, sweeping his arms across the table. "Please help yourself to whatever you like."

"I might need a little help understanding what everything is," said Frances.

"Certainly. That dish closest to my wife is a chickpea curry. Then working towards me is a saffron, basmati rice with peas and mushrooms. The next is a vegetable curry and then we have a plate of those triangular pastries called samosas which are filled with potatoes and peas. Next to them are vegetable fritters. They're made with chickpea flour and vegetables and then fried. Lastly we have dahl which is a lentil soup."

"It looks so lovely and smells so delicious. It's a good thing we hadn't eaten lunch yet isn't it, Alfred?" asked Frances.

"It is, my Lady, I can hear my stomach grumble already."

Amar beamed from ear to ear.

"Please, help yourselves. We have tea and water to drink, in case you find it a bit spicy."

"I have spent some time in India over the years, and I absolutely love your cuisine, though I understand you usually make it hotter for yourselves than what I might be used to."

"That is true," said Amar, chuckling, "though this week we are trying to make it milder for Mohandas. He prefers plainer food as part of his overall philosophy, so you might find it just about perfect."

Frances took a helping of rice and poured some of the chickpea curry over it. She took another small helping of vegetable curry and then put a samosa and vegetable fritter on her plate. She reached for a pitcher of water and poured herself a glass just in case. She had found she had a good tolerance for Indian food and spices, but she had never eaten with the Bhandaris before, so she erred on the side of caution.

Alfred heaped his plate with a little bit of everything that was available and he too poured a tall glass of water for himself. Everyone had already served themselves and started before Alfred and Frances had arrived so they tucked in.

"Are you working, Ajeet?" asked Lady Marmalade.

Ajeet shook his head.

"No, my Lady, I am at the University of London studying engineering. I hope to head back to India one of these days and work with the independent government."

Frances nodded, and looked over at Chandra.

"Please, call me Frances. And you, dear, are you at university too?"

Chandra nodded and smiled. She was a very attractive young woman with long black hair that curled naturally.

"I too am at University of London. I am studying medicine. Like my brother, I hope to go back to India and help with forming our new government."

"That's marvelous and ambitious," said Frances. "You know, my daughter recently graduated last year from the University of London, and she took medicine too. I wonder if you know her..."

"I was wondering that too," said Chandra, smiling. "She wouldn't be Amelia Marmalade, I mean, Lady Amelia, it's just that she was very informal with her title, everyone called her Amelia or Amy."

Frances nodded.

"Yes, that's my daughter."

"She was very well liked. I didn't know her that well, I mean, everyone knew her, she was very popular and very kind. Very helpful with the younger students. I had just entered my first year when Amelia, I mean Lady Amelia, was graduating."

It looked as if Chandra had blushed just slightly.

"Don't worry my dear," said Frances, "I find it hard to keep these titles straight. Stick with Frances and Amelia and you'll do just fine."

Chandra smiled.

"Thank you, Frances. You know, we all thought that Amelia would have been our valedictorian, except, well you know how it is, everything still isn't quite equal between the sexes in some parts of society."

"I do know what you mean. It's a shame really."

"I had heard it said that was why Amelia had chosen U of L rather than Oxford, because the medical faculty was treating women more equally. Is that true?"

Frances finished chewing on a bit of fritter before replying.

"Yes, my dear, that is exactly the reason she chose University of London over Oxford. Though my husband wasn't amused."

Frances chuckled and Chandra smiled in empathy.

"He's on the board with Oxford and they gave him every reassurance that her degree would be just as good as anyone else's. They said it would of course be better than the one she would get from the University of London. No offense, U of L is a terrific university."

Chandra nodded.

"But Oxford is only slowly coming into the twentieth century and they've only recently started offering medical degrees to a select few women. Amelia is a bit stubborn that way. She wanted a university that would treat her, or at least pretend to treat her equally, so the University of London it was. She loved it, Eric, my husband, got over it and all in all I think she got a very good education."

"We have been very happy so far," said Amar, "for both Chandra and Ajeet. Of course, for me, I can't complain about the price, Oxford would have been out of the question."

"I quite understand," said Frances.

They ate together in silence for a while.

"I imagine then, Frances, that your husband went to Oxford?" asked Ajeet.

Frances looked up at him and took a sip of water. The food was indeed mild, or moderate, depending on your palate's ability to handle Indian spice, but Frances found it quite enjoyable. She cleared her throat.

"Yes, he did. Eric attended Oxford and studied law. That was back in 1897 if you can believe it."

Frances smiled at the memory.

"Shortly after that he served in the Boer War in 1902 and when he came back he went into his father's business."

"Would it be impolite of me to ask what type of business?" asked Ajeet.

"Not at all," said Frances. "Mostly land holdings, real estate with some commercial business on the side, manufacturing mostly. We own a bit of London. Much of Fleet Street actually amongst other properties, and a few newspapers too, including The Guardian, The Observer, The Daily Telegraph, The Financial Times and The Daily Mirror, in addition to quite a few regional papers."

Ajeet nodded his head and turned his mouth and raised his eyebrows.

"Good heavens, sounds like you're richer than the king."

"Ajeet," said Amar, looking at his son with a frown on his face.

"I'm sorry," said Ajeet. "I just got carried away."

"That's okay, Ajeet, in truth we are richer than the King, though I don't usually like to brag and we live quite simply considering. Eric and I like it that way. I hope you'll be discreet with what I've shared with you today."

Ajeet nodded.

"Of course."

Frances wasn't sure why she had shared such detail with the Bhandaris, these were obviously people who had as intimate friends the likes of Mohandas Gandhi and he would certainly not be impressed by wealth.

Nevertheless, if Ajeet, or anyone else for that matter, was astute, all that Frances had shared was mostly in the public record if you knew how to look, and she hoped that opening up with them would accord her the same in return, especially in regards to this murder she was investigating.

They continued to eat in silence for a while, each enjoying their allotted portion of food. Frances was quite surprised that the whole family was so slim, considering how much food had been prepared.

"Please, Frances, have as much as you like," said Gita.

"It was absolutely marvelous," said Frances, "I feel as stuffed as a Christmas turkey."

They all laughed.

"Did you cook all of this yourself?" asked Frances.

Gita nodded and smiled.

"My daughter helped a great deal," she said, looking over at Chandra.

"She's fibbing, all I did was taste test really," said Chandra.

"Well, to both of you, my sincerest gratitude and compliments."

They both smiled broadly.

"Perhaps we should move to the living room where it is more comfortable to sit. I know that you have come in regards to the terrible events from last night. Let us retire to the living room where we can help you in any way we can," said Amar.

Amar got up from the table, and led the group into the living room. Alfred and Frances sat on a couch and Chandra and Ajeet sat on another couch. Amar took what appeared to be his own soft leather recliner, its brown skin looking like it had seen much use over the years. Sujay sat in another chair and there was a third left open for Gita, but she did not join them. Frances noticed that she was cleaning up the dining room table.

In the middle of all of them stood a squat wooden table with a glass face. It was covered almost to the edges with a large rectangular white doily. There was nothing on top of the table. In fact, as Frances looked around, the whole area seemed clean and uncluttered. Against the far wall was a bookshelf that held many books, neatly and orderly. She wasn't certain, but she might even have guessed that they could be in alphabetical order. By author or title she couldn't be sure. Next to Amar was a round wooden table which held the wireless and nothing else.

"How long have you lived here?" asked Frances, trying to make idle chit chat before getting to the meat of the matter. She was waiting for Gita to join them.

"My children were born here," said Amar, proudly. "We came when we were just newly married, almost twenty five years ago."

"And how do you know Mr. Gandhi?" asked Frances.

"Mohandas has been a family friend for a long time. My father knew him from Porbandar where they grew up together. They were young friends. Mohandas has always kept in touch with him, my father, and that is how I have come to know him too."

"That is interesting. I sometimes marvel at how small the world is," said Frances.

Amar nodded.

"Unfortunately, everybody needs Mohandas now, so much so that we get very little time to see him. He writes once or twice a year, but selfishly, I would like to enjoy more of his time. That's not going to be possible with this conference. Tonight for example, he'll be at a banquet with some of the leaders of the government. And now with this terrible incident at his lecture last night, I fear that I will see less of him."

Amar chuckled ruefully, though you could tell that there was part of him genuinely saddened by this inability to see more of his friend than he'd like.

"I can understand that," said Frances. "Mr. Gandhi seems like a wonderful man. Caring and considerate and friendly. It is no surprise to me that he is being eagerly pursued by all parties. And sadly, there is still only twenty four hours in each day for all of us."

Amar nodded.

"What can you do. It is an honor and privilege nevertheless, that he stays here in our home. I cannot ask for more than that."

Gita came into the living room carrying a tray with tea, teacups, cream and sugar and a small plate of biscuits. She lay it down in the middle of the table.

"This is tea grown in the area where we are from," she said.

"And where is that, not Porbandar, I didn't think they grew tea there?" asked Frances.

Gita nodded.

"You are right. This tea is from Nilgiri in Kerala. Nilgiri is the blue mountains close to where we are from. When Amar's father finished his training and education he moved his family to Thiruvananthapuram which is the capital city in Kerala. That is where we met."

"Fascinating. I'd love to try some of this tea," said Frances.

"It should be ready," said Gita. "I had it steeping for a few minutes already in the kitchen."

She poured a cup for Lady Marmalade and then for Alfred, her husband and everyone else. There was just enough for a cup for everyone. Frances poured cream and sugar in it, stirred it and tasted it. Gita looked at her for a response.

"It's very good," said Frances. "It has a floral scent and taste to it that is quite unusual."

Alfred nodded his appreciation as well. Gita smiled and nodded her head and then took her seat. Alfred took a biscuit from the plate and dunked it into his tea.

"Let us get down to business," said Amar. "You have been very patient with us, Frances. Now, how can we help you?"

Frances set her teacup down on the table in front of her and looked over at Amar and then to Sujay.

"I had come hoping to see Sujay or Mohandas. As you know, one of Mr. Gandhi's colleagues was shot dead last night after the lecture, and I'm helping the police determine who did it."

"Have they been able to come up with some suspects?" asked Sujay.

Frances shook her head.

"Not yet, but these things often take time. We have found several tickets from last night's event that were scattered around the general area where Mohandas was fielding questions, so we will know definitively who some of the audience was who were gathered around him."

"And how may we help?" asked Sujay.

"I wanted to get any more information from you about who you might think would want to harm Mohandas."

Amar looked up with a furrowed and worried brow.

"I thought the police felt the target was Ravi Meda?" asked Amar.

"Yes, that's what the police think at the moment. Personally, I think the bullets were meant for Mohandas."

"Really?"

Frances nodded.

"But why?" asked Amar.

It seems to me that Mohandas is a more likely target for a variety of reasons. He has a very high public profile and it seems from what Sujay has told me that he has received death threats in the past."

Amar turned and looked at Sujay.

"You have not said such things to me," he said.

Sujay looked down for a moment, and nodded his head slowly.

"Mohandas does not want to worry his close friends with this information. He did not want me telling you. He does not feel that it is important, only that it will get in the way of his important work."

"Well, if Mohandas doesn't think they are all that serious, then perhaps they aren't," said Amar, looking back at Lady Marmalade.

"I think, and I don't know Mohandas as well as the rest of you, that he is driven by his goal of Indian independence. I don't think he would want anything to derail that mission, especially death threats."

Amar sipped on his tea and leaned in to take a biscuit. He chewed it thoughtfully for a moment.

"I will defer to your expertise then," he said.

Frances nodded and smiled at him.

"If I might ask, Frances," said Sujay, "and I believe that the target of the shooter might have been Mohandas, but it seems that the bullets hit Ravi squarely, which would suggest that maybe they were meant for him after all?"

"I know, but there could be any number of reasons why the shooter didn't manage to hit Mohandas. The gun might have jumped awkwardly in his hand causing him to miss his mark. He might be a new shooter and thus inexperienced. He might have been jostled or it might have been as simple as him mistaking Ravi for Mohandas if he was a hired gun."

Sujay furrowed his brow.

"You think it might have been a hired gunman?" asked Amar.

Frances shrugged and looked down at her teacup.

"Not particularly, but one must always keep in mind several possibilities until one is more certain of the motive."

Frances picked up her tea and took another sip and then placed the teacup back down on its saucer on the table.

"But Mohandas is such a sweet man. A gentle man. Why would anyone want to hurt him?" asked Gita, looking at Frances. Frances looked over at Sujay.

"I think Sujay has some of those answers, and that's why I wanted to speak with you today, Sujay. These letters that Mohandas has received, what reasons do they give for threatening his life."

"There are three main groups who seem particularly upset at Gandhi for one reason or another," said Sujay. "The first, and perhaps surprisingly, are amongst certain Hindu factions. They believe that Gandhi is kowtowing to other groups and they're especially upset by his dogmatic approach to non-violence which they feel will leave Hindus weak."

Sujay took out a piece of paper from his pocket. It looked like a telegram.

"I received this telegram earlier today, after I had requested the names of the most recent writers of the death threats against Mohandas."

Sujay opened it up.

"There is a Hindu faction that has been particularly vocal in their opposition to Mohandas. They are led by Nathuram Vinayakrao Godse."

Frances listened intently.

"None of his names begin with the letter P," she said.

Sujay nodded.

"That is true, but very often we go by nicknames. I do not know his nickname but it might be worth looking into. The second group is a group of Sikhs who feel that Mohandas is not giving their religion or culture enough recognition or attention. The main advocate amongst them is Pitambar Singh. He has written of his displeasure with Mohandas before."

"There's a name that starts with P," said Frances.

"Why is that important?" asked Amar.

"Sorry, I thought you might have known. Ravi's last words to Sujay, Mohandas and I were 'Indian...p', and we're not quite sure what that meant, though I think we all agree that he was either trying to say 'Indian person' or 'Indian' and then trying to say the first name of the shooter."

"But how do you know that these men were at the lecture last night?" asked Amar.

"We don't. But if they were, then we have something to go on. If they weren't then we have three names that we can omit."

Sujay waited, looking from Amar to Frances and back again. Amar nodded his head but didn't say anything further.

"What was the third group?" asked Frances.

"There are some Muslims who are upset with Gandhi too. They have written of their displeasure more than once. Their basic dissatisfaction with Mohandas is that they do not believe he represents their ideas with sufficient, how shall I put this, vigor."

Frances nodded and kept her gaze on Sujay as he looked down at the telegram in his hand.

"The last letter, and I think all of them from the Muslim contingent were written by Parvez Dada."

"Hmm," said Lady Marmalade, "another man with a first name beginning with the letter P."

"If I might, my Lady. It seems strange to me that all these men would write letters and sign their names to them if they were really planning on killing Mr. Gandhi. I wouldn't have thought that very wise," said Alfred.

Frances looked at Alfred and then down at her teacup and picked it up and took a long sip. She held the teacup in both hands and turned to him again.

"You're quite right, but then I have often found crime to be quite unreasonable and unwise. You'd be surprised at how often a criminal will forget about some incriminating piece of evidence they had left weeks or months, sometimes even years before. And thank the Lord for that too. It makes my job, and dare I say the policemen's job that much easier."

Alfred nodded and tipped the rest of the tea into his mouth. He had been cradling the teacup all the while. He then put the empty cup and saucer on the table in front of them, and looked over at Frances.

"Yes, I suppose that would be quite possible," he said.

"You see, Alfred," said Frances, "very often crime is committed in the heat of the moment with the pulsing of passion coursing through the veins. Quite literally criminals have often lost their minds briefly during the committing of such acts. Reasonable and reasoning men don't commit crimes. Crimes are usually the last resort of an unreasonable or impassioned mind."

Alfred nodded.

"Quite. I guess it is difficult for me to imagine losing my faculties to such a degree."

"And that is exactly why catching them is sometimes harder than we imagine. Because we don't believe the depths of irrationality or anger or even hatred that some men, and dare I say women, will go to when caught up in the heat of criminal madness."

Frances turned to look at Sujay.

"I wonder if you've been able to determine the names of those two poor men who were murdered at Dharasana?" she asked him.

Sujay smiled a big, broad smile and his white teeth were as white and straight as a new parliament building.

"I did," he said. "I thought you might be interested in that, as we had spoken about it last night. I asked for that information from our people in New Delhi."

Sujay looked back down at his telegram.

"The two men who died from their injuries as the salt works were Chetan Panchal and Ajit Pai."

Frances nodded and pursed her lips.

"That makes four names staring with P."

"But those men are dead," said Amar.

"Yes, Amar, I know that, but the rest of their families are not. Sujay, do you know if either of these men had brothers or sons who would be old enough to commit such a crime?" asked Frances.

Sujay shook his head.

"I'm afraid I do not have the information, Frances," he said. "But I will request it for you."

Frances nodded and drank the rest of her tea.

"How safe do you think Mohandas is now that there's already been one attempt on his life?" asked Chandra, looking genuinely worried.

Frances looked at her and smiled.

"I think he is probably safer than he was before the attempt on his life, if it was in fact an attempt on his life as I suspect."

"How can that be?" asked Ajeet. "Surely they now know they didn't get him so they'll want to finish the job."

Frances shook her head and put her empty teacup back down on the table.

"No, I don't think so. You see, they had their one opportunity and they messed it up. There is too much focus on Mohandas now. The papers will be writing about this for the rest of the week, if not for as long as he's here in London, and the police will be investigating thoroughly. No, if I were the shooter I'd be hunkering down and trying to keep a very low profile."

Ajeet nodded.

"That is not to say that Mohandas shouldn't take extra precautions, but I truly believe that it would be very unlikely for anyone to try another attempt within the next few weeks."

Frances looked at Sujay.

"You will ensure that there is extra security for Mohandas, won't you?"

"I will try my best. Mohandas has already declined an offer from Scotland Yard for a policeman to follow him around, and Ravi and I were not security men for Mohandas, he doesn't believe in that. He thinks it will send the wrong message."

"I understand, but please do try and get him an extra body just to watch over him," said Frances.

Sujay nodded and smiled. Frances stood up and Alfred followed.

"You have all been very kind to me this afternoon by inviting me into your home for such a wonderful meal. I only wish it was under happier circumstances," said Frances.

Amar, Sujay and Ajeet stood up. Amar offered Frances his hand which she shook. She did the same with Sujay and Ajeet, as did Alfred.

"It is our pleasure. I hope you will get the man who did this to Ravi, regardless of whether it was meant for Mohandas or not, Ravi deserves justice," said Amar.

Frances nodded and smiled and said her final goodbyes, then she and Alfred left the Bhandaris' home and walked to the car. Faces reappeared peeking from behind curtains and around the corners of windows as she and Alfred left for home.

Thirteen

At just after four p.m. with her belly still comfortably full from the delicious Bhandari food, Frances and Alfred pulled up in front of Scotland Yard. It was a quiet Tuesday afternoon and as they entered the old gray government building there was not much going on inside.

A constable at the front desk looked up from the paper he was reading. He was an old man with gray wisps of hair and a haggard, drawn face, lined with wrinkles that wrote of hard times. He looked to be in his seventies though he was probably at least a decade or more younger.

"What is it?" he asked Frances as she walked up to him smiling.

His face was the color of cremated ash and he had dark sagging circles below his eyes. Looking at him you thought his eyes might roll right out of their sockets at any moment. He rested his head against his right hand. He was a man who had forgotten why he was alive, or perhaps he had just this morning woken up in a body so old and sick he was hoping to kick the bucket.

"Good afternoon," said Frances, her voice was bright and happy, which only made the old man feel worse. "I'm here to see Inspector Davison."

"And you are?"

His voice was as slow and monotonous as the unpleasant scratching of a needle at the end of a gramophone record.

"I am Lady Marmalade and this is Alfred Donahue. He'll be expecting us."

Lady Marmalade's voice had not lost its cheeriness, though her manner had become more professional. The constable got up as slow and with so much obvious effort that you might think he carried the weight of the world on his shoulders. He lumbered off slowly with a hunched back and a big sigh that lasted as long as a tire losing air.

He returned several minutes later, just when Frances had started thinking about sitting down, followed by Sgt. Pearce. Pearce walked out of the main door that separated reception from the rest of the offices and held out his hand.

"Good afternoon," he said, "we've been expecting you. Please come in."

His voice was rich, deep and warm like honey poured over hot stones. Pearce smiled and shook hands firmly and his mustache was immaculately neat.

He turned around and led them through the door he had just exited. Alfred and Frances followed him to the end of the hall where they turned left into a small office. Behind the desk sat Inspector Davison. He stood up and shook their hands without much warmth or friendship, but because it was expected.

"Please sit down," he said, waving his hands to the two moderately cushioned chairs that lay empty across from his desk. Pearce took a harder, wooden chair that was off in the corner and he carried it up to the side of Davison's desk, but sat closer to Alfred.

"So good of you to see us, Inspector," said Frances, trying to grease the dry cog of bureaucracy.

Davison nodded his head and grunted. Pearce twirled his mustache and then got out his notebook. There was a folder on

Davison's desk, off to his left and a desk calendar which had plenty of scribbles on it which Frances couldn't read upside down. Primarily because the penmanship was worse than a surgeon's. To Frances' right, against the wall, stood a wooden filing cabinet and on top of it was a picture of a younger Davison with his bride. It was a wedding photograph. Next to that was a more recent photograph with a thicker Davison and heavier bride and two young girls who Frances thought to be about ten or eleven. Close in age to be sure, slim and plain looking.

"Lovely family," said Frances. "Your daughters are very pretty."

Sometimes she told little white lies. This was one of those occasions. She could tell that Davison was still prickly from having been put in his place by her husband.

Davison looked over at the two photographs in their wooden frames on his wooden filing cabinet, and a smile almost creased his cheeks. He nodded.

"Jenny and Margaret are good girls," he said.

He looked back at Frances and stared at her for a while not saying anything. Frances decided to break the silence.

"I don't think you've been formally introduced to my butler, Alfred Donahue."

Alfred leaned over the desk and offered his hand which was begrudgingly shook.

"We had a wonderful lunch with the Bhandaris," said Frances.

"Who?" he asked, looking over at Pearce.

"That's the family that Mr. Gandhi is staying with in Ealing," he said.

"Right," grunted Davison nodding his head. His thick ham hock hands were knitted together resting on the desk calendar.

"I mentioned it earlier to you," said Frances. Davison didn't answer. He seemed to be in a foul mood thought Frances, but she persevered.

"I was hoping to see Mohandas, but of course he wasn't there. I thought there was an off chance that he might have come back from the conference to enjoy lunch with his hosts, but I imagine that the conference is taking up much of his time. In any event, Sujay Patel was there. You'll remember him from last night."

Davison nodded his head.

"He had intuitively determined what I might have come asking, and so he had the names of some men who might be worth looking into further as possible suspects for this crime."

"I see," said Davison, "and who might they be?"

"Sujay mentioned that there were three groups who were quite dissatisfied with Gandhi's approach to independence. Hindus, Muslims and Sikhs. The Hindus are upset because some of them think he's turning them into pushovers. The Muslims and Sikhs are both feeling disenfranchised."

Davison nodded again.

"Did he give you some names of anyone who had written threatening letters?"

"Yes, he did," said Frances. "A Hindu by the name of Nathuram Vinayakrao Godse, a Muslim by the name of Parvez Dada and a Sikh by the name of Pitambar Singh."

"That's a good start," said Davison. He put his left meaty hand on the folder that was next to him. Then he thought better of it and knitted it back together with his other hand. Then he looked back at Frances and frowned.

"You know this Gandhi chap has refused our help," said Davison and he sounded quite upset by it.

"What do you mean?" asked Frances.

"We've offered, at great expense to the taxpayers I might add, to have one of our finest look out for him. To offer some additional security. He said he won't have it."

"Did he say why?"

Davison nodded.

"It wouldn't set the right tone, he said."

"If I might argue on his behalf Inspector, it is unlikely that the shooter would try again so soon. That would be madness."

"It surely would, but it has happened before, and I'll be damned if I lose someone on my watch, even if he's not one of us."

Frances wasn't sure how to take that last comment, so she ignored it.

"Then the best we can do is to ensure that we catch the murderer as soon as we can."

Davison looked like he might say something, but he didn't. He looked over at the folder instead and then slid it in front of himself.

"Something that strikes me as odd. You say that this Sujay gave you the name of three men who had written threatening letters to Gandhi, isn't that right?"

Frances nodded.

"And you think that one of these three men would, after having identified himself in such a way, decide to shoot Ravi, or Gandhi in public?"

Frances nodded again.

"It is possible, Inspector. I agree that it would be unusual, but you must know that criminals are very often incriminating themselves, and if these letters had been written months ago, they might have forgotten about it."

"It is possible, Inspector," said Pearce, "we've seen this sort of thing before."

Davison looked over at his sergeant and barely nodded. He opened up the folder that was in front of him and it contained several pages of handwriting.

"What is that?" asked Frances.

"This contains the names and ticket numbers of all the tickets that were bought for the lecture last night. Unfortunately they're not in alphabetical order, but rather numerical order according to ticket numbers."

"Perhaps we can look at the tickets that you found last night or this morning scattered around the crime scene," offered Frances.

"That's what I was thinking," said Davison.

Davison slid open a desk drawer on his left side and pulled out the six tickets that were stored in there. He put them on his desk, to the right of the open folder and took some time to arrange them in numerical order. He looked at Pearce.

"We have six tickets, Sergeant. In numerical order they are 0007, 0031, 0055, 0112, 0193 and 0245."

He looked over at Pearce who had just finished writing them down. Davison looked back over at the pages containing the ticket numbers and the corresponding name. He dragged a squat finger down the column that contained the ticket numbers until he got to 0007. He drew his finger horizontally across until he got the corresponding name.

"Ticket 0007 was bought by Bijay Panchal."

"Another P," said Frances.

Davison looked up while Pearce scribbled in his notebook.

"I beg your pardon?"

"Oh, sorry Inspector, that's just the fifth Indian name I've come across today with a letter P starting either the first or last name. You'll recall that Ravi's last words to me were 'Indian...p'."

"Yes, I remember that. If you'll just let me finish this up, then we can discuss your amusement of it at length."

Frances smiled at him sweetly. He frowned and looked back at his papers and continued dragging his index finger down to the next ticket number."

"Ticket number 0031 belongs to Amir Pai. "He looked up at Frances. "That's a sixth name for you."

She smiled and nodded at him. Davison continued on.

"Ticket 0055 belongs to Patrick O'Malley. A seventh name with P for Lady Marmalade."

Frances was no longer smiling, she looked at the papers in front of Davison. Though they were upside down the handwriting was legible and she could make it out.

"Ticket number 0112 belongs to, um, Molapo Mathibeli."

Davison struggled in getting his tongue around the African's name, but he got it eventually with a bit of help from Frances.

"Ticket 0193 is Vivienne Eastwood's, and ticket 0245 belongs to Ryan Webb."

Davison looked up at Frances. If I recall, none of those names you gave me earlier are related to these six tickets. Davison looked back over at Sergeant Pearce. Pearce flipped through a page or two of notes and shook his head.

"No, Lady Marmalade gave us Parvez Dada, Nathuram Godse and Pitambar Singh."

Davison looked back over at Frances and smiled like the cat who had caught a mouse. Frances was not amused.

"Yes, that's quite right, but you hadn't let me finish, Inspector. Sujay had also found out the names of the two men who died from injuries sustained at the hands of the British at Dharasana Salt Works."

"Very well, what are their names."

Frances looked at Davison and smiled more broadly than he had earlier.

"That's were it gets more interesting," she said. "The names of the two men were Ajit Pai and Chetan Panchal. I believe that you just mentioned both those last names." Frances looked over at Pearce. "Am I correct?"

Pearce nodded.

"She is, Inspector. Ticket 0031 belongs to Amir Pai who could be related to Ajit Pai and ticket 0007 belongs to Bijay Panchal a possible relation to Chetan Panchal."

"I think, Inspector," said Frances, "that you would do well to interview both of those men. And I believe those names are male names. Of course you'll be interviewing all six as I'm sure they will all have something helpful to tell about the evening's events."

"Of course," said Davison, "I am well aware of how to investigate a murder."

"I didn't mean to sound unkind, Inspector, I am only here to help. We are on the same team and I would never presume to tell you how to do your job."

Frances was trying to offer an olive branch in the hopes that they might find some no man's land in order to better work together on this case.

"Very well," said Davison, "we might as well look at the three other names you've brought up and see if they are on this list."

"Thank you, Inspector. The first fellow is Nathuram Godse."

Davison started on the first page and dragged his thick finger down the column containing the names. He worked methodically through the first, second, third page, coming up empty. He plodded on. He was just about to give up when he found the name he was looking for on the last page.

"Ah, here he is," said Davison. "Nathuram Godse, ticket number 0279."

Davison looked up at Frances.

"I will be speaking with him too."

Frances smiled.

"The other two were Parvez Dada and Pitambar Singh."

"One at a time please. I can't keep two of these names in my mind at the same time."

"Let's start with Parvez Dada then," said Frances.

Davison once again scoured the pages with the ticket entries, dragging his finger down the column, slowly and surely. He came up empty with Parvez and he also came up empty with Pitambar Singh.

"May I have a look please, Inspector," said Frances. "Can't hurt to have a second set of eyes."

Davison turned the folder to face Frances and she took her time to carefully review all the names, but the inspector had not missed any. There was no Parvez Dada or Pitambar Singh on the registry.

Frances turned the folder around and pushed it back towards Davison. He took it and closed it and lay his big meaty hands on top of it as if that was the end of that.

"Well, I think that was a job well done. We have somewhere to go," said Frances.

"But Parvez and Pitambar were not on that list ,were they?" asked Davison, somewhat pleased with himself.

Frances shook her head.

"No, they weren't. You did a very thorough job of it, Inspector," she said, and she almost felt like standing up and patting him on the head like the good boy he was

But she didn't. She didn't need to make things worse between them.

"But in fairness, Inspector," she continued, "they might still be here in London and they might have snuck into the lecture last night. I wouldn't have thought that would be particularly hard to do."

Davison looked at her with a blank expression on her face. His fingers knitted together like unruly roots. He didn't say much for some time, and during that time Frances continued to hold his stare with kind eyes.

"You could be right," he said. "I'll make inquiries with the Home Office."

Frances nodded.

"I would do that."

Davison and Frances seemed locked in a stare, much like rams caught amongst each other's horns. Finally, Davison broke it first and looked over at Pearce.

"Give me the seven names of the men with a letter P in either their first or last name."

Pearce licked his index finger and pulled a couple of pages down from his notebook and looked over them. His eyes moved up and down.

"Pitambar Singh and Parvez Dada whom we aren't sure attended the lecture. Amir Pai with ticket number 0031..."

"I don't need the ticket numbers, Pearce," said Davison.

Pearce nodded.

"Right," he said. "Bijay Panchal and Patrick O'Malley. They were all at the lecture, then Frances mentioned the two deceased men, Ajit Pai and Chetan Panchal."

Pearce looked at Frances and smiled, then he looked at Davison. Davison was looking at Frances and she returned his gaze after smiling at Pearce.

"Well, two of those men can hardly be considered suspects seeing that they're dead. Of the remaining five, Lady Marmalade, who do you think did it?" asked Davison.

"Oh, Inspector," said Frances, "I wouldn't pretend to know who did it this early on. Though I think we have a good list to start with. Certainly Amir and Bijay have a strong motive if in fact either one of them or the both of them shot Ravi. Revenge is a very strong motive. Though I wouldn't put the case to rest yet. This Patrick chap might have something interesting to say, and

I'd suggest that we take a good look through the whole list, see if any of them have criminal backgrounds. Wouldn't you think that would be a good place to start?"

Davison smiled at Frances but it wasn't the smile of friends.

"You would make a very fine policewoman," he said, "if we allowed policewomen amongst our ranks."

Frances smiled at him.

"That's kind of you to say," she said, "and you'll get your policewomen soon enough. I understand there are currently Metropolitan Women Police Patrols, are there not?"

"Oh yes, quite. However, they have limited powers of arrest and aren't fully integrated with us. They take on womanly responsibilities, help out with juveniles and prostitutes. Nothing very serious."

"Perhaps more serious than sitting behind a fancy desk pushing papers around."

Alfred had to stifle a laugh, and coughed instead. Pearce raised an eyebrow and twirled his mustache, trying to keep the corners of his mouth from smiling.

"Is there anything else you'd like to help me with, Frances?" asked Davison, dropping formal address.

"Did you find anything of note in any of the other names on the list?" she asked.

He didn't open up the folder again but he shook his head.

"I haven't looked yet. But rest assured that I will. We're generally very thorough here at Scotland Yard."

"I have no doubt. What about that police whistle I found for you? Any word on who it might have belonged to?"

"We're looking into it," he said.

Frances smiled at him and then stood up. She offered her hand and he stood and shook it.

"You've been very kind, Inspector," she said. "I'll be certain to let the Commissioner know just how kind you've been the next time I see him."

Davison didn't like the tone in her voice for there was nothing to like about it. She held his gaze steady for a moment just letting him know she hadn't appreciated his tone either.

"Good day, Frances," he said.

Frances turned to face Sergeant Pearce and he shook her hand warmly. He had a mischievous twinkle in his eye and a smile on his lips.

"I'm sure we'll get this chap with your help, Lady Marmalade," he said.

"I have every faith in Scotland Yard," she said, though what she meant was that she had every faith in him specifically.

Pearce led them out and once they were in the reception area he placed a gentle hand on her shoulder. Frances turned to look at him.

"Don't mind Davison too much, he's one of the old boys, and he has a bit of difficulty adjusting to a civilian, especially a woman, if you'll pardon me for saying it, telling him what to do."

"Not at all, I'm sure he's looking forward to his upcoming retirement," she said, hiding the veiled threat exceedingly well.

"I hope not for a few more years, my Lady," said Pearce, "he has been a terrific mentor, and he really is one of the best here."

Frances smiled and nodded. She understood what Pearce was trying to suggest.

"I have no doubt of that," she said, "and please call me Frances."

With that, she and Alfred walked out of the main reception area of Scotland Yard and out into the warm, later afternoon sun. It was coming on five and many people were slowly making their way home. They climbed into the car and Alfred turned to her and smiled softly.

"You find him difficult to deal with, my Lady?" he asked.

Frances nodded.

"You have no idea, Alfred. I fear my tongue is bleeding from all the biting I've done to it."

"Perhaps though, as Sergeant Pearce said, he is a good copper after all."

"Yes, I imagine he is, and that is what will spare him from me speaking with the Commissioner about him."

Alfred started the car.

"I do believe, my Lady, that he will come around once he finds out how helpful you can be."

Frances looked over at Alfred as he turned out from the parking space and headed on into the traffic.

"For my sanity, I hope you're right," she said.

Fourteen

There's a pub in London's East End called the Bare Knuckles. It got its name honestly. In 1734 James Figg regained his title as the English bare knuckle boxing champion when he won against Ned Sutton at the back of this old ale house which then became known as the Bare Knuckles.

It's the sort of place that ladies don't visit, whether with a small l or big L, and women aren't welcome except for the prostitutes who can be found outside milling around like stray cats looking to rub up against one of the drunk exiting patrons.

Most nights, at least most weekend nights some sort of bare knuckles fight will erupt between two drunk and disorderly patrons. They're escorted out where it sometimes carries on into the street.

This pub is the sort of place where the working poor spend their hard earned money on cheap beer and loose women. Where it's hard to tell if the stains upon the wooden floors are from urine, beer or vomit, and if truth be told it's likely to be a combination of all three.

And it's busy, this ale house. Almost packed to the rafters, full of men smelling musty and sweaty and dirty. Men of all colors and sizes, the only thing they have in common is the paucity of their earnings and their quickness to temper.

In the corner, squashed up against a wall are two men drinking a third beer for the night, and it won't be their last.

They're squashed into two chairs with a small square wooden table between them. They're so close that their knees are almost touching.

It's warm outside on this Thursday evening in September of 1931, but it's at least a few degrees warmer inside the public house. Men are bumping up against the table and beer splashes down the sides of glass mugs. The sound is a dull roar, and it's hard to hear anything especially as the two men try to talk to each other.

Their faces are glowing with sweat and their cream colored shirts are damp and stained. Their wool pants are too hot but they don't notice. The first man is taking a big swig of his ale. The light inside is incompetent, worse yet, it's useless. A candle upon each table, and there aren't that many tables about, would brighten the place up.

"How could you miss?" he said.

"Easy when you bumped into me," came the reply.

The two men lock eyes over their beers. A rowdy patron stumbles back and knocks into the table and into the first man, spilling some of his beer down his shirt. The man at the tables stands up. He's short and, not muscular.

"You stupid bastard," he says.

The stumbler turns around and grins at him. He's one of the few happy drunks, or so it seems, that find their way into this place by mistake.

"Sorry, mate," he says, and offers the short man a second, full beer in one of his two hands. The short man takes it and nods, but he's still upset.

"Watch where you're banging," he says, and he sits down. He now has two mugs of beer in front of him. One is half empty, that's the way he sees it. The other is the full one just offered to him. His tall friend looks at him.

"That's a clever trick," he said.

"Don't you start, you botched the shooting," said the short man.

"You should have done it yourself. You were the one who thought we should have killed him earlier."

The short man nods his head and takes a long drink from his fresh beer. He wipes his mouth with his free hand.

"And we should have, that way we wouldn't be in this situation now, would we?"

It's a rhetorical question that he doesn't need an answer to.

"Then why didn't you?"

"Because you talked me out of it. I wanted to kill him in India but you were opposed to that. I should have just followed through with it then. Would have saved myself a whole pile of problems."

The short man's friend looks at his companion through steady, hard eyes. He's as blank as polished steel. He sips his beer more carefully.

"I'm going to have to finish this up myself I guess," said the short man.

"I guess so," said the companion. "My heart's no longer in it. We shouldn't have been carrying this grudge this long to begin with."

He sips more of his beer. The stumbling man is swaying and wobbling, it looks like he might come back knocking up against the table again. That's sure to set off the short man. And that's the problem with him, thinks his companion, he's too sentimental and emotional. Everything is an insult. He's too hotheaded and that's what's got them both into trouble.

They've botched up the one attempt at murdering Gandhi and now he wants to take another go at. That's not just dumb, it's utter madness. The police are investigating, they've Scotland Yard on the case and he thinks now is the time to try again. If he hadn't been so excitable and anxious at the time, he wouldn't have bumped into him, causing him to miss his shot, and they'd be in here celebrating, or probably in a fancier establishment.

This was going to be the end of their relationship, but he still had to keep an eye on him, because he was liable to do something crazy.

"Yes," said the short man, "I'm going to have to do this myself. First opportunity I get."

"I think you should think about it when you've got a clearer head."

"I've never felt so sure of anything in my life."

And that's part of the problem. The arrogance that surely will be the downfall of them both. The tall companion stares at the table and then at his beer. It's time to get going soon, he figures, right after this beer. He drinks from it a little more deeply, and looks over at the short man across from him. His two beers are in competition now as if it's a race to see which one will get drained quickest. Both mugs are half empty, and even in this dimly lit hovel of an ale house, the short man's tall companion can see the bloodshot eyes of the short man.

Then the next thing that happens is stumbling man banging into their table again. Both of the short man's mugs of beer spill large tongues of the liquid onto the table, and it quickly spills onto the short man's pants.

The short man gets up quickly and knocks the table over, but not before grabbing one of his mugs of beer. His companion was expecting this, and he quickly slid his chair back as far as it would go. The table doesn't land on his lap, rather it thuds heavily against the wet and musky smelling floor.

The short man takes a swing at the stumbler's head, but the stumbling man is wobbling backwards and the short man is too drunk to compensate quickly enough. The mug in the short man's hand glances off the stumbler's eyebrow but doesn't break the skin.

The stumbler's two friends reach for the short man and they start fighting with him. It's a big mess. Clenched fists are flying everywhere, mostly glancing off hair and shoulders, but some are landing solidly on the short man's face. He's taken to being defensive.

They knock him down and start with their boots to his face and ribs. That's when his companion stands up. He decides he's had enough of this. He takes one of the men and brings his head down onto the edge of the table and knocks him out cold. The second fellow he makes use of the man's momentum and drives him head first into the wall where he then proceeds to slide down to the floor and collapse partially on his friend already lying down there. The companion slips his foot behind the stumbler and swings his forehand towards from him and makes contact with the stumbler's throat and he trips over the companion's foot and collapses on top of his two friends.

The companion reaches down and picks up his short friend and helps carry him out into what seems like a cool evening. The short man is stumbling and clutching at his broken nose. He's pretty banged up but he'll survive. This is not the first time that the companion has had to help his friend out of a pickle. But he starts to think it might be the last time.

Fifteen

Sergeant Pearce had telephoned Lady Marmalade earlier in the day to let her know that he and Davison were going to pick up Amir Pai and Bijay Panchal. They had received word that they were at a men's hostel. Pearce wanted to know if Lady Marmalade was interested in joining them for the interview, so long as she allowed Davison and Pearce to do the talking.

Pearce hadn't said as much, but Frances had the suspicion that her being there was likely Pearce's idea, and that keeping her quiet was Davison's. Nevertheless, it was an opportunity she wasn't going to turn down. Panchal and Pai were both at the lecture and both of them had motive to injure Gandhi or Ravi. Ravi had after all been involved in the Dharasana Salt Works' march and could be someone they wanted revenge against.

Alfred drove her off to the police station and they arrived shortly after two in the afternoon. It was Wednesday, September the 9th. A sunny, warm summer day as she and Alfred stepped out onto the side street and made their way up towards the main entrance to Scotland Yard.

The whole day seemed to be a repeat of the day before. Only they were a couple of hours early, but the same bored and bedraggled constable was at the reception desk. He pretended like he didn't know them, or perhaps he was that dimwitted that he didn't recall them from the day before, Frances couldn't tell.

And just like the day before, he came back out followed by Sergeant Pearce. Pearce was just as chipper and warm as he usually was. He shook their hands warmly and led them through the door and down the hallway. He turned and spoke to Frances.

"I must urge you to let Davison do the talking, he's adamant about that, and he can get easily flustered if he's interrupted during an interrogation. I'm sure I'll hardly be saying anything myself."

Frances nodded good naturedly, though she knew that being quiet was hardly within the realm of possibility, especially when there was an opportunity to interview potential suspect. But then again, if Davison asked all the right questions, there would be no need for her to speak at all.

Pearce stopped outside Davison's office and knocked on the open door. Frances and Alfred stood out in the hallway with Pearce. A constable came by and they stepped aside.

"We're ready when you are, Inspector," said Pearce.

Davison got up from his desk and walked over to the doorway. He stopped for a moment, considering whether or not he should wear a jacket. He decided against it. His sleeves were rolled up and his thick, hairy forearms were showing. He wore gray suspenders over his shoulders which held up his pants.

Davison came out and greeted Frances and Alfred with what was quite a warm handshake coming from him.

"Please let me do the talking," he said, and Frances nodded.

They followed Davison and Pearce as they marched off at a good pace down the end of this hall and then taking a left and then a right down a couple of others. Eventually they came to an interview room where a constable was stationed outside. The constable moved aside as Davison got there.

Davison looked through the window on the door and grinned.

"Good," he said, "looks like he's been stewing a bit."

Davison turned around and faced Frances, Alfred and Pearce.

"Well, let's wrap up this bit of business then," he said.

Frances smiled at him, but she wasn't convinced. If she'd learned anything at all about crime and the solving of it, it was that arrogance was your surest enemy to the truth.

Davison opened up the door and walked in followed by Pearce, Frances and then Alfred. The young Indian man inside looked up at them from his seat behind a small table. He seemed tall and lanky sitting there and his ankles and wrists were chained. There were two chairs on the opposite side of him which Davison and Pearce sat down in.

Pearce opened up his notebook, pulled out his monocle and attached it to his eye. He started flipping through the pages until he found what he was looking for. Davison looked at the young man, staring at him intently. The Indian looked down at the table and slumped in his chair. Davison kept staring at him for a while, a long while, and Frances had an urge to start the interview already, but she bit her tongue.

"Bijay Panchal," said Davison, spitting out the name as if it were distasteful and hot curry.

Panchal looked up at the inspector.

"Is that your name?" asked Davison.

Panchal nodded his head, slowly and surely.

"Son of Chetan Panchal?"

Panchal nodded his head again, just as slowly as he did the first time.

"What of it," said Panchal.

Davison leaned in across the table, his forearms, prickly with black hair, his fingers like interlaced sausages reaching towards the Indian.

"Your father is dead, is he not?"

Davison kept his gaze on the Indian, not letting it slip for even a moment.

"Killed by policeman like you," said Panchal, with hatred and anger balled up tight in his belly like a curled snake.

"That's right," said Davison, "and you're angry, and you hate me."

Panchal looked up at Davison again. His eyes flashed flames of anger but he controlled himself.

"I do not know you," he said.

"Just like you did not know the men who beat your father to death. Your cowardly father, who would not stand up for himself."

Panchal got up out of his chair faster than Frances thought he'd be capable of. He struggled to pull his hands up, but they were constricted by the chain around his waist. They barely made it up against his belly. His fingers stretched and curled towards Davison, he wanted to reach out and throttle the inspector.

"I'll kill you!" he yelled, and his voice carried loudly and angrily around the room.

Davison stood up and with this big meaty hand he pushed Panchal hard against his chest, pushing him back into his chair where he slid backwards and toppled over. Davison stood watching silently until Panchal slowly picked himself back up and pulled his chair towards the desk where he sat back down. He was breathing hard, and his eyes looked at Davison under a furrowed brow.

"Inspector," said Frances, "you'll catch more flies with honey than with vinegar."

She couldn't help herself. Even if Panchal were guilty of trying to assassinate Gandhi, or the murder of Ravi, she felt that the law, and British law especially should conduct itself with proper decorum.

Pearce looked over at her with a look of astonishment on his face. Davison didn't look round, but he did sit back down. He watched as Panchal got his breath back.

"Why are you here visiting my country?" asked Davison.

Panchal looked up at him, hate still hot in his eyes.

"To visit friends," he said.

"And why are you not staying with these friends then?"

"There isn't any space."

You could tell he was lying. The answers were too quick, too rehearsed. They had to have been practiced.

"I'll give you one last opportunity to tell me the truth," said Davison, "before I start getting mean. Where were you on Monday evening?"

"I was having dinner with friends."

"Tell me their names?"

"I forget."

Pearce was looking at Bijay and then at Davison. Davison was starting to get decidedly hot under the collar. He lifted his hand up and smacked it back down on the table hard. The table jumped and shook as did Bijay. Frances got quite the shock too.

"I can make your life a living hell!" said Davison, with spittle erupting from his mouth as he spoke. "I can lock you up in here and throw away the key and there isn't anything that anybody can do about it!"

Davison got up and walked around the room and stood behind Bijay. The veins in his next stood out like ropes. Frances was worried that he was going to come unglued.

"Where were you on Monday night?" Davison asked again, his voice steady and measured, trying his best to reel himself in. Panchal didn't turn around to look at him.

"At friends," he said.

Davison wound his arm up behind and smashed his open hand against the back of Bijay's skull. It was a terrible thud and crack and left him dazed.

"Inspector!" said Frances, not willing to stand this sort of treatment any longer. "A word outside."

Her voice was cool and determined. Pearce's monocle dropped from his eye and dangled on its chain like a hangman. Davison looked at her with a hard face which softened quickly upon seeing the severity and sincerity written all over her face. Frances walked out the room and moments later Davison met her.

"Inspector," said Frances, with the crisp tone of authority. "I cannot stand and watch you abuse a criminal let alone a suspect..."

"But..."

Frances put her hand up.

"Let me finish."

Davison hung his head down and ground his teeth.

"Your prejudice towards Indians is apparent, but your abuse will not be tolerated. I am loath to use my title and authority, but if you continue with this course of action I will report this event to the commissioner, and I'm certain that come Monday you will no longer have a job. I am going to try and go in there and see if I can undo the damage you've done, and find anything of value. Is that understood?"

Davison looked up at her and nodded. He took in a deep breath through his nostrils and exhaled the same way. He ground his teeth some more and thought better of saying anything further and getting himself into more trouble.

Frances walked into the interview room and took what had been up until then, Davison's chair. Davison stood outside the interview room for a while and tried to compose himself.

"I hope you'll forgive the inspector," she said, smiling at Bijay, "he's been under a lot of stress, and we're dealing with a terrible loss at the moment."

Panchal didn't say anything for a moment.

"He didn't have to hit me," he said, whining.

France nodded.

"Quite right, and I can assure you, Mr. Panchal, that so long as I am here, there will be no further violence tolerated."

She looked over at Pearce and he nodded with great vigor.

"I am Lady Marmalade, and this is Sergeant Pearce. You can call me Frances."

Panchal smiled a very thin and tenuous smile and nodded at her.

"Thank you, I am Bijay Panchal and you can call me Bijay."

"Did they tell you why the brought you in, Bijay?"

Bijay shook his head.

"They said they wanted to ask me questions, but when I got in here they put me in these chains, and then he started asking me these questions just now."

Bijay looked up at Davison as he entered the room and then went and stood by Alfred, his hands across his chest.

"Well, I am here as a friend of Scotland Yard and of Mr. Gandhi's. I am certain that you are well aware that Mr. Gandhi is here in England at the moment."

Frances stopped and waited for Bijay. He nodded his head.

"And, as much as you might feel like you should lie to the police, it isn't going to be helpful. I am certain that when you think about it, you know why you are here, don't you, Bijay?"

Frances looked at Bijay and he looked down at his lap and fiddled with his fingers. He nodded just barely.

"So why do you think you are here, Bijay?" asked Frances in a very warm and grandmotherly tone.

He kept looking down at his fingers, fiddling with them as if they were something new he had just found. Davison was glaring at him from the wall, with his hands crossed in front of him and his face all upside down in a big frown. But he was quiet. He wanted his job and he was close enough to pension that he'd play very nice right now.

"Must be about something that happened at Mr. Gandhi's event," said Bijay, just sneaking a glance at Frances before looking back down in his lap.

"Yes, you're very perceptive, Bijay. Tell me what happened at Mr. Gandhi's lecture that might get the police involved?"

Frances was trying to lead him slowly to a waterhole, like you might do with a timid horse. Though Bijay didn't strike her as being timid as having to try regain his trust after Davison had torn one strip off him from one side and then the other.

"Someone was shot."

It was barely a whisper.

"Do you know who was shot, Bijay?"

Bijay shook his head.

"Well, it was one of Mr. Gandhi's colleagues. A man by the name of Ravi Meda. Do you know Mr. Meda?"

Bijay looked up at her and shook his head again.

"Not well. My father knew him."

"That's good, Bijay," said Frances. "The more honest you can be with us, the sooner you can get out of here. If you had nothing to do with it."

He looked at her through sad eyes.

"I swear, I had nothing to do with it. I didn't shoot Mr. Meda, I hardly even knew him."

Bijay was leaning in against the table, trying his best to show how sincere he was.

"Well, perhaps you can tell me what happened then," said Frances.

"Me and a friend were standing around Mr. Gandhi when I heard this shot. Two shots, and we just ran out of there. I didn't wait to see what happened. I just ran away."

"Who is your friend?"

Bijay glanced down, and then back up at Frances.

"Amir Pai. The police brought him in with me today."

"Now you and Amir have both lost fathers, correct?"

Bijay nodded.

"Our fathers were beaten by the British at Dharasana. It was a peaceful march, my father was not a violent man. He never even laid a finger on me."

Bijay looked at Frances and his eyes were wet. A tear rolled down his one cheek.

"I'm very sorry for your loss, and Amir's," she said, with kindness and genuine compassion.

"My father just wanted a free India. He didn't hate the British, he just wanted us to be able to govern ourselves."

Bijay looked away.

"I can understand that," said Frances. "As hard as it may be to believe you have a lot of sympathetic ears here in England too."

He looked at her furtively and then dabbed his eye into his shoulder and then the other eye into the other shoulder.

"Help me understand, Bijay, why you were there to see Mr. Gandhi. I can imagine that you must have a lot of anger towards the British and Mr. Gandhi especially."

Bijay shook his head, and looked at Frances.

"Amir and me met through one of Mr. Gandhi's friends. He thought it would be helpful for us to perhaps become friends as we had both lost fathers. And we did, for the past year or more, we've been very close. Mr. Gandhi came to visit us shortly after we had been introduced to each other. He had come to visit both families. I couldn't stand the sight of him. I spat at him and I cursed him and said some very angry things to him. Same with Amir."

"And you wanted him to pay for your pain," said Frances.

"Yes, at the beginning. I wanted him to hurt like I was hurting. But being angry at him, and saying what I said to him, it didn't make the pain go away. It made it worse. And recently I had received a letter from Mr. Gandhi, so did Amir, and in it he apologized for what happened and how he had no idea something like that was going to happen. How he would have taken my father's place if he had known. At the end of the letter he said he hoped that one day I'd be able to forgive him. That my father had forgiven the British..."

Bijay choked on his words and tears fell from his eyes. He swallowed hard, trying hard to stifle the tears.

"How did he know your father had forgiven the British for what they had done?" asked Frances.

Bijay coughed and dabbed his eyes on his shoulders again.

"Mr. Gandhi said that the doctor who was present and who had treated the wounds of the protestors had heard my father say that he forgave them. He told the doctor to tell his family to forgive them too. So I came here to tell Mr. Gandhi that I had forgiven him. That both Amir and I had forgiven him, and how much better it had made us feel."

"You had come all this way just to tell him that you forgave him?" asked an incredulous Pearce.

Bijay nodded.

"It cost a lot of money, but we had both worked hard this past year to save up. We have the full support of our community and families. Everyone was behind us. We even had a few extra pounds we were going to donate."

Frances looked at him and felt his authenticity. Though he had a good motive, he had somehow managed to overcome the pain without resorting to revenge. A rare, but beautiful bird that helped the spirit soar above man's petty dealings.

"If you came in the spirit of forgiveness, why didn't you tell the police you were there? Surely you must have known that the police would be looking for witnesses?" asked Frances.

Bijay looked up at her and smile a thin wisp of smile from his thin lips.

"The British police had just a year ago beaten my father for nothing more than peacefully marching. I have come to forgive Mr. Gandhi and them, but I have not yet forgotten."

Bijay kept his gaze steady with Frances' and then looked at Pearce.

"I hope though, now that you're here, that you will help us try and determine who it was who killed Mr. Meda?" asked Frances.

Bijay nodded.

"Can you tell us about anything that seemed strange about the group you were with while you waited to speak with Mr. Gandhi?"

Bijay looked off to the side of the room for a moment and then turned back to look at Frances.

"Everyone seemed quite well behaved as we waited for our turn, even though this one African kept talking on and on with Mr. Gandhi about how the Africans should be considered equal partners with the whites and Indians of South Africa. Mr. Gandhi agreed, and said he had regretted his earlier stance when he was just starting his civil rights movement in South Africa. Eventually it seemed that the Africans were happy with Mr. Gandhi's apology and stance, when this Englishman started shouting nasty things about Mr. Gandhi and Indians in general. That's when the shots went off."

Pearce popped his monocle back in, wet his fingers and twirled his mustache. Then he flipped back and forth in his notebook a bit.

"Did this Englishmen have a different accent to most others you noticed in the group?" asked Pearce.

Bijay looked over at Pearce and nodded.

"He had a different accent to yours, but I can't say. I didn't really pay attention to it."

"Did he talk like this when he spoke," said Pearce, doing his best Irish accent, "or did he talk more like this when he spoke," putting on a Scottish accent.

Bijay smiled at him.

"More like the first one," he said.

Pearce looked over at Frances and pointed his finger at a name in the notebook. He looked behind him then and raised his notebook with his finger still stuck under the name and showed it to Davison. Davison leaned in and nodded his head. His arms still folded in front of him.

"Was that helpful?" asked Bijay.

Frances nodded and smile at him.

"It was, it has certainly given us something else to consider," said Frances.

"This Irishman," said Pearce, "that was the accent you picked. Was he carrying a gun or anything like that, that you might have noticed?"

Bijay shook his head.

"No, there were only walking sticks that some of the men were carrying. He was carrying one too, but I didn't pay much attention to it. I only turned around and noticed him when I heard the shots. By that time everyone had started to scatter. There were arms and sticks all over the place."

Pearce nodded. Frances turned around in her chair and looked at Davison.

"Inspector," she said, "did you find any weapons on Mr. Panchal or at the men's hostel where you found him."

Davison looked at Frances and shook his head. It seemed as if his arms were permanently stuck in a straight jacket that his mind had created.

"We did not find any weapons in the hostel or in Mr. Panchal's room. That is not to say he couldn't have gotten rid of it before we came for him."

Frances smiled at the Inspector and nodded at him.

"I assume then, that there were no weapons found on his friend Mr. Pai either?"

Davison shook his head again.

"I'm just thinking then, out loud," said Frances, "that perhaps after we've interviewed Mr. Pai, and if it turns out that he had nothing to do with this murder either, perhaps you might find it wise to let them go, holding onto their passports of course."

Davison looked at her for a long while without speaking.

"Perhaps," was all he said.

Frances turned around then and looked back at Bijay.

"Well, Bijay, that wasn't too bad was it?"

Bijay nodded.

"You've been most helpful. If your friend Mr. Pai corroborates your story then I imagine you'll not have much more to do with the police."

"So I can go now?"

"Not yet, but if the inspector is feeling generous, you might yet get home in time for dinner."

Pearce finished jotting down some notes as Frances stood up, she turned to face Davison again.

"If you'd be so kind as to show me to Mr. Pai. I don't have any more questions of Mr. Panchal, unless of course you do?"

Davison looked at her for a moment and then wearily shook his head.

"Mr. Pai is in the next room," he said.

Davison led the group out of Mr. Panchal's interrogation room and into the next one which held his friend Mr. Pai.

Sixteen

It was just after three in the afternoon when everyone settled into the interrogation room that held Amir Pai. They had taken a quick break for refreshments and use of the bathroom.

Pearce and Davison had settled into the chairs opposite Amir, a table identical to the one that was in Bijay's interrogation room stood stolidly between Amir and Pearce and Davison.

Amir was dissimilar to Bijay in many ways. Where Bijay was tall, Amir was short. Frances thought he might be as short as Gandhi, but she couldn't tell for sure. Though unlike both Gandhi and Bijay, Amir was thick set with a round, fat belly and round face. If his head had been shaved, he could quite easily pass for a statue of the smiling Buddha. He wasn't smiling though, in fact he looked quite upset.

"Why have you put me in here. I have done nothing, as Allah is in my witness, I have done nothing," he said.

"You are Muslim?" asked Davison, trying to keep his tone flat and even.

Amir nodded.

"How does a Muslim like you and a Hindu like Bijay meet?"

"We met over shared loss. Our fathers were murdered by British swine," said Amir, his tone getting angry.

Davison sat with his forearms on the table in front of him. They looked like logs with hair like black moss covering them.

His hands were flat and open, palms down on the table, and he tapped his fingers.

"Keep your tone up like that, and I'll be sure to keep you here all week," said Davison.

Amir looked away, and then back at Davison.

"Why did you bring me here?" he asked, his tone gentler this time, the anger gone.

"I think you know why we brought you here," said Davison, "it's about Monday evening."

Amir looked away and fiddled with his fingers. He bit his lips and twisted his lips about as if they were itchy and his teeth bringing relief.

"So you do know?" asked Davison.

Pearce had his notebook out and his pencil ready. He was taking notes intermittently. Frances and Alfred stood behind Davison and Pearce, against the wall. Alfred had his hands clasped behind his back. Frances had hers in front of her and they clutched her handbag. Amir nodded without looking up at anyone.

"Were you trying to shoot Gandhi or Meda?" asked Davison.

Amir looked up then with wide eyes. He shook his head vigorously.

"No, no, you don't understand, we didn't go to shoot anyone."

He looked at Davison and then at Pearce with sad, pleading eyes.

"The way I see it," continued Davison, ignoring Amir's last remark, "is that you're angry at the police and you're angry at Gandhi. And why are you angry? You're angry because you've lost your father, and I can understand that. But considering that there were no police at Gandhi's lecture on Monday night, I'm assuming you were there to take out your anger on Gandhi. Is that right?"

Davison looked at Amir with hard eyes, his face a stone mask of uncaring police justice. Amir started shaking his head like a dog trying to wring the water from itself.

"No, no, no. No, no, no. We didn't go to hurt Mr. Gandhi..."

"Then you must have gone to kill Meda. Why did you want to hurt Meda?"

More shaking of his head. Frances was starting to get dizzy just watching Amir shake his head.

"No, no, no. Not Mr. Meda, no, no, no."

"Don't lie to me Mr. Pai. Don't lie to the police. Mr. Panchal has already said you were upset at Meda because he set up the Dharasana march. Mr. Panchal has already implicated you in the matter."

Amir was beside himself. He tried to clutch at his face with his hands, but they were handcuffed at his waist just like Bijay's were. He started crying and he looked up at the ceiling.

"Merciful Allah, please have mercy," he said, then he looked back down at Davison and squeezed his eyes shut to rid them of the residual tears. "I swear to you I didn't shoot anybody. I didn't come to hurt anyone. If Bijay said that, it is untrue. I don't know why he would say that."

Davison looked at him.

"I can help you," he said, "but only if you tell me exactly what happened. If you continue to lie to me then I will make sure that the full weight of the law is brought down upon you. And you know what we do with murderers here in England?"

Davison kept a steady, hard gaze on Amir. Amir shook his head softly and slowly this time, afraid of the answer.

"We hang them from the gallows for everyone to see."

Amir started practically shaking. He looked terrified and his head shook from side to side as he kept repeating, "no, no, no," over and over again. Frances wasn't going to stand for much more of this treatment. Although no longer being physically abusive, she was disturbed by Davison's continued harassment of the suspect, Amir. In addition, gibbeting hadn't been practiced in England for almost a hundred years.

"So Mr. Pai, just tell me the truth and I'll be able to help you," said Davison.

"Yes, yes, yes, I will tell the truth. I swear to you, I will tell you the truth."

Davison looked at Amir dispassionately and Pearce got ready to write in his notebook.

"Bijay and me went to hear Mr. Gandhi speak because we wanted to talk to him afterwards. We wanted to accept his apology and offer him our forgiveness which he had asked for. You see, both Bijay and I had been very unkind to him when he had first come to visit us. He had a friend of his bring Bijay's family and my family together in shared mourning, and when he had come to visit we had not been ready for him and we had said some regrettable things."

Amir was looking keenly at Davison and then at Pearce as Pearce wrote down what he was saying in his notebook.

"A few months later, Mr. Gandhi wrote a letter to Bijay and me. I know Bijay got one because he shared it with me, and I shared mine with him. Mr. Gandhi said he took responsibility for my father's death and said that if he had known he would have gladly taken his place. He asked only that one day we might be able to forgive him."

"Did your father have any last words that you know of?" asked Pearce.

Amir nodded, looking a little surprised.

"In Mr. Gandhi's letter he said he wanted to share the last words that the doctor had told him my father had said. My father had said 'we must fight on to defeat them'. Those were his last words..."

Amir took a moment to compose himself and swallowed.

"Bijay and me took a long time to talk about it over the months that followed, and we both thought we should come and offer Mr. Gandhi our forgiveness. We recognized that the real enemy was the British."

Amir looked a little sheepish when he said that.

"But we do not hold any anger towards the British anymore. Mr. Gandhi showed us how to let go of it and move towards forgiveness. So when we were ready to offer Mr. Gandhi our forgiveness, we found that he had already made plans to visit England, so we bought tickets to come and see him here."

"You just happened to have the money available at the time?" asked Davison.

"Yes, because Bijay and I had gone into business together and we had been saving money for our mothers so they didn't have to work and for our brothers so they could finish school. But our families said that coming here to forgive Mr. Gandhi was the first thing we should do. So we did."

Amir looked eagerly at Davison and then at Pearce. After a while, Pearce looked up from his notebook and nodded at Amir.

"Have you had a chance to offer your forgiveness to Gandhi?" asked Pearce.

Amir nodded.

"No, we were very close. We were probably the next two or three in line to speak with Mr. Gandhi after the lecture when we heard the gunshots."

"How many did you hear?" asked Pearce.

"Two."

"Are you sure?"

Amir looked away for a moment, recollecting the events. He closed his eyes and then nodded is head. He opened them and looked back at Pearce.

"Yes, two loud gun shots."

"If you did not go to shoot Gandhi or Meda, then who was it?" asked Davison.

"I swear, I don't know. I never saw who did it. But before I heard the gunshots there was this Englishman shouting horrible things to Mr. Gandhi. When I turned to look at who it was, that's when I heard the gunshots."

"So you saw this man shoot Meda?" asked Davison.

"No, I didn't see it. It happened so fast. When I realized that I had heard gunshots I then saw this man run off. But by then everyone had started running away. Bijay and I ran the opposite way from him."

"Did you notice him carrying a gun?" asked Davison.

Amir shook his head.

"Did you notice anyone carrying a gun?"

Amir shook his head again.

"Was anyone carrying anything that you noticed?" asked Pearce.

"Yes, there were several men carrying walking sticks. This Englishman was carrying a walking stick too."

"Did this Englishman sound like this when he spoke, or did he sound more like this when he spoke?" asked Pearce going from his Irish accent to his Scottish brogue.

Amir smiled at Pearce. It seemed both he and Bijay both enjoyed Pearce's use of accents.

"He sounded very much like the first one," said Amir.

"Did you hear anyone else arguing with Gandhi, or being combative with him?" asked Davison.

"Not really. There were these two Africans who kept talking about something to do with South Africa. I wasn't paying attention. They were speaking loudly but I didn't think they were angry."

"And you're sure you saw no guns whatsoever?" asked Davison.

Amir nodded his head.

"Maybe there was a gun, but I didn't see any. It was very scary. You just don't think something like this will happen. Mr. Gandhi is a very peaceful man. We were just waiting around to talk to him and then this one man starts shouting slurs and then there's these two gun shots. Everyone got very scared and started running away all over the place."

Davison furrowed his brow and nodded. He turned to Pearce.

"We have a murder without a murder weapon and no shell casings."

Pearce nodded and took a moment to twirl his mustache.

"I think we're looking at something well planned out. I would guess that whoever came to shoot Mr. Meda wanted to leave very few clues. Which is odd, because they chose to do it in a crowd."

"So how do you suppose they did it then?" asked Davison.

"They probably took a moment to pick up the casings before they went. Or perhaps they had a bag or some sort of thing attached to the gun to catch the spent casings. Could also mean that they were using a revolver like you said."

Pearce looked over his shoulder at Frances. Frances smiled at him.

"I am open to all manner of methods. It didn't sound like a revolver to me as I said before. But that shouldn't steer us off the possibility that it might have been."

Frances saw the back of Davison's head nodding. He turned to look at Pearce again.

"I'm going to go with a revolver. I think that seems like the most likely method."

"I'd have to agree, Inspector," said Pearce. "Additionally, the shooter was in the thick of it. The crowd that is, that might have changed the sound of the gunshot."

Pearce turned around and looked at Lady Marmalade.

"Could it not?"

Frances had to admit that although she knew the difference between a revolver and a pistol and a rifle, and had indeed fired all kinds over the years, she wouldn't put money on it that the weapon used was not a revolver. She rather preferred to collect the evidence and see where that led.

"I am sure that is quite possible, Sergeant," she said. "As I said before, we must go where the evidence leads, and perhaps due to the lack of shell casings that anyone found, maybe the lack of evidence suggests a revolver."

"I agree," said Davison though he didn't turn around to look at Lady Marmalade.

"Hopefully we will find the murder weapon," said Frances, "for if we don't, it shall be much harder to determine who killed Mr. Meda."

"If I could ask a question?" asked Amir, timidly.

Everyone looked at him as if they had forgotten that he was in the room with them.

"If the person who shot Mr. Meda was trying to shoot Mr. Gandhi, why did he do such a bad job of it? We were after all so close together in this circle that was around Mr. Gandhi."

"We're not all convinced that it was Gandhi that the shooter was after," said Davison.

"That's true," said Frances, "though I still believe they were after Mr. Gandhi, and there could be any number of reasons why they shot Mr. Meda instead."

"Such as?" asked Davison.

"In a small group like that, it could be quite easy to be jostled and bumped just at the wrong time. They might also have been trying to shoot from further off than we suspect."

"Which would be dangerous," said Davison, "with the crowd around Gandhi."

"Very true, Inspector. I'm just offering suggestions since you asked, not promises."

"You think there was more than one person involved?" asked Amir, looking at Frances.

"Not necessarily," she said, "what gives you that impression?"

"You keep saying 'they'."

"Oh, I see, that's just a figure of speech I use. If I used the singular then I'd probably use 'he' or 'him', but what if it turns out to be a woman, that way I'm training my mind not to see that possibility. Also, if there is one, then 'they' covers it. If it is more than one then 'they' covers that too. One needs to keep a wide open mind."

"I doubt a woman would do this," said Davison.

Frances looked at the back of his head but didn't say anything. She held a similar position on the matter but that didn't mean a woman didn't do it. Until the evidence suggested otherwise, it was important not to hold favorites. She looked back up at Amir.

"Who do you think the shooter was aiming for?"

"Mr. Gandhi," he said. "I only knew of Mr. Meda because his name came up as someone important in organizing the march, but I never heard that he actually went on the march himself."

Frances nodded.

"I agree with you."

Davison stood up and turned around to face Lady Marmalade.

"Do you have any more questions for this man?" he asked.

Frances shook her head.

"I can go then?" Amir asked.

Davison turned around to face him.

"No, not for a while. And we'll be keeping your passport when we do let you go. I'm not convinced of your innocence yet."

Pearce stood up and followed Davison out of the room. They were followed by Frances and Alfred. They walked down the hallway for a while, out of earshot of the constables when Frances touched Davison's shoulder. Davison stopped in the middle of the empty hallway and turned to her.

"You still have some questions you'd like answered?" he asked.

Frances nodded her head and smiled at him.

"I do. I was wondering about a few things actually. Firstly, have you had any word on who that whistle belongs to?"

Davison shook his head.

"No I haven't. And I'm not sure why you're pestering me about a police whistle when we're investigating a murder. I'm sure it'll turn out to be one of my men's who attended the scene."

"Well, I'd still like to know. Secondly, have you had a chance to speak with the coroner to determine what type of bullets were used to shoot Mr. Meda?"

Davison shook his head again.

"I'll be making a call to him this afternoon as soon as I'm finished with this visit."

Frances nodded.

"Please keep me informed. Lastly, when are you going to interview Mr. Godse?"

"When we can find him," said Davison. "My men haven't had much luck with that yet. Seems he's a bit of a slippery fish. But what I am doing, just so you're aware that I am actually trying to solve this murder, is interviewing that African chap, what's his name?"

Davison looked over at Pearce.

"Mr. Mathibeli, Inspector," he said, without having to refer to his notes.

"Yes, that's the fellow. I'll be interviewing him tomorrow, along with Ms. Eastwood and if we can find him, this O'Malley chap who seems to have an issue with Indians."

"Good, if you don't mind, I'd like to hear what he has to say."

"Who?"

"Patrick O'Malley, the Irishman that both Mr. Panchal and Mr. Pai identified as shouting slurs at Mr. Gandhi before the shots were fired."

"Right."

Davison looked at Pearce.

"Put that in your notes. When we get him and we're ready to interview him, make note to call Frances."

Davison looked back at Frances as Pearce jotted it down in his notebook.

"He's unlikely to be a pleasant chap, I'm not sure you'll like what he has to say or how he says it."

"I appreciate your consideration Inspector, but these ears have heard the worst that humanity has to say."

"Anything else then?" asked Davison.

"No, thank you, Inspector, you've been most helpful and today has been quite informative."

"I don't see how," he said. "I've still got my eye on those two."

"And yet without any weapon found anywhere near them, and their similar stories, I don't think how they might be involved."

"Motive, Frances, motive. Please see them out," he said, looking at Pearce.

Davison walked off down the hall and disappeared into his office. Pearce looked at Frances.

"I don't necessarily agree with the inspector," he said, "but we can't completely rule out Mr. Pai or Mr. Panchal yet."

"Quite right," said Frances. "Though I think our focus is better pointed elsewhere until we have any additional evidence to suggest that they might yet be involved."

Seventeen

A tall man in a long overcoat and carrying a cane walks up to a row house in Hackney. He limps as he walks, leaning on his cane for balance and support He looks into the windows in the living room and doesn't see anyone. He goes round to the front door and uses the handle of his cane to rap on the wooden paneling. He waits a long while and then raps again, loudly so that whoever's inside might clearly hear him. He waits along time, but no one comes to answer his knock.

He hobbles down the front steps and decides to miss the house right next to the one he's just knocked at and goes to the third house. He hobbles up the stairs and brings his face up close to the large front windows of this house, just as he did the first. He shields his eyes from the overcast light so he can see into the house better. There's nobody inside.

He moves round to the front door and he knocks on it with his cane, just like he had not minutes before on the first house. He waits patiently for the inhabitants to answer, but nobody comes. He tries it a second time, louder this time and he waits longer. He looks into his waist pocket and pulls out his watch and times himself. He gives it two minutes.

He puts his watch back into his waist jacket and leans back heavily onto his cane and walks down the stairs, hobbling as he goes. He walks up the stairs to the middle house he had previously walked by. He doesn't look into the window, but rather goes straight up the front steps and knocks on the front door. This man, in addition to wearing a long overcoat is wearing a Windsor cap, and gloves, everything is in black as if he were attending a funeral.

He waits for a long while, but he doesn't knock again. In time a short man opens up the door. He's disheveled and pushes his hand against his temple. He's wearing rumpled clothes. There's dried blood crusted on his upper lip and a bruise forming across his cheek and eye.

"Come in," he said.

The tall man in the overcoat walks into the house, no longer limping and no longer needing the use of his cane. He keeps his coat and hat on. They walk into the living room where they sit down. The man with the headache reaches for a wet cloth which he places across his forehead.

"How are you feeling?" asks the tall man.

"Like hell," says the other.

"Shouldn't have drunk so much."

The tall man looks at the other man and notices his bruises.

"You wouldn't have gotten into a fight you couldn't finish," he adds.

The man with the cloth over his face looks up at him, and he's not amused. He grunts.

"That's what you're for."

"No, not really. I'm not here to finish up your dirty work."

"Then why are you here?"

"I wanted to talk about our conversation last night. I want to see if you're still determined to go after Gandhi."

The tall man looks over at his bedraggled friend. The friend is looking up at the ceiling with the damp cloth cool upon his forehead.

"Yeah, I'd like to, just as soon as I'm feeling right as rain."

"We discussed this last night," said the tall man, "I think it is a bad idea. The papers are full of it and I don't see how we'll get away with it."

"Well, if you'd just done the job right the first time we wouldn't be in this bloody mess."

Each conversation is hard on the man with the headache. The words seem to batter against his temples like shards of sharp glass before coming out his mouth.

"I would have if you hadn't bumped me. Anyway, we didn't get it done and we can't try again now. Perhaps we can go back to India towards the end of the year when this has all settled down and finish it then."

The man with the headache sits up and he takes off the damp cloth. He looks at the tall man and winces and frowns.

"We'll bloody well finish it now. I'm not going back to that god forsaken land of curry eaters and their stench. We'll do it today, bloody hell."

He takes his head in his hands and starts to massage his temples. The headache has just been made worse by his friend's sniveling cowardice. The tall man stands up.

"I was hoping you wouldn't say that," he says.

The man with the headache looks up at him.

"Bloody hell," he says, "you can't be serious."

The tall man nods, and he points his cane at his friend. What hadn't been noticeable before were two small triggers under the handle.

"The neighbors will hear, you'll never get away with it."

"The neighbors have gone off to work," says the tall man, "I checked."

He pulls both triggers and a couple of soft bangs, close together make noise in the living room. It would be hard to hear them from outside, the cane had been modified to suppress recoil and sound. The man with the headache looks down at the two small red dots on his chest. He clutches at them with his hand, and then looks up at the tall man.

"Sorry about that, old friend," the tall man said.

He walks up to the man who no longer has a headache and closes his eye. Then he walks to the end of the living room and looks out the window. He looks carefully and takes his time. Nobody seems to have heard anything, so he leaves the house, closing the door softly behind him and disappears down the street and into the day.

Eighteen

It's eight in the morning on September the 10th as Lady Marmalade makes it down to the living room. Both Declan and Eric are sitting at the table eating their breakfast. Frances comes over and kisses Eric on the cheek, and she does the same with her son. They all exchange salutations before Frances sits down wearily in her chair with an audible sigh.

Eric looks up from the sports section of the paper.

"Everything alright, love?" he asked, taking a bite of toast with marmalade jam.

"Yes, I suppose so," she said, placing a napkin across her lap.

"Mother dear," said Declan, "that is the biggest fib I think I've heard you say in years."

Declan is grinning at her, and on his fork is a piece of sausage and he puts it in his mouth. Frances looks up at both of them and grins.

"You know me to well," she said to Declan. "It's this murder that is bothering me. It's been almost three days now, and it doesn't seem as if I or the police are getting any closer to finding out who did it."

Frances sighs again as Ginny comes into the living room carrying a silver tray covered to keep the contents warm. In front of Lady Marmalade is an empty plate. Ginny comes up and takes off the silver cover and places it nearby on a side table.

"I've cooked sausages, bacon and poached eggs this morning, my Lady. Though I can make you fried or scrambled or boiled eggs if you'd prefer."

Frances looks up and smiles at her.

"Smells marvelous, Ginny. Just a couple rashers of bacon and an egg should be plenty."

Ginny places the still hot bacon and egg on Lady Marmalade's plate. Frances reaches for the salt and pepper shakers and shakes them both liberally over her food. She takes a bite of the bacon and then of the egg. Eric gazes at her with some concern, as does Declan in between his bites of food. Ginny pours a cup of tea for Frances before she leaves the living room.

Frances adds some lemon to it and takes a sip. It is hot and tangy.

"Sometimes these things take time," said Eric.

Frances looks up at him, but she's not finding his words comforting.

"Sometimes," he said, "murders don't get solved at all. I mean look at the Ripper case from last century. They still don't know who did it."

Eric means well, but it's not really helping.

"That's true," said Frances, "but I've always been able to determine the elements of the crime."

"Perhaps you're putting too much pressure on yourself, Mum," said Declan.

Frances nods her head.

"Could be," she said, and takes another bite of bacon.

"What is it specifically that's bothering you about this?" asked Declan.

Frances finishes chewing before she speaks.

"There are a number of factors, I suppose. The first is that Inspector Davison and I are not seeing eye to eye. I don't think he's happy with having a woman around trying to help, and frankly, I'm not very happy about his policing abilities."

Eric looks up from taking another bite of toast.

"I'll speak to the commissioner then," he said.

Frances shakes her head.

"No, that's not necessary. I had strong words with him. I just find him quite abrasive and focused on the wrong things. Wouldn't you say, Alfred?"

Alfred is standing against the far wall, opposite from where Frances is sitting.

"Quite, my Lady," he said.

"What do you mean?" asked Eric.

"Well, he found two of the Indians who were at the lecture Mr. Gandhi gave on Monday evening. Mr. Panchal and Mr. Pai. They were the two sons of the two men who died at the hands of the British police in India at Dharasana."

Eric nodded at her.

"That sounds like they've got motive," said Declan.

Frances nodded.

"Exactly. I was very interested in talking to them and hearing what they had to say."

"So what as the problem then?" asked Eric.

"Well, Davison came on too strong right from the beginning. He was convinced they did it, even though no weapon was found on them or in their vicinity when he picked them up."

"Hmm, I see," said Eric.

"On top of that, he was rude and racialist, and he shut Mr. Panchal down. I eventually had to intervene, and that's when we got into hot words."

"What happened?" asked Declan.

"I took him outside and basically told him that if he didn't watch himself I was going to report this incident to the commissioner."

Declan smiled and put the last of his sausage into his mouth. He nodded and grunted.

"So we went back in, and I finished the interrogation of Mr. Panchal. He denied it, so did his friend, Mr. Pai, but more than that, I believe them."

"Uh huh," said Eric. "So the two best suspects don't appear to have anything to do with it. What did they say that convinced you they were innocent?"

"Well," said Frances, finishing a forkful of egg, "it was more that they both admitted to almost the identical story. Additionally, their telling of it was very persuasive."

"And that was?" asked Declan, buttering a slice of toast and spreading some marmalade over it.

"They said that Mr. Gandhi had put the two of them in touch as he thought it might be helpful for them to get together over a shared loss..."

"That sounds reasonable," said Declan.

"Yes it does, though they both admit to mistreating him and saying some regrettable things to him."

"Mr. Gandhi?" asked Eric. Frances nodded.

"But then Mr. Gandhi wrote them a letter a short while later asking for their forgiveness and expressing his sincerest regret that their fathers had lost their lives during the march."

Frances took a moment to take a sip of tea.

"They told me that the letter had in impact on them and they were determined to try and set things right. They've become business partners and they decided that they should spend their savings to come over to England and offer Mr. Gandhi their forgiveness."

Eric nodded and put the last bit of toast into his mouth. Declan took a bite from his and Frances cut up the remaining slice of bacon and speared it with her fork and put it in her mouth.

"Well, that seems reasonable," said Eric.

Frances nodded and finished chewing.

"Yes, it does. Reasonable, plausible and honest actually. But this begs the question, who did it then?"

"Well, what I've always found odd about this is why Mr. Meda was shot. I know you think it was meant for Mr. Gandhi, but how could you miss at such close range?" asked Eric.

"That's just the thing," said Frances. "Neither Mr. Pai or Mr. Panchal knew Mr. Meda well, other than that he was involved in setting up the march. And I have to believe that the shooter or shooters were aiming for Mr. Gandhi, because if they weren't and they really were trying to kill Mr. Meda then we're on the wrong track."

"What do you mean?" asked Declan.

"Because of what Mr. Meda said to me just before he died. He told me it was an Indian person or an Indian with a name starting with the letter P. And the only names we've come up with that start with the letter P are those who have been antagonistic to Mr. Gandhi."

"And no one else?" asked Eric.

"Well, there is this one Irishman that I'm hoping to speak to if the police can find him. His name's Patrick O'Malley. He was shouting racialist slurs at Mr. Gandhi according to the two men I spoke with today."

"That's good news, isn't it?" asked Eric. "I mean if it's not the two men you spoke with today then perhaps it's this racialist chap. Could be he didn't care who he shot as long as it was an Indian."

Frances finished up her egg and put her fork and knife together on the plate. She pushed it off to the side and then put a slice of toast on her side plate and buttered it. She put marmalade on top of the butter.

"I wish it were so, though somehow I fear that it might not be as neat and simple as that."

"Why not?" asked Eric. "It has been that simple on some occasions before."

"That's true," said Frances, nodding, "but it just doesn't seem to fit this picture. I think this was a deliberate and planned attack aimed at Mr. Gandhi."

"And Patrick O'Malley could be your man who planned it and pulled it off. I mean, if you think that it was aimed at Mr. Gandhi and whoever tried to shoot him missed, then that man could easily be this Irishman," said Eric.

"Very true," said Frances, "but something just doesn't feel right about it. I mean why bring attention to yourself by shouting out racial slurs if you're intent on killing someone? Why not shoot them quietly and obtrusively?"

"Because as you've said to me before, my love, there is sometimes no understanding the passions of the criminally deranged," said Eric.

"Dad's got a point," said Declan.

"He does indeed," said Frances. "Using my words against me."

She smiled at him and took a bite of toast. Then she sipped on her tea.

"Then there's also this police whistle that I found at Abbot House on Tuesday morning when Alfred and I headed back out to the crime scene."

"What about it?" asked Eric.

"Well, it just seemed odd and out of place."

"Not really, there are a lot of police at a crime scene, especially one of this nature. What did Davison say about it?"

"He thinks I'm wasting his time having him follow up on it."

"Maybe with good reason. Perhaps one of his men dropped it getting in or out of one of the police cars."

Frances nodded, holding her piece of toast above her plate.

"Yes, that's probably the likely situation, but I'd sooner just have it tied up. I don't like any loose ends."

"Did he say he'd look into it?" asked Eric.

Frances nodded and took another bite of toast.

"Then you'll find out in good time. In the meantime, you've got this Irishman to interview and these Indian chaps with names starting with P. That seems like a lot to go on. I imagine you'll have a good idea by the time you've finished interviewing all of them."

"And that's another pickle. There were two men who have a P in their first or last name. A Sikh by the name of Pitambar Singh who had written of his displeasure with Mr. Gandhi and a Muslim with the name of Parvez Dada who wrote of similar complaints."

"Sounds terrific," said Eric.

"No, not really. Neither of them were on the registry for the lecture. They either didn't attend or used false names."

"Which would be smart if you were planning on killing someone," said Declan.

"Yes, except eyewitness accounts only suggest that there were three Indians in the midst of the group looking to speak with Mr. Gandhi when the shots were fired. And we know who the third is."

"Who is it?" asked Eric.

"It's Nathuram Godse, a fellow Hindu who is unhappy with Mr. Gandhi and has written as much."

"Oh, I see. The problem is, he doesn't have a P in any of his names."

Frances smiled and looked at her husband.

"Exactly."

"Perhaps you misheard when you leaned in to listen to Mr. Meda's last words."

"Perhaps, but I find that quite unlikely."

Frances bit off more of her toast and glanced down at her teacup.

"Must be this Irish racialist then," said Declan, trying to be helpful.

Frances looked at him and smiled.

"Or this Godse chap. I mean, on a dying man's lips a G and P might sound similar," said Eric.

"But if it's neither of them. Then what?"

Eric took a sip of his tea, and looked over at Declan. He thought for a moment.

"Then perhaps the answer isn't in England at all, but in India."

Frances smiled at her husband and ate more toast and then sipped more tea.

"I think you could be right, though I have no desire to travel off to India to solve a murder here."

Eric shook his head and grinned at his wife.

"That's not what I meant. I don't think you'll have to. The murder took place here, so unless the culprit has already taken the boat abroad, he might still be here. What I really meant was that whatever the reason for shooting Mr. Meda, or trying to shoot Mr. Gandhi, might be tied to events that happened in India."

"Thanks darling, but I think we're already agreed that this is tied back to India, Mr. Gandhi and Mr. Meda are both Indians and it must quite likely have something to do with Mr. Gandhi's satyagraha or Dharasana march. I haven't lost focus on the fact that this has probably spilled over from the political reformation movement in India."

Eric shook his head.

"Just trying to be helpful," he said, "and I know we're all aware of the Indian connection, but perhaps we're looking too closely, that's all. Listen, this sort of thing isn't my specialty, I have faith that you'll sort it out."

Frances nodded. Eric stood up and came over to her and kissed her, then he looked at Declan.

"I think we should be getting to the office," he said to his son.

Declan nodded, stood up and kissed his mother on the cheek. They said their goodbyes and left Frances alone with her thoughts, crumbs left from her toast and her half full teacup. She was looking at her bread crumbs and thinking of Hansel and Gretel. She wondered if she'd lost track of the trail that would lead her to the murderer. She sighed.

"Everything alright, my Lady?" asked Alfred.

Frances looked up at him and smiled.

"Not really, Alfred, I feel as if I'm losing track of this murder. The investigation doesn't seem to be getting anywhere."

Lady Marmalade took a sip of her tea, and stared into the red colored liquid.

"If I might, my Lady," said Alfred.

"Of course, Alfred, your opinions are always valued," she said, looking up at him and smiling.

"Perhaps you're being too hard on yourself. It hasn't even been a week and we've already ruled out two of the most likely suspects. Hopefully today we'll hear from Scotland Yard and get a chance to listen to this Irishman tell his tale. Perhaps he might even have done it, and if so, then by tonight the whole affair will be behind us. If not, there's still Mr. Godse who might be good for it, even if his name doesn't have a P in it. And if neither of them, well then, we've just narrowed the field even more. We'll catch him, I know we will."

Frances smiled and took the last sip of her tea.

"Yes, I suppose you're right. We are making headway in the case. It could also be that I'm quite anxious to finish this up as quickly as possible so that Mr. Gandhi doesn't have to worry about anything of this sort happening for the remainder of his stay."

Alfred nodded.

"I am sure he is comforted by knowing that England's best police department, complemented by His Majesty's very best sleuth are working hand in glove."

Frances smiled at him. She wasn't sure Gandhi even knew who she was, let alone that she had had some success with sleuthing. Nevertheless, Alfred's words were comforting and she allowed them to cheer her up.

"Well, I do hope we hear from Inspector Davison later today. I'd like to find out if we can pin this on Mr. Godse or, God forbid, Mr. O'Malley."

"You would find that more distasteful?" asked Alfred.

"I'd find whoever did it, quite distasteful enough, but to think that one of our very own in England, would allow such racialist sentiment to get the better of them such that they kill a man. That would be a ghastly horror. England looks bad enough with how she conducted herself at the Dharasana Salt Works incident. The foreign press would have a field day if they thought we were generally a bunch of racialist thugs."

Alfred nodded.

"I find the whole idea of murder to be quite abhorrent. The last resort of the midget minded."

Frances looked up at Alfred and smiled at him.

"That's a very poetic way of putting it," she said.

Nineteen

The phone rang and Alfred answered it. In the living room Frances was just finishing up her lunch of French onion soup. Alfred put the receiver down on the table in the alcove of the hallway where the telephone was and walked back into the living room.

"It's for you, my Lady," he said.

"Who is it?"

"Inspector Davison."

"Oh, that could be a spot of good news," said Frances, pushing her chair away from the table and getting up.

"I certainly hope so, my Lady," said Alfred.

Frances went into the hallway and picked up the phone. She sat down at the table.

"This is Lady Marmalade," she said into the receiver.

"Frances. Inspector Davison here."

"Good afternoon, Inspector."

"We've picked up both Godse and O'Malley if you'd like to come down to the station."

"Have you spoken with either of them yet, Cameron?"

"Not yet, but I'm about to pop in and have a go with them. I'll see you when you get here."

Davison hung up and Lady Marmalade put the receiver back down on its cradle. She got up and returned to the living room where Alfred was standing. He looked at her with a questioning face.

"Scotland Yard had picked up both Mr. Godse and the Irishman, Mr. O'Malley. I'd like to get going. Inspector Davison said he was about to start interrogating them. Though I'd wish he'd wait for me."

"Then we mustn't waste any time, my Lady," said Alfred.

Alfred walked out of the living room, following Frances and they made their way to the front door. It was just after two in the afternoon. It had started raining, and Frances put on a cardigan and took an umbrella.

Alfred opened the door for Frances and closed it behind them. He helped her into the Rolls and got into the driver's seat. He started it up and drove them out of the garage and onto the street where he slowly made his way towards Scotland Yard through the light rain.

"I'd recommend girding the loins, my Lady," said Alfred, keeping his eyes on the road ahead of them as the windshield wipers thumped quietly across the windshield.

Lady Marmalade laughed out loud and laughed for a while. Alfred stole a glance at her, not sure what was so funny.

"Oh, Alfred, where do you come up with these little gems?" she asked.

"That's from the bible, my Lady. It means we should prepare ourselves for the task to come."

He was puzzled by her amusement, trying his best to explain the sincerity of the message. Frances attempted to stifle her laughter.

"My dear Alfred, I'm not laughing at you. I understand full well what the idiom means. It just came out so unexpected when you said it, that's all. We've practically been silent the whole way and then as we're getting there you throw out that gem. What precisely should we prepare ourselves for?" asked Frances looking at him with a smile on her face.

"I'm just a little worried about this Patrick O'Malley, my Lady. It would appear that he's quite uncouth and I hope that you won't be upset by that."

Alfred looked over at Frances quickly. Frances nodded.

"I'm quite prepared for it. Though one never knows how such uncouth men will react in the company of a lady. Perhaps we shall find him on his best behavior."

"But if we don't, I just hope you're prepared, my Lady."

"Thank you for your concern, Alfred. I'm well aware of the uncouthness in some parts of our modern society. If he becomes unbearable we'll leave."

Alfred nodded, comforted that Lady Marmalade would not put herself in the company of too much unpleasantness.

"Perhaps we'll find that our usefulness for this case will come to an end," he said.

"You mean that perhaps Mr. O'Malley might be the murderer?"

Alfred nodded.

"That would indeed wrap it up in a nice and neat little bow. I can't say I'd be unhappy with that outcome, other than for the black mark it'll leave on England's visage."

Alfred pulled up across from Scotland Yard and then got out of the car. He helped Frances out of her side and they walked across the road to the front entrance.

"Perhaps I should inquire about getting an office here for myself," Frances said to Alfred as he opened the door for her.

"They would be lucky to have you, my Lady," he replied.

The front desk constable was someone new. He was a young man with a very efficient manner. A wonderful contrast from the older unhappy man they had suffered through on the previous trips here.

"Good afternoon," said the young constable, looking up at Frances very bright eyed.

His uniform was impeccable and he was smartly dressed. His skin was smooth from a recent shave and white as porcelain.

"Good afternoon constable," said Frances. "I'm Lady Marmalade, and this is Alfred Donahue. We're here to meet with Inspector Davison and Sergeant Pearce. They're expecting us."

The young man stood up and smiled at her.

"Yes of course, my Lady," he said. "If you'd just like to take a seat, I'll go and get one of them for you. Shouldn't take long."

He smiled and walked off as had the older constable Frances had seen before. Only this young one was brisker in his step and more upright in his deportment. He wasn't gone long before he returned with Sergeant Pearce. Pearce came through the door and out into the reception area and greeted them warmly.

"Perhaps we should get you your own desk here, you're practically here every day," said Pearce, smiling.

Frances smiled.

"I was just saying the very same thing to Alfred as we came in."

"Well, I for one would be happy to have you helping us. Inspector Davison is in the interrogation room with O'Malley as we speak."

Pearce turned around and led them through the door that separated the reception area from the main offices and they headed down the hallways as they had done before. When they neared the interrogation rooms that Frances had just been in the day before, Pearce turned around and faced them both.

"Just a word of warning. It appears that O'Malley is about to confess to the murder."

"Really?" asked Frances.

Pearce nodded.

"I'm afraid so."

He turned around and led them the rest of the way down the hall. He stopped outside the interrogation room where another smartly dressed constable stood watch. Pearce looked in through the window in the door and knocked on it. He stepped back.

"The inspector is coming," he said.

Frances wasn't sure why they didn't just head in. Perhaps it was protocol. She understood protocol all too well, but she didn't trust it when it came to Davison. Davison opened the door and stepped out. For the first time that she could remember he was smiling. His pencil thin mustache curled like a lazy U above his upper lip. It also appeared as if he hadn't changed since yesterday. He wore the same shirt and the same pants. The shirt was also rolled up to his elbows almost the same way it had been before.

He looked at her and then at Alfred.

"I think you might have wasted a trip," he said. "I've just gotten a confession from O'Malley."

"You did?" asked Frances.

"I did," he replied.

"And you're happy with it?"

"What's not to be happy about it. It's a confession and this case is all but closed. We can wrap it up with just a bit of paperwork."

"When did he confess?" asked Frances.

"Just moments ago."

"Without coercion?"

Davison looked at Frances and furrowed his brow.

"Of course. He seemed almost quite pleased to be able to tell the tale. I hardly had to tell him why he was here before he started blabbering on like a baby."

"Well," said Frances. "If it's all the same to you I'd like to speak with him myself."

Davison looked at Frances but didn't say anything immediately.

"Are you sure?"

"Why wouldn't I be?"

"Well, he's not very polite, and I'm not sure you'll like hearing some of the things he has to say."

"I've girded my loins for the occasion, as my butler Alfred suggested."

Frances smiled broadly, she wanted to laugh, but she didn't want to have to explain herself to Davison. He looked at her, but there was no sign of frivolity on his face.

"Very well, if you insist."

"I do, Cameron. I insist."

This whole discourse between Davison and Lady Marmalade had wiped off the smile from Davison's face. He opened up the door to the interrogation room and walked in, followed by Frances, Alfred and then Pearce.

A rough looking man in blue overalls sat opposite them behind a table. He had a scar above his right eyebrow and another one on the right side of his chin. He wore several days of growth over his face, a face that was lined and weather beaten. He had small blue-gray eyes that looked at you with a blank stare and his brown hair was cut short, speckled gray in places. Frances would put him in his forties, but he had a hard face that had seen rough times, and he could easily have been ten years younger.

Davison pulled out a chair for Lady Marmalade and she sat down in it, across from Patrick O'Malley. Davison took the seat to her left. Pearce walked behind O'Malley and stood to his left, facing Frances.

"Oy, what 'ave we 'ere?" asked O'Malley, grinning wickedly.

It was a face that masked emotion, even the smile was humorless and cold.

"You don't look like a copper," he said.

Frances smiled at him. He was an ugly man, not so much in physical appearance, though he certainly wasn't handsome, but more so in manner and personality. Her back bristled just hearing him speak. He had a way of turning words into shards of glass. His tongue was poison and his manner coarse.

"There are few female police officers Mr. O'Malley. If you had spent much time breaking the law I'm sure you would be aware of that."

He squinted at her and grin only got bigger.

"I've spent plenty ah time with coppers miss. Did the copper 'ere forget to tell you I've got a foul temper and tongue. 'Specially when it comes to women."

"And you'll watch that tongue of yours while you have a lady present," said Davison.

O'Malley looked over at Davison and nodded his head at an angle.

"But of course," he said.

"But I'm not here to visit with you, Mr. O'Malley. I'm here helping the police investigate the murder of Mr. Meda."

"What, that stupid curry eater? Don't bother, I've already confessed."

Frances wouldn't be moved by his spurious tone or racialist remarks.

"I am curious, Mr. O'Malley, before we get to the nuts and bolts, why you have such distaste for Indians."

"Why?" he asked rhetorically, rolling his eye and looking up at the ceiling. "Because they're stupid, dirty and stink like the backside of a latrine. And that's just for starters. They're thieves, liars and bloody snakes."

"I see, and I presume you know this because you've spent some time in India?"

O'Malley looked at Frances for a while but didn't say anything.

"Oy, you're funny you are. Do I look like a gentleman of means? I've never spent a day in that hell and neither would I if you paid me a 'undred pounds."

"Then pray tell, Mr. O'Malley, how you've informed your opinion of Indians then?"

"You can jus' tell by lookin' at 'em. You should know, you've seen 'em. They're dirty and unclean and reek to 'igh 'eaven."

"I do know, Mr. O'Malley, for I have met many in person and I've spent some time in India. Indians are exactly the opposite of what you've suggested. They're more like us than not and their food is delicious and their culture rich."

"Bloody curry lover," said O'Malley, under his breath.

Davison's hand slammed down against the table, making an incredible racket.

"You watch your mouth, O'Malley, or I'll smack some sense into you right here, right now. Apologize to Lady Marmalade."

O'Malley looked from Davison to Frances and then back again.

"A real Lady, so royl'ty is interest in a scoundrel like me eh? My most 'umble apologies, your 'ighness."

Frances wasn't smiling.

"It's nobility, not royalty, Mr. O'Malley, and the proper form of address is 'my Lady'."

O'Malley didn't say anything.

"We've discovered that you're a racialist, O'Malley, but what I'd really like to know is why you wanted to kill Mr. Meda."

"I take except'n to that, mah Lady. I'm not a racialist, I just believe we're betta' than 'em, and I don't want 'em 'ere in our beautiful country."

"Semantics, Mr. O'Malley, semantics. You might be surprised to know that we are the minorities on the global stage and perhaps we should act with more restraint and empathy."

O'Malley leaned in, but he couldn't put his hands on the table. He was chained at the waist. But he did his best to stare hard at Frances. She met his eyes with equanimity.

"Seems like you've given me 'nother reason for getting rid of as many of them animals as possible."

Pearce had taken a step forward as O'Malley had leaned in to try and intimidate Lady Marmalade.

"If you don't mind, Mr. O'Malley, I'd like to get to the underlying reasons, or motive for you killing Mr. Meda. Inspector Davison advises me that you did indeed kill Mr. Meda, did you not?"

O'Malley nodded his head and grinned wickedly.

"I sure did. An' I'd do it again."

Frances kept her eye on O'Malley and nodded her head.

"I'd like to go back to the beginning. Why were you at the lecture? A lecture about pacifism and vegetarianism."

"To kill an Indian, that's why."

"Tell me Mr. O'Malley, what sort of work do you do?"

O'Malley looked at Frances and furrowed his brow. The question confused him. He didn't know what it had to do with anything.

"I get odd jobs when I can."

"So you don't have stable employment at the moment?"

O'Malley shook his head.

"Not that you'd un'erstand. Times are tough for 'ard working people, your majesty."

Frances wouldn't be baited.

"Yes, I know. Things are quite tough at the moment, and I'm sorry for that. But what I do want to know, is if you have at best, intermittent employment, then pray tell, Mr. O'Malley, where you got the five pounds to pay for the ticket. That's quite a substantial amount of money for someone in your position I'd imagine."

"I didn't know it five pounds. I got the ticket from another fellow."

"I see, and who was this fellow?"

O'Malley shrugged his shoulders.

"Can't tell you. He jus' ask'd if I wanted to go and raise some trouble at the talk is all."

"How did you meet this man?"

"At a pub in the East End."

"What was the name of his pub?"

"The Bare Knuckles. Not the sort o' place you'd be interested in."

"So if I understand you correctly, this man just came up to you and offered you a ticket?"

"Not exactly. I was talking to my mates abou' 'ow much we 'ate these curry eaters, and he come up and asked if we wanted to attend this talk by that one Indian who everyone thinks is so 'igh and mighty."

"You're talking about Mr. Gandhi."

O'Malley nodded his head.

"Yeah, that's 'im. He wanted to know if we'd be interested in creating a disturbance at it. Of course we said yes."

"And so he just happened to pull out a ticket for you then and there."

O'Malley shook his head and grinned at Frances.

"No. 'e took our names and said he'd be back with the tickets the next night."

"And that's what happened?"

"Yeah, that's wot 'append. 'Cept he said he could only get the one ticket which he gave to me 'cos it was in my name."

"Did you see this man again?"

"I did, I saw 'im at the talk that curry eater gave. I told my mates I'd make 'em proud, and I did."

O'Malley was smiling like a proud Cheshire cat with a mouthful of mouse tails.

"If this man wanted you to make a scene at the lecture, why did you wait until it was all over to make a scene when half of the audience had gone home?"

"Because this gentl'man asked me too. 'Sides, it suited me fine. If I'd 'ave made a scene too early I'd 'ave been kicked out and then I couldn't 'ave shot that dirty bastard now could I?"

O'Malley was enjoying the conversation now that he could talk about the hatred he felt in his heart and how he'd killed one of those no good Indians. He was proud of it, he was, and if he ever got out of jail he'd keep telling this tale for a long time. He hadn't had many proud moments. In fact, life had been hard and unfair to him, but this was something he could own and take pride of. He looked at Frances, grinning from ear to ear.

"You think it's funny killing a man, Mr. O'Malley."

Still grinning.

"I didn't kill a man, mah Lady, I killed a dirty rat. They're not people, ask the Inspector 'ere, he understands."

O'Malley looked over at Davison, still grinning with this stupid smile stuck on his face like gaping gash.

"Watch your mouth," said Davison. "Everyone's treated equally under the law of His Majesty."

And he would ensure that everyone was treated equally, because he didn't see Indians as animals, but as people, even if he didn't quite understand them or like them. Davison wouldn't condone violence against anyone just because they had a different color skin, but he had to admit that he preferred them to stay out of England. England was for the British after all, or so he thought.

This was not a view shared by Frances. She liked to think of all people as God's people on Earth, and if they should like a chance to make a go of it in England, and they were law abiding, hard working people, then why should anyone stand in their way.

"This man who brought you the ticket, he asked you to make the scene at the end of the lecture, when Mr. Gandhi was outside taking questions?"

"That's right."

"Did he say why?"

"No he didn't."

"And you thought it prudent to make a scene just before shooting a man to death?"

O'Malley shrugged.

"Did you want to get caught, Mr. O'Malley?"

"Listen, Lady, I isn't ashamed of what I done. I'd do it again, a lot of people think what I done is good."

"And yet these men were not even living here in England, but rather just visiting. Why do it to one of them?"

"To send a message that none of 'em is welcome 'ere."

"I see. So were you trying to kill Mr. Meda or Mr. Gandhi?"

"Don't matter to me, they all look the same anyway, don't they? I still don't know who's who."

"Well, the man you shot and killed was Mr. Meda, a friend and assistant to Mr. Gandhi. If you'd really wanted to make a bigger scene which the papers would have written about extensively, you'd have gone after Mr. Gandhi I'd think."

O'Malley's smile turned upside down and he leaned in again towards Frances.

"The papers, they wrote about it plenty. I got the message out."

"And yet you could have made a much bigger scene. Mr. Gandhi is one of the current leaders for a independent India, I'm surprised you wouldn't have tried to shoot him."

"Listen, I shot who I was closest to, and who I had a better shot at. Do you think I'm lyin'?"

Frances nodded.

"I think you are, Mr. O'Malley, I don't think you have the guts to kill anyone, despite how full of bile you are."

O'Malley got up quickly from his chair and tried to topple the table over onto Lady Marmalade. Davison was prepared and he had this big meaty arms on the table holding it down firmly.

"You don't think these 'ands can kill anybody? Come 'ere and I'll snap your spine like a twig."

O'Malley's eyes sparked with anger and hatred. Pearce came up behind him quickly and pushed him hard back down into his chair. Too hard for O'Malley fell out of his chair backwards hitting his head against the concrete floor. It made a horrible dull thud.

Pearce leaned down and helped the dazed O'Malley back up into his chair. O'Malley's nose was bleeding and he hung his head down limply. Then he looked back up at Frances and licked at the blood on his top lip.

"I killed the bloody curry eater, I did," he said, strongly but without a lot of anger left.

Frances shook her head.

"No, I don't think you did, Mr. O'Malley, as much as you might wish you did."

"Hang on, my Lady," said Davison. "He's just given a confession, just like the one he gave me earlier."

Frances turned to look at Davison.

"Yes, I know that. But he's just a small man with a large hatred against people he's never met and never known. He's just hoping to get a little bit of fame at the expense of another's life.

No Inspector, Mr. O'Malley might be hateful and spiteful, but he's no murderer."

"I've seen no evidence to the contrary," said Davison.

"I'm about to offer it. Mr. O'Malley gets offered a ticket to an event he knew nothing about from a stranger. A stranger offering to pay five pounds to let the likes of Mr. O'Malley into a lecture to create a scene. I find it incredulous to believe that Mr. O'Malley then decides to take it upon himself to murder an innocent man in cold blood."

"I did too," said O'Malley licking the blood still leaking from his nose.

"No you didn't, Mr. O'Malley. You were used as a decoy for the real murderer to perform his task."

"And who do you suppose that fellow was then?" asked Davison.

"Why, the fellow who brought Mr. O'Malley his ticket. Tell me, Mr. O'Malley. What did this man look like?"

"He was tall. Taller 'an that man over 'ere."

Mr. O'Malley was looking at Alfred who stood up against the wall across from him.

"Was he an older man?"

"No, I'd say he was about my age."

"What did he look like?"

"Hard to say, I only saw 'im in the dark of the pub, but he didn't 'ave any features that stood out."

"What was he wearing?"

"He wore a long coat both times and a funny 'at. He also walked with a cane."

"What did his hat look like?"

"It was one of them that's folded onto itself on the top."

"A Windsor cap perhaps."

"If you say so. Listen, like I said, I did it. This man wasn't one to do a dirty job like 'at. He was too well dressed."

"Alright then, how did you kill this man?" asked Frances.

"I shot 'im."

"With what?"

"A gun."

"What kind of gun, Mr. O'Malley?"

"It was one of 'em Tommy guns like Machine Gun Kelly."

O'Malley said it as if it was the truth, and he had actually used a machine gun to kill Mr. Meda amongst a group of witnesses.

"Not only did you not shoot Mr. Meda," said Frances, "but you're too dimwitted to realize that a machine gun like that would easily seen by just about anyone with any eyes."

"I ain't dimwitted, I hid it under a long coat, just like the one that the other men 'ad."

"Which other men?"

"Well the man that got me that ticket, he 'ad a mate with 'im who was there too. Both of 'em 'ad on these long coats."

"And where is the machine gun now?" asked Frances.

"I got rid of it."

"How?"

"I just got rid of it."

"Mr. O'Malley," said Lady Marmalade, "if you'd like us to take your story seriously, you're going to have to produce the weapon."

"I can't."

"What do you mean you can't?"

"I gave it to some bloke who wanted it."

"That's an expensive weapon just to give away."

"Well, 'es been good to me."

Frances looked over at Davison.

"You can't seriously be entertaining the idea that this man shot Mr. Meda with a Tommy gun?"

Davison looked over at her and shrugged. Frances looked back over at Mr. O'Malley.

"How many times did you shoot Mr. Meda?"

"I dunno, a bunch of times. I just pulled the trigger for a bit. Maybe a second or two."

"I see, and what did you do about the shell casings?"

"The wot?"

"The shell casings, Mr. O'Malley, the casings that are ejected once the bullets have been fired."

Mr. O'Malley looked away for a moment.

"I didn't do nothin' with them. I ran off as soon as I'd done what I'd set out to do."

Frances looked back at Davison who wasn't looking very comfortable anymore.

"Did you find out what kind of bullets killed Mr. Meda?"

Davison looked up at Pearce. Pearce started flipping through a few pages of his notebook back and forth until he found what he was looking for.

"The cartridges extracted by Dr. Williams were .38 Special."

Pearce looked back up at Lady Marmalade and then at Davison.

"Did you know, Mr. O'Malley, and this hasn't been shared yet, that there were no shell casings found at the scene whatsoever. So what do you suspect might have happened to them?"

"Couldn't say. I guess the police aren't as good as we'd like to think."

Frances turned to look at Davison again.

"If I were a betting woman, Inspector," she said, "I'd put money on the bet that the Tommy gun doesn't shoot .38 Special bullets."

Davison looked at her again and shrugged.

"I don't know about that, Frances," he said. "I'll have to get my men to look into it."

"Please do that."

"That won't be necessary, my Lady," said Alfred, standing back against the wall. "I took an interest in the St. Valentine's Day Massacre that happened in '29 in Chicago."

Alfred looked at Davison and then at Frances who had both turned around to face him, to see if they recalled the gangster massacre. Frances nodded her head.

"I remember hearing about it vaguely," she said.

Davison shrugged.

"Well, I was quite intrigued by the whole idea of mobsters and gangsters at the time in America. But what's relevant to this conversation is that the Tommy gun or more specifically the Thompson Submachine Gun uses .45 Auto caliber bullets. Those are quite different to the .38 Specials that killed Mr. Meda."

O'Malley looked up at Alfred and his face grimaced. His mouth turned upside down and he glared at him. Frances and Davison turned around and looked back at O'Malley.

"Looks like your story is unraveling, Mr. O'Malley," said Frances.

"Well, I woulda done it. And I'm 'appy for whoev'r did do it. We've got too many of 'em Indians 'ere anyway."

"Let's see if we can't dig ourselves out of the lies, Mr. O'Malley, and shine some truth on this whole event. Can we get your cooperation?"

O'Malley tried his hardest to glare at them some more. But he was a popped and deflating balloon. The whole facade he'd created about being a murderer had just blown up in his face. He was defeated. He lowered his head in defeat and shrugged.

"Now listen here, O'Malley, if we don't get full cooperation from you, from this point on," said Davison, "I'll lock you up just for wasting our time. Do you understand?"

Davison was squinting and his eyes were furrowed. He was starting to get upset for having been mislead. He slammed his hand back down on the desk.

"Do you understand me, O'Malley!" he exclaimed.

O'Malley looked back up at him and nodded.

"Yes, Inspector, I understand."

"Good!"

"So why were you really there?" asked Frances.

"To make a scene like I told you. That man who bought me the ticket 'e said 'e wanted me to make a scene after the talk when people were gathered around that Indian."

"Why did he want you to do that?"

"He didn't say, an' I didn't ask. He said 'e liked my attitude about 'em Indians and 'e wanted to know if I'd be interested in causing a disturbance. I told 'im I was."

"And you said you only met him three times is that right?"

"I think it was twice."

"No, Mr. O'Malley, you told us you met him the first time at the Bare Knuckles pub when he asked you and your mates if you wanted tickets to Mr. Gandhi's lecture. Then you met him again the next day or shortly after to get the ticket where he told you he only had the one for you. Then you said you saw him at the lecture with another man also in a long coat."

O'Malley started to nod his head.

"Yes, that's right. I remember now. It was those three times."

"Have you seen him since?"

O'Malley shook his head.

"No, it was jus' those three times. Yes, I'm certain of it, just those three times."

"Did you speak to him when you saw him at the lecture?" asked Frances.

"I tried to, but he seemed all 'igh and mighty then. I waved at 'im from across the room but he jus' turned away. Same with 'is friend."

"Did you see them after the lecture, were they amongst the audience who were gathered around Mr. Gandhi after the talk was over?"

"Yeah, they were both there. I don't know why, 'e didn't seem like a bloke that wanted to talk to any Indians."

"Did you see him shoot Mr. Gandhi or anyone else for that matter?"

"No I didn't. He didn't have a gun, 'e was just waving 'is cane around. But I wasn't that close to 'im. I started yelling things to 'em Indians, so I was looking at 'em when I 'erd the shots go off."

"And what happened to this man and his friend at that time?"

"I didn't really take a look, I ducked my 'ed and ran off."

"Tell me what this man's friend was like. Was he tall like the chap who bought you your ticket?"

"No, 'e was much shorter. 'Bout my 'ight, but slim like I'm, the tall one."

"What did he look like?"

"'Ard to say, I didm' take a close look. He 'ad a beard if I recall."

"And the man who bought you the ticket, did he have a beard or mustache?"

"Yes 'e 'ad a mustache."

O'Malley turned around and looked at Pearce and then back at Davison.

"But not like 'em. His mustache was thick but stuck to his lip, not twirled out."

Frances nodded.

"What did he sound like when you heard him speak? Did he have an accent? Was he working class or posh?"

209

O'Malley shook his head.

"No, 'e didn't 'ave an accent much. I didn't see 'im as a working man but he fancied 'imself as a bit of dandy, but 'e didn't 'ave a posh voice."

"Thank you, Mr. O'Malley. Wasn't that much easier?"

O'Malley didn't say anything to that.

"I woulda killed 'em Indians if I'd 'ad a chance."

He was trying to sound determined and committed but his heart didn't seem into it.

"I wouldn't go around saying things like that, Mr. O'Malley, especially not in a police station. If you want to get yourself locked up for life then you're going about it the right way. But I can promise you, that's no life for any man. Worse than what you think you're going through now."

"'Ow would you know anything 'bout that?"

"I've been around the poor, Mr. O'Malley, and I've been around those locked up. The poor have it better, because if nothing else, they can change things in time."

Frances stood up.

"I don't have any further questions for Mr. O'Malley. Do you, Inspector?"

Davison stood up and shook his head. Pearce closed his notebook and came over their side of the table.

"There's the other chap we have next door that you might like to speak to then."

"I would, Inspector."

"Wot about me, do I get out now?" asked O'Malley.

Davison turned around and looked at him for a moment before speaking.

"If you behave yourself, I might let you out today."

"Listen, I told you everything I know, I told the truth I did."

Davison opened up the door and led everyone outside into the hallway where he closed it behind them again.

"As you can imagine, I haven't had a chance to speak with this Godse chap, what with O'Malley confessing when we got him in."

"I quite understand, Cameron. I don't expect that Mr. Godse did it either, though he might be someone to watch. No, I think who we're looking for is a pair of Englishman. One tall one and one shorter one. Just like Mr. O'Malley said, I think they used him as a diversion for carrying out the murder. I imagine it likely that everyone was focused on the racialist, thus giving them a chance to shoot Mr. Meda, or to try and shoot Mr. Gandhi as the case may be."

"Very well, let's go and see if he can add anything to the scene of the crime."

Twenty

They walked into an almost identical cell to the one that had just held Patrick O'Malley. It had the same table in the middle of it with two chairs on the side opposite to the one that seated the prisoner. Davison pulled out the chair for Lady Marmalade and held it while she sat down. He took the one next to her. Pearce went and stood behind Godse as he had done with O'Malley, and Alfred stood up against the wall behind Frances.

"Nathuram Godse?" said Davison.

The thin Indian looked at Davison and nodded ever so slightly. He appeared to be of average height with a reasonably nondescript face. His mouth though full was hard and straight. His eyes were flat without much emotion and his nose was hooked and pinched with a slim bulbous end that drooped towards his upper lip, much like a hawks beak. He was a young man, barely having entered adulthood and his face had not yet discovered it could grow facial hair. The hair on his head was black, short and slightly wavy.

"Why am I here?" he asked.

He spoke with the accent of his people but his intonation was good and his command of the language excellent.

"You're here because we are investigating the murder of Mr. Ravi Meda."

"I had nothing to do with that," said Godse, shaking his head back and forth quite vigorously.

213

"That's what they all say," said Davison.

"I swear to you, I had nothing to do with it."

"Are you denying that you were there at the lecture that Gandhi gave?"

"No, no, no. I was there, but I did not do these things. I did not shoot Mr. Meda."

"So you knew he was shot?"

"Yes, of course. You would had to have been blind and deaf not to realize what had happened."

"Let's get back to the beginning, Mr. Godse. Why were you at Gandhi's lecture?"

"I wanted to talk to him, it was the only opportunity I had to speak with him of late."

Davison held Godse's gaze until Godse looked away, down at the table. Godse fiddled with his fingernails in his lap.

"As I understand it, you have written of your displeasure with Gandhi before, have you not?"

Godse looked up and his eyes closed a bit and his mouth turned into the smallest snarl.

"You people have no idea what it's like for us. I'm not going to tell you about it, but Mr. Gandhi is on the wrong path and he needs to understand that."

"Quite," said Davison. "And you were the one to put him onto the right path or to kill him if he didn't change."

Davison, sitting here listening to Godse, started to think that Frances could be right about who the real target was. Namely Gandhi. Perhaps Ravi Meda wasn't who those bullets were meant for, but rather they were meant for Gandhi.

"Kill him, you must be joking. I didn't plan to kill him at all."

"We have those letters, Mr. Godse, and they clearly suggest that you were threatening to kill Gandhi if he didn't repent from his approach towards Indian independence."

Davison was reaching, he didn't know exactly what the letters had said, he was hoping they had indicated such threats, but it was a bluff he thought worthy of pursuing.

Godse smirked and looked at Davison.

"You don't have those letters. Because if you did, you'd know that I never mentioned killing Mr. Gandhi, only that he was losing a lot of support amongst a good majority of Hindus, and that it was dangerous for him to continue on the path he was taking. That's all. That is in no way a threat upon his life."

Davison looked over at Frances, and she shrugged at him. She leaned in and whispered in his ear.

"I'm afraid, Inspector, that he has called your bluff. We don't know exactly what those letters said."

Davison nodded.

"Very well, Mr. Godse, what was it exactly you wanted to say to Gandhi that couldn't wait for India?"

"You don't understand, Inspector. It wasn't that it couldn't wait, but rather that Mr. Gandhi would not speak with me face to face. I have tried for months now to have a meeting with him, but he won't meet with me. He thinks I am too young and foolish. But he doesn't know that there are lots of young Hindus who are very interested in a different direction for India. We belong to the Rashtriya Swayamsevak Sangh, or RSS..."

"Which is?"

"We are a group of seriously concerned Hindus who are opposed to Muslim separation and determined to develop a free and independent India for all Indians, Muslims included, but not a separate Muslim state."

"Tell me more about this group, Mr. Godse? Why does Mr. Gandhi not wish to talk with you?" asked Frances.

"I don't know why. That is part of the problem, we are trying to get him to see that the RSS is an upcoming group that should be party to the independence talk. Maybe it is because I am young and he doesn't think I have very much to say, but it is us young Hindus who will go on to lead a free India, and day by day the RSS is growing in strength. Already we have over one hundred thousand members."

"Are you a militant organization?" asked Frances.

"No, no, our founder. Dr. Keshav Baliram Hedgewar is a peaceful man. He is a doctor dedicated to helping the poor. Yes, it is true that he has been involved in the struggle for independent India, but he has only done so by non-violent methods. This is our way, our approach. We are made up of volunteers who are working for a free and independent India, but not with a separate Muslim state."

"And did you have a chance to talk with Mr. Gandhi?" asked Frances.

Godse shook his head.

"No, I did not. There was a quite a large group gathered around Mr. Gandhi and I was not amongst the first to be asking the questions. Additionally, there were a couple of Africans who were taking a long time to discuss the politics of South Africa with him. It seemed they would never stop, until this Englishman started yelling racialist slurs at Mr. Gandhi, and then moments later there were these two gunshots, very close together."

"Did you see anybody with a gun who might have shot Mr. Meda?"

Godse looked steadily at Lady Marmalade.

"No, I'm afraid I didn't. It might have been that Englishman who was yelling terrible things at them, but I didn't see him because I was in front of him. It sounded to me as if he was behind me and to my right. I was just behind the Africans, on the right of the one who was long winded."

"So you would have had a good view if it was one of them then?"

Godse nodded.

"But it wasn't. They were gesticulating with their hands, both of them, as they took turns talking to Mr. Gandhi, and neither of them had anything in their hands."

Davison looked over at Frances.

"I thought you just said, before we came in here, that we were looking for a tall Englishman?"

Frances smiled and nodded at him. She had her hands folded over her handbag in her lap, and she was sitting straight as a bolt.

"You are correct, Inspector, but one must never rest one's laurels until the suspect is caught and confessed. In the meantime, Mr. Godse might have additional information that could be of great help. We have no weapon, we've only just found out the caliber of the bullet, and we're narrowing in onto who he or they were, but we should still keep a broad view in mind."

Davison looked away. He was more like a bulldog than a terrier. When he got ahold of something he wanted to get right at it, and perhaps that was both a blessing and a curse. But what he wanted to go for right now was to find out who this tall Englishman was. But he looked back at Godse and rested his hands on the table in front of him and let his mind chew his patience into a tired and tight ball.

"Mr. Godse, as the inspector has mentioned, there were a few Englishmen around. You've mentioned the one, the racialist. I'm wondering if you happened to notice two others. One of whom would have been tall and the other shorter. Both of them appeared to be wearing long overcoats. Do you recall seeing anyone like that?"

Godse looked off towards the corner of the room and fiddled with his fingers. His eyes looked up towards the ceiling. He slowly nodded his head.

"Yes, I believe so, now that you mention it. There were two men in long dark gray overcoats. They are also wearing what I think you call Windsor caps. They didn't say anything but I noticed them because at one point while the Africans were taking up so much of Mr. Gandhi's time I looked around me to see how many of us there were gathered around him, and I noticed them. The tall one especially."

"How would you describe him?"

Godse looked around and then behind him and saw Pearce standing off his left shoulder. Godse nodded his head towards Pearce.

"His mustache was similar to that. Not as long with the handlebars though, I think you might call it an English mustache. Just very slightly curled up at the bottom, and mostly flat against his lip."

Frances nodded and watched Pearce as he took notes.

"He didn't have a face that you could recognize. I didn't look at him too long because he glared at me so I looked away. He was tall though, probably taller than that man over there."

Godse nodded towards Alfred standing against the wall behind Frances.

"He had a cane too, though it was an odd sort of a cane. Looked thicker than most of the others there, but I didn't really pay attention to it."

Frances nodded and smiled.

"I think we know what our murder weapon was."

Davison looked over at her and nodded.

"Yes we do, .38 Special rounds are fired by a revolver, which doesn't eject the casing, which is why we didn't find any."

Frances looked at him.

"Yes, Inspector, though I always thought the sound was more muted than what I would have expected from a revolver. I believe this cane that our Englishman had with him was likely the weapon. It would explain the more muffled sound that I heard."

Davison shrugged. He wasn't willing to argue with her, not in front of Godse especially. Nevertheless, he would savor the moment of satisfaction when they found this Englishman with his revolver. He'd never heard of someone using a cane as a modified gun. Perhaps in fairytales and Sherlock Holmes stories, but this was reality, and reality was much more pedestrian than fanciful tales.

"What about the shorter Englishman? Can you describe him in any detail?" asked Frances.

Godse had been looking back and forth from Davison to Lady Marmalade, quite intrigued by their banter.

"I didn't pay very much attention to him. The taller man caught my eye. I only remember seeing his companion out of the corner of my eye and noticed how similarly they were dressed."

"Anything else, anything at all that you found interesting, or odd, or strange about them?" asked Frances.

Godse took a moment to recollect his thoughts and to think back to the incident.

"Uh, not really, though...it was strange, they seemed out of sorts with the rest of us. Like they didn't quite fit in with the group."

"In what way?"

"Can't say for certain, though they reminded me of the military and the police I've seen in India. They were brisk in their manner, and something about them just seemed like they were used to order and routine. They just seemed to stick out a bit in that more relaxed atmosphere of Mr. Gandhi's talk. I can't really put my finger on it more than that."

"Thank you, Mr. Godse, I think you've been most helpful."

Godse didn't smile.

"I'd like to leave if it's all the same to you then," he said, looking at Davison.

"In a while," he said. Then he looked at Frances.

"Are you finished with your questions?"

Frances nodded and stood up, grabbing her handbag and slipping it into the crook of her left arm. Davison got up and opened the door for her and led her out followed by Frances, Pearce and then Alfred bringing up the rear. Frances turned to Alfred when they were outside in the hallway.

"How tall are you Alfred?"

"Six foot one on a good day, my Lady," he said, smiling.

She smiled back, and turned to face Inspector Davison.

"So we're looking for an Englishman over six feet tall with a much shorter companion."

"That doesn't really narrow it down very much does it? There must be hundreds of thousands of Englishmen who fit that description here in London alone," said Davison.

"That is true, Inspector, but we aren't looking for just any tall Englishman in London."

"We're not?" asked Davison, raising an eyebrow.

Frances shook his head.

"If I were you," she said, when what she really meant was that she was about to tell him how to carry on his investigation, "I would be looking for tall Englishmen who had recently served as police officers in India. To make it even easier, I'd start with those who were involved in any incidents related to Mr. Gandhi's marches with perhaps a focus on this most recent one at Dharasana."

"And why do you suppose I should do that?"

"Because that's a good place to start, Inspector, especially in light of what Mr. Godse just told us. I think these two men are ex police or military, and I've always thought that this murder had something to do with Mr. Gandhi and that Dharasana march specifically. In addition, is not the .38 Special a favorite amongst the British military and police in India?"

Davison shrugged again.

"I don't know."

"Well, Inspector, I suspect you might find that it is."

"Very well, I'll see if I can't find out who was in charge of the police contingent at the Dharasana Salt Works."

"Thank you Inspector," she said. "I'd also like to urge you to take a more active interest in the police whistle I found. I have a suspicion it might belong to one of our murderers."

Davison looked at Frances for a moment.

"Perhaps you're right. I've found out that it doesn't belong to any of my men."

Frances nodded and smiled at him.

"That would mean they were here in London," added Davison.

"It most certainly would."

Twenty One

The row homes in Hackney were nondescript. They all looked very much the same. Dour and long with sad faces. It was a working man's row of homes where the wives stayed at home and tried to stretch farthings further than pennies, and if she was any good, she might stretch it to within nodding acquaintance of pounds.

There was a constable outside the front door of the home. He nodded at Inspector Davison and Sergeant Pearce as they walked up the stairs. Pearce twirled his mustache as they walked into the house. They both wore light rain jackets, though it wasn't raining this afternoon.

It was Friday just after noon, and they had been called out by the postman who had found a man's body slumped up against the couch. He had seen the body through the large windows as he had walked up to deliver the post. The coroner was inside the living room kneeling over the body.

"Doctor," said Davison as he entered the living room.

Standing to one side were a couple of the coroner's men, ready with a stretcher to take the corpse away when Dr. Williamson was done with it.

Williamson looked up at Davison and Pearce.

"Inspector, Sergeant," he said.

"What can you tell me?" asked Davison.

"Well, Inspector, looks remarkably similar to the Indian chap, Mr. Ravi Meda, who was shot at Mr. Gandhi's lecture on Monday night. Two bullet holes, as you can see. Only this chap seems to have gotten into a fight too."

Williamson pointed to the two bullet wounds that were on the man's chest.

"From the cursory look that I've taken, they look to be of similar caliber and to have been delivered at a similar distance to the murder from Monday."

"Except this man is not Indian," said Davison.

Williamson looked up at Davison, a little puzzled.

"Yes, Inspector, that's quite obvious. He's not Indian, he's British."

"Yes, Doctor, I can see that, I was wondering why a similar murder is committed against two different people."

"That's for you to determine isn't it, Inspector?" asked Williamson.

Davison didn't say anything, and continued to look at the dead body. It was hard to tell the size of the man as he lay slumped in the chair, but Davison would guess he was shorter rather than taller.

"How do you know that, Doctor?" asked Pearce, looking down at the body of the dead man."

"I don't understand what you mean?" asked Williamson.

"Well, couldn't he just as likely be American, or Australian? Perhaps even South African?"

Williamson looked back over at the dead body and nodded. Then he looked back at Pearce.

"I suppose so, Sergeant," he said, "we'll find out soon enough once we've identified him."

"What about the bruising on his face. Is that related to the shooting?" asked Davison.

Williamson looked back at the dead man, and shook his head.

"Doesn't look like it. Looks more like that happened the night before. There wouldn't be as much bruising otherwise."

Davison nods thoughtfully and taps his chin with his finger.

"I've just had a thought," said Pearce as he walked away.

Pearce went out into the hallway and picked up the mail that was still strewn over the floor, having spilled through the mail flap of the front door. The postman had delivered the mail, even though he had seen the dead man in the house. Perhaps a creature of habit. Pearce picked up the mail. There were only a few pieces of it. They were all addressed to a Mr. Trafford Leak. Pearce walked back into the living room and showed the letters to Davison.

"I think we might have an idea who the dead man is, Doctor," said Davison.

Williamson stood up and gathered around Davison and Pearce.

"Mr. Trafford Leak," he said. "Well, that certainly makes my job a lot easier, Inspector. If that's all you need from us, I'll have my lads take the body away."

"Just a minute if you don't mind, Doctor," said Davison. "I want to know if you've disturbed anything in here at all."

"Not at all, Inspector, your constable let us in and we went straight into the living room where the body was. We haven't touched anything except for the body, and we might have stepped on the post when we came in, but that's all."

Davison nodded.

"Can you give me any idea of when he might have been shot?" asked Pearce.

"Hard to say without getting him to the hospital, but probably two to four hours ago if you pressed me to answer it."

"This morning then," said Pearce.

Williamson nodded.

"I can tell you with greater certainty once I've had a better look at him," said Williamson.

"Very well, thank you Doctor, you can take him away."

Williamson nodded at his staff and the two men put Mr. Leak's body onto the stretcher and carried him out, as Davison and Pearce moved out of the way. Davison looked at the letters and opened up the first one. It appeared to be from his fiancée.

Dear Traf,

I can't bear to write this, but ever since you've been back from India, you're a changed man. I don't understand what happened to you there, but you've become terrible angry and distant.

I have to call off the wedding, and I'll return the ring whenever it's convenient for you.

I'm sorry,

Mabel Walmsley

"That's interesting," said Pearce, "looks like we have an Indian connection here. We should tell Lady Marmalade right away."

Davison looked up Pearce with an arched eyebrow.

"In time, Sergeant. This is a homicide, and as far as I remember, homicides are the domain of the police."

"Yes, of course, but we have been encouraged to keep her aware of any developments."

"Indeed we have. And we will, in due time. Let's first finish up our investigation."

Davison opened up the second letter. It was from a firm of barristers and solicitors. The return address was to Wallace and Bigsley.

Dear Mr. Leak,

We have reviewed your case, and determined that there is not sufficient evidence to pursue. It appears that the British

Indian Police, acting with the authority of the British Government has discharged you dishonorably well within their rights.

You may retain us to pursue it if you wish, but we advise you that you would be wasting our time as well as your money.

Regards,

William Wallace Esq.

"Looks like we've found our couple of killers, Inspector," said Pearce.

Davison folded the letter back up and put it in the envelope. He looked up at Pearce.

"Looks like we've found one of them. The shorter one, and the one with the smoking gun seems to be the taller chap who isn't anywhere to be seen."

Pearce nodded.

"It would appear we have two British Indian policemen who might have been involved with our murder from Monday night," said Pearce.

"It would appear that way," said Davison, "though we're going to have to try and find out where this taller chap is, and where he might be hiding."

"A name would help."

Davison nodded.

"Go and knock on a few doors and see if you can't come up with anything."

Pearce left the room and headed outside to see if there were any neighbors who might have something to offer about the mysterious second man.

Davison took a look at the third letter. It was from the electric company. On the outside were stamped in large blue lettering 'Overdue'. He looked at the invoice. It appeared that Mr. Leak was about to lose his lights if he didn't pay up. The bill was a final one for three months being in the arrears. Mr. Leak owed twenty pounds and thirteen shillings. Not only had he recently been discharged, but it appears he had come into some financial difficulties too.

Davison looked around the rest of the house. It would appear as if the taller man was a friend of the now deceased. Nothing seemed disturbed or out of place. There wasn't even any sign of a struggle between the two of them. This was a tale that would be interesting to hear, and he planned on hearing it.

He walked up to the arm chair which had just recently held Mr. Leak. It was dry as if it had been out in the sun all day. The bullets had not exited his body. The coroner would have checked for that, but it was information that Davison needed for his report in any event.

Upstairs were two bedrooms, the one obviously being Mr. Leaks. On top of the tall chest of drawers by the bed was a picture of a man and a woman. It appeared to be reasonably recent, probably within the last few years. Davison could tell because he recognized the man. It was Mr. Leak, and he stood next to an attractive woman with short hair and a hat on her head. She was about his height, and they were holding hands and smiling at the camera. It was a black and white photo taken outdoors. They were in front of the Thames with Big Ben behind them. Mr. Leak was dressed in his police uniform.

There was a second photograph on the chest of drawers which was a group shot of a dozen or so policemen. The men appeared to be in a dry and hot climate. It wasn't England. Davison guessed it was India, but it might have been Australia or perhaps even South Africa. He hadn't visited any of those countries and the scene was minimal, dry and barren except for a few clumps of bushes and a couple of trees behind the men.

Davison picked up the photograph and looked at it more closely. He could see Mr. Leak in the first row on the far left.

There were two rows of men, staggered. A front row and a rear row where the tallest men stood.

There was one chap in the middle of the back row who was the tallest. To his left was another taller chap. Those two were the only obviously tall men in the group. Davison stared at them closely. The photograph must have been at least half a dozen or more years old. He could tell by the uniforms they were wearing. The cut of the jacket was a little longer in the waist than it had become about six or seven years ago.

Davison looked at the bottom of the photograph where the initials and surname of each of the men were, he took note of their names and put the photograph in his jacket pocket.

The second room was practically barren, except for a shorter chest of drawers. Each drawer was empty and there was nothing else in the room except for a bed that was covered in a threadbare white sheet.

Davison left the room and headed back downstairs. He exited the front door and stopped to talk to the constable stationed outside.

"I want the front door dusted for fingerprints, and anything inside the living room that might have had fingers upon it."

The constable nodded and Davison trotted down the front steps and looked up the road and then back down. He saw Pearce knocking on a door kitty corner from where Davison was. He crossed the street to meet up with his sergeant.

An old woman in a dress that was too tight for her and made her look like a fat sausage opened the door. She had curling rolls in her hair and wore no makeup. She had a bulldog's face with an upturned mouth. Pearce looked over at Davison as he joined him. He then looked back at the woman and smiled at her.

"Good day, madam, I'm Sergeant Pearce, and this is Inspector Davison."

"'Ullo," she said.

"We're investigating a murder over at twenty six Houlsen Road," said Pearce.

He turned away and nodded his head towards the home where the constable still stood stiffly outside. Then he looked back at her.

"You don't say?" she said.

"Sadly, yes, madam. We're wondering if you happened to see anything this morning across the road? A man coming and going, or anything at all?"

"Wot time?" she asked.

"Anytime this morning, whenever you might have been up until now."

The older woman puts a fat finger to her sad looking mouth and looks up towards the sky. Then she nods.

"Yes, I do b'lieve I saw a tall man leave that 'ouse 'bout nine thirty, maybe b'fore."

Pearce nodded and jotted down the information in his notebook. He then looked back up at her and twirled his mustache, holding the pencil in the same hand.

"How would you describe him?"

"'E was definitely tall. I didn' take a good look. I don't make a 'abit of spyin' on my neighb'rs."

Pearce nodded.

"We understand that, madam, but anything you might be able to share with us. Anything at all would be truly helpful. Scotland Yard would be in your debt."

The older woman liked that, her sad mouth turned happy for a moment. She liked to feel important.

"'E was tall. Taller 'an you," she said, looking at Pearce.

"I'm not that tall madam," he said.

"I 'spose not, but 'e was tall. Definitely over six feet 'e was."

"How can you be so sure?"

"I saw him exit the 'ouse over there. And 'e was up to 'ere."

The woman turns to face her doorframe and puts her hand up towards the top of it to indicate his height.

"'E was dressed in black too. 'Ad a black cane and black coat. A long black coat almost down to 'is ankles. He also wore a 'at that was squashed on 'is head and 'e 'ad on black gloves."

Pearce took down the notes as quick as she could speak them.

"Was there anything else about him that you can think of?" asked Pearce.

The woman looked over at Davison and smiled at him. She had taken a fancy to the older policeman. Davison nodded at her and pushed an uncomfortable, painful smile onto his face.

"Well, when 'e left the 'ouse, 'e took a moment to look up and down the lane, like you did," she said, looking at Davison. "Then 'e walked quite quickly down the lane that way. I didn't pay much attention to 'im after that."

"So he didn't look out of place. You didn't see him carrying a gun or anything like that?" asked Pearce.

"'E's unusual because 'e's tall, but I've seen 'im visit that 'ouse before. Seen the two of 'em together. Last night 'e actually 'elped carry 'is friend, the short one, into the 'ome."

"Are you sure about that?"

"Quite sure. The short one was 'olding onto 'is friend. 'E looked pretty drunk."

"What time was that?" asked Pearce.

"Just after midnight I'd say."

"Did it look if they'd been in a fight?"

"Couldn't say. It was dark, Serg'nt, and they were walking across the road to that 'ouse you pointed to."

"Did he stay or did he leave shortly after?"

"I saw 'im leave. 'E wasn't in 'is friend's 'ouse very long."

"Did you see him return this morning?" asked Pearce.

The old woman looked back over at Davison and smiled. Davison wanted to get going, to check on any of the other neighbors.

"No, I didn't. I 'eard a couple of soft bangs. Like a car might've backfired far down the street. I went to see, but there were no cars around. I did see 'im, the tall one looking out 'is friend's window. Then shortly after 'e left."

"And this morning then, when you saw the tall friend leave, did he look like he'd been in a fight?"

The woman shook her head slowly.

"No, 'e looked very well put together, like 'ed 'ad a good night's rest."

"And did you or did you not see him carrying a gun or other weapon?" asked Pearce.

"No 'e didn't 'ave no gun. Just that walking stick I told you about."

"Thank you, and what's your name madam?" asked Pearce.

"Mavis Beecham," she said, looking at Davison, and tilting her head and smiling at him.

"You've been most helpful, Mrs. Beecham?" said Pearce.

"I 'ave? You can call me Mavis," she said, still looking at Davison.

"Quite," said Davison.

Pearce nodded, and turned around, they walked down the steps of Mavis' house and stood on the sidewalk by the road. Mavis watched the two of them, holding the door half ajar. Davison turned to look at Pearce and noticed Mavis standing in her front doorway. He looked up at her.

"Thank you, Mavis, that will be all."

She gave him a coy little wave and closed the door slowly.

"I think she likes you," said Pearce.

"Yes, well, I'm married, and she's quite a bit older than me."

"Oh, I don't know about that, not that much older, Inspector," said Pearce smiling.

"That'll be all, Sergeant," said Davison. "What else can you tell me about the other neighbors?"

"Nothing, I'm afraid. Both neighbors on either side of Mr. Leak's home are away, and anybody else I was able to interview didn't see or hear anything. Thank God for nosy neighbors like Mrs. Beecham."

Pearce was looking down at his notebook, flipping through a couple of pages. He put it back into his jacket pocket with the pencil and then twirled both sides of his mustache.

"We should contact Lady Marmalade this afternoon, Inspector."

Davison grunted. She was an annoying stone stuck in his shoe, but he had to keep her informed because he didn't want to have to talk to the commissioner about it.

Twenty Two

Pearce had called Lady Marmalade up at just after four p.m. She was just finishing up tea outside on the patio, by herself when Alfred had come in to tell her about the call. She wasn't expecting Declan or Eric to be home for some time, though she had been expecting a call from Scotland Yard on that particular day.

Lady Marmalade was particularly concerned that Davison hadn't yet found out who the whistle belonged to. The longer it went without finding out who it belonged to, the more she was inclined to think it had something to do with the murder. And she wanted this solved before the week was out, if only to offer Gandhi some sort of solace and comfort.

Alfred drove them both over to Scotland Yard, and this time when they entered the main reception area, Pearce was speaking with one of the constables on duty. He looked up at them as they walked in and smiled.

There were a few other citizens there on that Friday, late afternoon, on police business. None of which really interested Frances, and neither did she have the time to listen in to what any of it was about. Pearce stepped right out from behind the reception area and gave her and Alfred a warm shake of the hand.

"So good of you to come," he said.

"I'm delighted you decided to call," answered Frances, "I was starting to get a little worried that you had been resting on your laurels."

She smiled at him, because she was only half teasing.

"Not I," said Pearce warmly, "I give you my word, Frances, that I am dedicated to solving this heinous crime just as quickly as we can. There have been some good developments in the case I think, over the last several hours. Come along and we can talk about it in Inspector Davison's office."

Pearce led them behind the reception area and down the hall as they had visited before. They were soon ensconced within Davison's office.

Davison was seated behind the desk and he chose, in his gruff way, not to get up when Lady Marmalade and Alfred walked in behind Pearce. He pointed his hand to the chairs in front of him and Frances and Alfred sat down. Pearce walked out of the small office and came back a few moments later with a hard wooden chair which he sat on.

"Pearce told me that you've had some promising events occur today, Inspector," said Lady Marmalade, deciding to start the conversation on pleasant terms.

Davison looked at her and blinked.

"Well, we went to a murder first thing this morning, if you find that pleasant..." he thought about his tone for a minute and decided that a bit of friendliness wouldn't hurt. "A murder related to Mr. Meda's, we believe."

Lady Marmalade looked from Davison to Pearce and Pearce nodded at her.

"Quite right," he said.

"Yes, that's not quite pleasant, but hopefully this will be the end of it then," she said.

Davison nodded.

"I hope so, if we can find the murderer quick enough. If he's killed his mate, I'm certain he might be off to get Mr. Gandhi again."

"Tell me how you think this is related to Mr. Meda's murder?" asked Frances.

"Well, we arrived at this modest home in Hackney shortly after noon this afternoon. We find a short man, you'd say he was short wouldn't you Pearce?"

Pearce nodded.

"Quite short I'd think."

Davison looked back at Frances.

"We found him shot dead. Two bullets to the chest, very similar to how Mr. Meda was shot. I've also received confirmation from Dr. Williamson, the coroner," Frances nodded, she knows the coroner well, "that the bullets he took out of this fellow's chest are .38 Special, and they were fired by the same gun, or cane, as was used with Mr. Meda.

"A cane you say?" asked Frances. Davison nodded. "That would explain the more muffled sound that I heard as compared to a revolver."

Davison nodded again.

"Yes indeed. It appears that we didn't find a revolver because there was no revolver to be found, and all eye witnesses that we've spoken to so far confirm that the only thing they noticed were canes or walking sticks."

"Still, I suppose a revolver could hide in a jacket," said Frances.

"True, but I believe when we find this chap, we'll find a cane modified to shoot .38 Special bullets."

"And what was the name of this man who was murdered today?"

"I wanted you to see this. It gives great insight into who we're looking for and who this lad is."

Davison opened up his drawer and pulled out the photograph of the dozen policemen as well as the three letters Pearce had retrieved from the house earlier in the day. Davison slid the photograph over towards Frances.

France picks it up and looked at it.

"The chap on the far left, the short one, is the fellow who was murdered," said Davison.

Frances looked at it more carefully and then down at the names inscribed at the bottom of the photograph. She looked up at Davison.

"You're saying it was a Mr. T. Leak?" she asked.

Davison nodded.

"Trafford Leak," he said.

Frances picked up the three items of post and looked at them, reading the letters and looking at the invoice.

"He was having some difficulty it would seem," she said.

"Yes. He's about to have his electricity cut off and his fiancée has called off the wedding and he doesn't have a claim against the Indian Police."

Frances nodded.

"I see. That's particularly interesting about being discharged with dishonor from the police. It makes me wonder if it had anything to do with Dharasana."

"That's something I want to find out," said Davison.

"Speaking of which, have you found out anything else about the whistle?" asked Frances.

"I have. This is another interesting bit. It likely belongs to a policeman from the British Indian Police. Those numbers aren't our members' regiment numbers. A chap I know at the Foreign Office says he's seen others like it. It's slightly slimmer than ours as you can see."

Davison pulls out his own police whistle from the drawer and takes out the one that Frances had found, from his pocket, and places them on the table midway between the two of them. Davison's whistle is indeed thicker as well as shorter. The number on his has four digits whereas the police whistle Frances found has five digits.

"Do all Scotland Yard whistles have only four digits, Inspector?" she asked.

Davison nodded and picks up the whistles and puts them away.

"This is really, very good work, Inspector," said Frances, and she notices Davison starts to smile even as he tries hard not to let it grow. Frances looks back at the photograph and notices the two taller men in the middle of the back row. The one is quite a bit taller than any of the others but a second man is also noticeably tall.

"You noticed these two tall men at the back?" she asked Davison, keeping her eye on the photograph.

"I did, and I'd assume that one of them is likely to be the killer of Leak and perhaps of Meda too."

Frances nods her head slowly.

"I think you could be right, Inspector. We're looking for an R. Webb and K. Hudnall."

"We are indeed. I've already asked a colleague at the Home Office to find out if either K. Hudnall and/or R. Webb are in London. If they are, or if one of them is, I'll bet my pension we've got our murderer."

Frances looked up at Davison and smiled at him.

"I think you will have, Inspector, I think you will have."

"I've also sent a telegram to the British Indian Police to try and find out who that whistle belongs to. And speaking of which Frances, I'd be remiss if I did not congratulate you on that find. It is proving to be quite helpful."

"I am happy to be of service to Scotland Yard. I only hope that we can finish this up in due course and give Mr. Gandhi some comfort. I am planning to visit him tonight at his friend's home for dinner. This is great news that you've been able to uncover."

"Agreed. We had an eye witness who heard a couple of soft bangs earlier this morning and went to investigate. She saw a tall chap peer out from the living room window of the deceased's house before leaving. He was carrying a cane, wore a long coat and gloves."

"So you likely won't be able to get any fingerprints then, I imagine?" asked Frances.

"Doesn't look like it, though I'm having them look for them in any event. Regardless, this women...what's her name, Pearce?"

Davison looked up at Pearce as he quickly opened up his notebook and flipped back a few pages. He took out his monocle and stuck it in his eye.

"Uh, Mrs. Mavis Beecham," said Pearce.

"Right, Mavis said she's seen this tall chap around the Mr. Leak's house a fair bit. Appears they were friends. She saw him bring him home last night at around midnight. The tall one helping the shorter fellow along."

Frances nodded.

"I assume she'll be able to identify him then if needs be?"

Davison nodded.

"I'm quite certain. Something else that was odd about the deceased, Mr. Leak, is that he appeared to have been involved in a fight the night before or several hours before he was shot dead. We found bruising on his face to indicate as much."

"And Dr. Williamson confirmed it was prior to his death?" asked Frances.

"He did. Additionally, there were no signs of struggle. I'd suggest the whoever shot Mr. Leak, and I'm assuming it was his tall colleague, surprised him."

Frances nodded.

"I agree. This has been most helpful, Inspector, we can only hope now, that if our suspect is Hudnall or Webb, that they haven't left the country."

"We'll have a whereabouts on them tomorrow at the latest, and as always we'll keep you informed."

"I hope that we might get a confession tomorrow, Inspector. I'd hate to see this case take a week or more to solve."

"As would I," said Davison.

"Would I also be correct in assuming that if both Webb and Hudnall are in London that you'll be picking both of them up for questioning?" asked Frances.

"You would, and before you ask," said Davison, "we'll make sure that you are here when we interview them. You have shown yourself to be worthy in that regard from previous interviews you've helped us with."

"Thank you, Inspector, that would be most kind."

Frances looked over at Alfred, then at Pearce and finally at Davison.

"Is there anything else that I might be missing?" she asked.

"I think that's about all that happened today. Quite a lot I should think. Pearce?"

Davison looked over at Pearce and he flipped through a few pages of his notebook.

"Correct, Inspector, there isn't anything else of note. We knocked on doors up and down both sides of the street and the only one who saw anything was Mrs. Mavis Beecham. Interestingly, neighbors on both sides of Mr. Leak's home were not in. If this fellow is professional, which it sounds like he might be, having been in the police, then I assume he checked the neighbors before going to Mr. Leak's to insure some privacy."

"That's what I would do if it were me," said Frances.

Frances stood up, and this time both Davison and Pearce stood up with her out of respect.

"I hope I'm not rushing," she said, "but I do have dinner at six thirty with Mr. Gandhi and his hosts Mr. and Mrs. Bhandari in Ealing. They're wonderful people and she's a marvelous cook."

"Not at all," said Davison, "Pearce will walk you out. I hope you enjoy your dinner."

"I will, and it will be all the more enjoyable knowing that I can now share this good news with Mr. Gandhi, we are within sight of the finish line, Inspector, I'm sure of it."

"I do hope so, Frances, I do indeed."

Frances left Davison's office followed by Alfred and Pearce, and Pearce led them back out into the reception area where they said their warm farewells.

"Who do you like for this murder, Alfred?" asked Frances when they were outside walking towards the car.

"For Mr. Leak's murder?" he asked.

"Well, I think it's the same man for both Mr. Leak's and Mr. Meda's."

"Then I'd have to say I fancy the taller of the two men."

"Why is that?"

"It seems to me that whenever we've heard anyone talk about this chap, they always comment on his height. So I'd imagine he's quite a bit taller than average."

Frances paused by the car and looked at Alfred.

"I like your deductive reasoning, my dear Alfred," she said smiling at him.

"Though if you might permit me to put a spanner into the works."

"Go ahead."

"Are we certain that these two murders are related?"

"You would have made a fine sleuth, Alfred, perhaps even a finer sleuth than butler, and you know that's saying a lot."

Alfred smiled and nodded.

"But you're correct, I suppose we don't know for certain that this murder is directly related to the first one. However, I believe the evidence is very compelling. For example, all we've heard tell of the events so far is that there were a short and a tall man in the group who were gathered around Mr. Gandhi. We also know that nobody saw any gun of any kind at both scenes, but witnesses identified canes and walking sticks."

Alfred nodded, holding the door open for Frances.

"The coroner has also told us that he believes the same weapon fired the bullets that killed both Mr. Meda and Mr. Leak. That in itself, my dear Alfred, is quite damning."

"I quite agree," responded Alfred.

"And lastly we have the letters found in Mr. Leak's home. His fiancée is leaving him, likely because he no longer has the means to support her as can be deduced from his inability to pay his electric bill, and lastly, and perhaps most importantly, is the letter from his barrister. Our suspect, Mr. Leak, and I believe him to be equally guilty of Mr. Meda's murder, was recently dishonorably discharged from the British Indian Police. Alfred, if we can tie that to the Dharasana incident, I think we have as solid a case as I've ever seen."

"I can't argue with that, my Lady," said Alfred, as Frances sat down into the passenger seat and Alfred closed the door behind her.

Twenty Three

Alfred pulled the Rolls Royce up to the curb. He got out of the car and opened the door for Lady Marmalade. He offered his hand and she took it and stepped out of the car. She was dressed in a pale blue full length dress with matching shoes and pale blue scarf around her head. She held a white handbag in white gloved hands. She looked stunning and elegant at the same time.

"Are you sure you wouldn't like me to keep you company?" asked Alfred.

"I'm certain, Alfred. Thank you for asking. This will just be a social visit. It would certainly be fun to have your company, but I fear that my husband and son would be at a loss for this evening without your company."

Frances smiled at him. Alfred smiled back at her.

"I think you jest. They're probably delighted for a moment of peace and quiet."

"You're probably right. But if you don't go back, I'm sure I'll hear about it from Eric later this evening."

"As you wish, my Lady. What time would you like me to come for you?"

"Eight thirty should give me enough time for a good meal and warm conversation."

Frances put her hand on Alfred's forearm, and smiled at him.

"Thank you for bringing me, Alfred."

"My pleasure, my Lady."

Frances stepped away from the car and Alfred closed the door behind her. He stood and watched as she walked up the stairs to the home of Amar and Gita Bhandari. Amar answered it and waved warmly at Alfred. Alfred put up his hand. Frances shook hands with Amar and then walked inside as Amar closed the door behind her. Alfred got back into the car and drove off.

"We are honored to have you with us again, Lady Marmalade," said Amar as he took her light white jacket and hung it up for her.

"Please call me Frances. It was wonderful of you and Gita to invite me over again. You spoiled me the last time with your cooking."

Frances grinned at him, and he returned the smile.

"Then I hope you will enjoy this evening's repast. Something similar. We haven't gone to great lengths," he said, "Mohandas is a light and simple eater. Come, let us join them."

Frances nodded and they walked together down the hall and into the living room. Mohandas Gandhi was seated on the couch that Frances had sat in before with Alfred. Next to him was Sujay Patel. They both stood up when she entered, as did Gita who was seated at the far end in an armchair.

Mohandas smiled at her.

"It is a great honor to have you with us," he said.

"It is a great pleasure to be invited within such esteemed company, Mr. Gandhi," she answered.

"Mohandas, my Lady, please call me Mohandas."

"Only if you'll call me Frances, and that goes for the rest of you," she said smiling warmly at them.

"Please come and sit down, Frances," said Gita, offering Frances the chair she had just sat in. Amar came back into the living room bringing with him a chair that he had brought. He put it down across from the couch. Frances sat down in what was Gita's chair. Gita went to sit on the hard dining room chair, but Amar gestured for her to take his more comfortable armchair, which was opposite from where Frances now sat.

"Can I offer you something to drink?" asked Amar. "I'm afraid that we are all teetotalers. But we have orange juice as well as mango juice and soda water as well as milk if you'd like."

Frances looked around. Gandhi had a glass of what looked like mango juice, as did Patel.

"If I could be a bother, I would love some mango juice diluted with soda water."

"Not at all," said Amar.

He took note of everyone's drinks, but they were mostly full, so he went off to get Frances her beverage. He came back not long after and offered it to Lady Marmalade. She took a sip.

"Marvelous, simply delicious," she said, smiling at him. He smiled back and then took a seat.

"So what made you decide to invite me back for another one of your famous meals?" asked Frances. "Besides my engaging manner."

Amar chuckled softly.

"Actually, it was Mohandas' idea."

Amar looked over at Mohandas, and he looked over at Frances and smiled.

"It is true, Frances, I had asked my dear friend Amar, as a special favor if he would mind having you over for dinner again. I was sorry to have missed you when you came by on Tuesday. If truth be told, you give me confidence in your manner, and I am comforted that you are helping Scotland Yard solve the tragedy that befell my dear friend Ravi."

"So it could be my engaging manner," she said smiling.

Mohandas chuckled and nodded.

"Exactly."

"Well, I couldn't be happier to have been invited round this evening. Just when I was feeling a little stymied by the events of this case, namely coming up with dead ends, which I'll tell you about, I met with Inspector Davison. You remember him from Monday evening?"

Mohandas nodded.

"It appears that there has been a good deal gathered just today that I am confident will help us solve this case by the end of the weekend."

"That is very good news," said Amar.

"Agreed," said Patel.

"But I don't won't to be rude," said Frances, "I'd love to hear how the negotiations are going at the Round Table. I hope you're winning some hard fought concessions."

Gandhi shook his head sadly.

"It appears that I am not cut from the politician's cloth," he said. "There are some things I find difficult to negotiate upon. Perhaps the most pressing being that all Indians should be protected under the Congress, especially the disenfranchised untouchables, who for some reason, their representative believes should be treated as a minority."

"I must claim a large body of ignorance when it comes to matters of internal Indian politics. Could you help me understand your position. Specifically, why you feel that the untouchables should not be granted minority status?"

Frances was leaning in towards Gandhi. She found him very easy to listen to. He had a quiet, warm and calm voice, and he was particularly well reasoned.

"I will certainly try and explain it to you to the best of my ability, Frances. But first I feel that a little bit of background information is important."

Frances nodded.

"The caste system in India is similar to what you have here in England, but it is much more egregious. You have the lower classes and the upper classes with a middle class in-between."

Frances listened intently.

"But unlike in England, where there is what I would consider an ability to climb the classes, it is almost impossible for outcastes or untouchables to rise beyond their caste. In India there are four main castes or what are called varnas. In order of importance they are Brahmins, which are generally considered the priestly class. Kshatriya which makes up the warrior class and includes kings, soldiers and governors of various sorts. Vaishyas which are general merchants and businessmen, and lastly are the Shudras. The Shudras are laborers and service people. At the lowest end of the Shudras are the untouchables or what some call the Dalit. I call them Harijan which means children of God. The Harijan are ostracized like no other group in India. To be touched by one of them is to become polluted, hence the name untouchables, and requires vigorous cleansing. The Harijan are not allowed to partake in religious rituals, have historically been kept on the outskirts of civil society both literally and figuratively. Anything that a Harijan uses, can not be used by anyone else. It is a systemic and heinous blight on India, and Hinduism."

"But is there not any pride in honest work and labor?" asked Frances. "We have the working class or lower class as you mentioned, and yet they are not shunned as it seems your Harijan are. And any class system, if I am to be honest with you, Mohandas, is a black eye to any civilized society."

Mohandas smiled at Frances and slowly nodded his head.

"I quite agree. But to answer your first question. The Shudras, or lowest caste are not as a whole shunned. Rather it is the sub-caste within, the Harijan who are. Part of the difficulty that I am experiencing at the Conference is that my dear friend, Mr. Bhimrao Ambedkar, who is himself Harijan, and I disagree with the approach that should be taken regarding alleviating the suffering of the Harijan. You see, the Harijan, as part of the

Shudras are laborers, but they labor in roles that are considered the worst, ugliest and most menial of occupations that nobody wants. They are the leather workers, the butchers, the sewer workers, and those responsible for disposing the dead, and so on."

"And yet how would society run if not for men who performed those duties."

Mohandas nodded.

"I agree, but we need to understand Hindu society in order to understand the full picture. In Hinduism, the cow is honored as a symbol of unselfish giving. We enjoy her milk and she provides much service on the farm. Killing cows is illegal in India, and most Hindus are vegetarian."

"I see," said Frances. "My son's friend is vegetarian for philosophical reasons, and that is why we were invited to attend your lecture, which was very informative."

Mohandas nodded and smiled again, looking at Frances with kind eyes.

"And this is where Bhimrao and I differ on opinion. Bhimrao believes that the caste system is inherent within Hinduism, and one can see this argument from that perspective of some forms of labor such as leather workers and butchers. My perspective however, is that it is more of a societal convention that has been attached to Hinduism to allow for the performance of certain jobs conveniently. You see, we cannot determine with certainty when the evolution of the caste system began, and there are very few texts in Hinduism that address this caste system directly. In summation, my position is that the Harijan should be included within the greater Hindu community without special protection. I find that paternalistic. We must excise untouchability from Hindu society, as well as the caste structure in general so that all Hindus can live peacefully side by side."

"And Mr. Ambedkar disagrees?"

"Yes, because as I mentioned above, he believes the caste system to be an intrinsic aspect of Hinduism, he wants the Harijan, or Dalits as he calls them, to be removed from Hinduism altogether and to be given special considerations."

"And you feel that is wrong?"

"Not specifically, I understand his position, my wish is rather for a greater unified India and Hinduism rather than a fractured and splintered one. If the Harijan get special treatment, then the Jains, Sikhs, Christians, Buddhists and Muslims will all want special treatment and I can't see how that will help Indian independence in the long term."

"And Mr. Ambedkar has a different take. I suppose I can understand where he's coming from," said Frances, "he is after all, as you said, from that caste. Perhaps the injuries he's suffered from that have put great pressure on his political opinions."

Mohandas took a sip of his mango juice and looked into the cup for a moment.

"You are quite right," he said. "Yet, these are things that we disagree about, and which we disagree openly about at the Conference. I fear it will not help us in the long run. Or perhaps I am not the politician that my fellow Indians have thought I was."

Mohandas smiled ruefully at Frances and then took a last sip from his mug of juice.

"But your heart is in the right place, and with that being said, I don't see how your position is wrong, and I suppose neither is Mr. Ambedkar's. I believe Mohandas, that time will iron out these wrinkles. So long as we're fighting the good fight, the future will take care of itself. That's what I believe, but then again, I have stayed far away from politics as much as I can, for these very awkward and difficult positions that politicians seem destined to wrestle with."

"They are indeed awkward and difficult. I have great respect for my friend Bhimrao. But friends can often disagree upon many points of philosophy and politics, as can twins I'm sure."

Frances drank from her mixed drink. It was fizzy and lightly sweet, and reminded her of India and the many times she had spent there.

"Would any of you like to add to the discussion?" she asked. "I do find it very intriguing and educational."

"I have lived here for so long," said Amar, "that I fear it is not for me to offer opinions on India from whom I am so far removed."

Frances looked at him and smiled.

"Though I trust in Bapu's opinion."

"Who is Bapu?" asked Frances.

"Oh, I am sorry, Frances. Bapu is a term of endearment that many of us have for Mohandas. It means 'father', and in Mohandas' case we use it to refer to him as the father of India."

Frances looked over at Gandhi and smiled.

"It is too much," said Gandhi, "but it is kind of my people to offer me such a great honor."

"I don't think that you will find dissenting opinions here, Frances," said Patel. "We are all great friends and admirers of Mohandas, and part of that has to do with shared beliefs and political leanings."

"Yes, I very much understand," said Frances. "But do you feel that Mr. Ambedkar's position as compared to Mohandas' will be something that can be negotiated?"

Frances looked at Patel.

"Yes, I do believe that all Indians will come to live under one India regardless of caste or belief. But from what Mohandas tells me of this Conference, I am not certain that the two of them will see eye to eye. But if you ask me, I can foresee the day when

India is independent that we might have a Dalit or Harijan for president."

Frances looked over at Gandhi, and Gandhi nodded.

"I think that is quite possible," he added.

"Perhaps that is enough talk of politics," said Gita smiling around at everyone in the room. "Dinner is ready, and we must not let it be ruined."

Amar nodded in agreement and he stood up with this wife. Everyone else stood up with them and walked into the adjoining dining room. Amar pulled out a chair for Frances which she sat down in. Amar sat at one end of the table, and Gandhi, their honored guest sat at the other end. Frances was on Amar's left and to her left was Sujay Patel. Patel was seated to Gandhi's right. The side opposite Frances was empty.

Gita came in and out of the kitchen, carrying trays with an assortment of curries on them. Most of them Frances remembered from her previous visit. Finally, when Gita had brought all the food out and the utensils, she sat down across from Frances and smiled at her.

"You've gone to a lot of trouble Gita," said Frances, "and I want to thank you for that."

"It is an honor to have you with us," said Gita.

Gita looked over at her husband. Amar looked up at Gandhi.

"Would you do us the honor of saying the prayer?"

Mohandas smiled, and then closed his eyes. Everyone followed suit. He said something in Sanskrit and then opened his eyes. He looked over at Frances.

"That is a verse from the Bhagavad Gita. It speaks to how the four foods that we are about to enjoy will become the life essence of who we are, intermingled with our breaths. It asks us to take a moment and think upon the immediacy and intimacy of this food which we take into our bodies to feed our spirit. This is one of the many reasons why I am vegetarian. If we are feeding our spirit, I feel that food of violence, which animal flesh by necessity entails, cannot uplift this spiritual condition."

Frances nodded her head.

"I can certainly understand and respect that position," she said.

Everyone looked at her for a moment.

"Please, Frances, you must take your portions first," said Gita.

Frances took a little bit of everything, including the pakoras and samosas which she had greatly enjoyed previously. Everyone then went and helped themselves. A jug of water was on the table which Gandhi used to pour himself a glass, as did Patel and Amar. Frances noticed how little food Gandhi had put on his plate. Perhaps a half of what she had managed to put on hers.

"Are you not particularly hungry, Mohandas?" she asked.

Amar smiled at Gandhi, and Gandhi in turn smiled at her.

"Hunger is something that one can control. I feed the body what is necessary for health and satiety. I also try and remember that many of my people are lucky if they get this much to eat all day. But this is sufficient. This will be enough for me."

Frances nodded at him and took a forkful of curry with some rice and put it in her mouth. Everyone started to eat.

"We have heard a lot about the Conference, but you promised that there was good news to be shared about Ravi's murder," said Gandhi.

"I did, and there is," said Frances, finishing a mouthful of food.

Everyone tucked into their food as they waited for Frances to start speaking. She took a sip of her drink.

"But first," said Frances, "where are your wonderful children?"

"Chandra is at the university studying along with Ajeet. Though I suspect there might be some socializing with friends involved too," said Gita smiling.

Frances smiled.

"Please do send them my warm wishes. I'm sorry they're not here with us."

"Of course," said Gita.

Frances took another sip from her drink.

"Alright, onto more serious matters. I'm not sure if I had mentioned that on Tuesday, when I went back to the scene, I found a whistle."

Frances stopped and looked at Amar and Gita for a moment. They shook their heads.

"It was odd. This was certainly a police whistle that I found, and I wasn't sure if one of Inspector Davison's men had dropped it the night before or that morning. I had Alfred give it to the inspector. I was hoping it might give us something to work with. I wasn't sure how it might be involved, but I had a suspicion that it wasn't one of Scotland Yard's."

"What gave you that impression?" asked Patel.

"Looking at it, it looked older as if it might have been there earlier than Tuesday. It wasn't anything definite, just a suspicion more than anything. I can't put a name on it, but I've been doing this sort of thing for some years, and I've learned to trust my intuition. Most often, it leads me in the right direction. Though not always."

Frances smiled at him and took a bite of her food.

"On that Tuesday, the police had found six tickets scattered close to the scene where Mr. Meda was shot. I believe I mentioned this in passing to Sujay on Tuesday." Patel nodded politely. "I thought this to be quite helpful, if we could find out who the tickets belonged to, we might have some idea of potential suspects or at least witnesses."

"And were the police able to determine who the tickets belonged to?" asked Gandhi.

Frances nodded.

"They did, and this is where things became hopeful for me. On Monday when I was here last, you had mentioned to me, Sujay, those who had written threatening letters to Mohandas. You had also told me the names of the two men who had died from their injuries suffered at the hands of the British Police in India."

Patel nodded.

"To refresh our memories, or mine as the case may be, there were three names you offered me. If I recall correctly they were Parvez Dada, Pitambar Singh and Nathuram Godse."

Patel clapped his hands together in delight, and smiled at Frances.

"You have a great memory," he said. "Do you remember who the two men were who died at Dharasana."

Frances smiled at him.

"I do. They were Chetan Panchal and Ajit Pai. Ajit Pai was easier to remember because his name is similar to your son's, Amar."

Amar smiled at her.

"You will all remember that Mr. Meda's dying words to me were 'Indian p'. That got me to thinking that he was either trying to tell us his killer was an 'Indian person' or an Indian with a name starting with P. I liked the latter idea as it seemed more likely to me. And I thought, having spoken with Sujay, that we likely had two strong candidates, namely Parvez Dada or Pitambar Singh, as both of their first names started with P. I was quite confident that once we learned who those six tickets belonged to, that either or both of their names would be included in that list. Sadly, sometimes things are not that easy."

"None of them were on the list?" asked Amar, putting a forkful of food in his mouth.

Frances looked over at him and nodded.

"That's right. I was really expecting one of them at least, either Parvez Dada or Pitambar Singh to be one of the owners of one of the six tickets that were found. The good thing is that the Vegetarian Society kept excellent records about who bought what ticket. Inspector Davison was able to obtain those records, and when I visited him we looked at the six tickets."

"And none of them belonged to either Parvez or Pitambar?" asked Patel.

Frances nodded before taking another bite of food.

"Hmm," said Patel, "that is very interesting. I too would have thought they would be on that list."

Frances nodded.

"They weren't, and that's probably because, at least I assume, that they aren't in England. But there were three names out of the six that were attached to the tickets who had Ps in their names."

"Do tell?" asked Gita.

"An Irishman by the name of Patrick O'Malley. You might have known him as the man who was shouting unpleasant words before the gunshots came."

Frances paused and looked over at Sujay and Mohandas. They both nodded, remembering him.

"I remember him," said Gandhi, "though I don't remember seeing any gun on him."

"Because there wasn't," said Frances. "He might be a racialist, but he's not a murderer. We interviewed him yesterday. I thought he was a good prospect, but I wasn't convinced it would be him. Why create such a scene if you were intent on murdering someone. Didn't make sense to me, and as it turned out, he was offered a ticket by the men who did commit the murder, but that comes later. He was a pawn."

"Who were the other two?"

"This is where things got very interesting, and I really felt we were on the right path when we found this out. The two other men were Bijay Panchal and Amir Pai."

"The sons of Chetan and Ajit," said Gandhi, looking sadly at Frances. Frances noticed that he had not eaten much of his food. Frances nodded.

"Yes, unfortunately. However, from a police perspective, they too looked like decent suspects. They both had what I considered to be strong motives."

Gandhi shook his head sadly.

"They were angry the last time I visited them. I helped them find each other. I thought that through shared loss they might find space of healing, but their anger was strong."

Frances looked at him kindly and smiled, nodding her head softly.

"I know, this all came out during the interviews. We interviewed both of them, independently, on Wednesday. They explained that they had come to London to offer their forgiveness to you."

Frances paused and looked at Gandhi. He held her gaze for a moment and then looked back down at his lap, nodding sadly.

"Forgiveness helps move past the suffering, at least in my experience," he said, softly.

"And I believe them. They both gave independent statements that were corroborated. They acknowledged feeling angry at you at first but came to appreciate what you had done for them. They have started a business together and with some of the profits they bought tickets to London to come and give you their forgiveness in person."

Gandhi looked back at Frances and smiled at her, the corners of his eyes crinkling.

"I must make time to see them," he said to Patel, who nodded his head. "I am pleased that it was not them."

"I was too," said Frances, "I much prefer seeing men and women with significant pain taking the high road, but it left me in a dilemma. I no longer had a good grasp of who might have committed this heinous act."

"All the men with the letter P in their name were no longer viable suspects," said Amar.

Frances nodded.

"I was, and remain very eager to finish this case for you Mohandas, as I am appalled that a close friend and colleague of yours was brutally murdered in cold blood here on England's soil."

Gandhi looked at her and smiled.

"I knew that the first time we met by the questions you asked. I knew then, that Ravi's murderer would not go unfound."

"And yet, here I was without any further evidence to pursue. The other three names associated with the remaining tickets found at the scene didn't seem to be strong candidates. One was a woman, and I don't feel that this murder was committed by a woman, the other chap was an African, who we were going to interview before we found what we did earlier today."

"That would have been one of the South Africans talking to me at the time, I imagine," said Gandhi.

Frances nodded and sipped her drink.

"I can't see how it would have been either of them. They were both very close to me and I would have seen one of them pull a gun out if they were the shooters," said Gandhi. "They couldn't have done it. They were still gesticulating when I heard the gunshots and Ravi fall to the ground."

"That was my suspicion too, when I heard both Bijay and Amir state that very same thing. The third person was a man by the name of Ryan Webb, which I didn't give much thought to, until now. I think we'll be talking to him, as I'm sure he's the same Webb that I saw earlier today in a photograph, which I'll get to in a moment."

"Was there anything that was helpful from that list?" asked Patel.

Frances finished chewing a mouthful of food she had just taken. She nodded to buy herself some time.

"Nathuram Godse whom you spoke of on our first visit was also on the list of those who had bought tickets. His ticket wasn't found scattered at the scene, but he was in the registrar."

"Did he do it?" asked Patel.

Frances shook her head slowly.

"No. We interviewed him yesterday too, and we don't believe that he had anything to do with it. Naturally, as you know, he is not the biggest fan of Mohandas," she said, talking to Patel, "but there were no weapons found on him or where he lives. He said something else that was interesting, and this is where we start to narrow it down to the real suspects."

Frances paused to scrape another forkful of the delicious curries onto her fork and put it into her mouth. Godse, confirmed what we had already heard from Bijay, Amir and Patrick, namely that they had all seen two men in long overcoats. They were an odd pair, because one of them was quite tall and the other was shorter than average. They also had the bearing and deportment of military men, and one of them had with him a long cane."

"But that by itself does not mean they are guilty of anything," said Amar.

Frances smiled and nodded.

"Quite right, Amar, but it was a start, and now it gets better. You see, the coroner, Dr. Williamson determined that Mr. Meda was shot with .38 Special caliber bullets. Not particularly large caliber but quite sufficient for murder as we know. .38 Specials are usually fired by revolvers and that was one conundrum that I hadn't quite figured out. We found no shell casings at the scene, which isn't surprising when you realize that Mr. Meda was shot with .38 Specials. After all, a revolver doesn't eject the shells. But my quandary was that the gunshots that I heard, sounded more muted or muffled than what I had come to expect from a revolver."

"So with what was he shot?" asked Gandhi.

"That is where it gets very interesting. He was shot with a rifle, or more accurately a modified cane that appears to act as a rifle, and that is why the gunshots sounded more muffled."

Gandhi nodded his head ruefully.

"But there were many men at the lecture with canes. I saw them myself," said Patel.

Frances nodded and cleared her throat and then took a sip from her drink.

"I know, but what happened this morning was another murder. And this murder is associated with Mr. Meda's murder. We know this, because the coroner has confirmed that today's victim, a Mr. Trafford Leak, was shot with .38 Specials, that Dr. Williamson strongly believes were delivered by the same weapon as that which shot Mr. Meda."

Patel nodded.

"That is indeed, very good news," he said.

"It is, and it gets better. Mr. Trafford Leak, it appears, from correspondence found at the scene, was recently dishonorably discharged from the British Indian Police. We're just waiting for confirmation as to why, but my suspicion is that this will be related to the Dharasana Salt Works incident. And if it is, then we're looking for his accomplice who is either an R. Webb, who I believe to be Ryan Webb or a K. Hudnall."

"Why those two exactly?" asked Amar.

"A photograph as I mentioned earlier, was found in Mr. Leak's bedroom. It was a group photograph of police officers wearing Indian police uniforms. Mr. Leak, who is shorter than average can be seen in the foreground. In the background, the tallest two are the men I just mentioned."

Frances went back to eating a bit of food while she let that bit of information settle into the minds of her listeners.

"That is fascinating. Is there anything else you have?" asked Patel.

Frances nodded.

"That whistle I found," she said, and Patel nodded. "Inspector Davison finally got around to investigating it. It doesn't belong to anyone at Scotland Yard, in fact it is a slightly different shape. And from preliminary inquiries at the Foreign Office, it appears to be British Indian Police issue. We're waiting to hear back from them as to who it belongs to. If I were to bet, I'd suggest it belongs either to Webb or Hudnall, and if it does, that is terrific news. It puts them at the scene of Mr. Meda's murder."

"Thank you, Frances," said Gandhi. "You have put great effort into this and it inspires my confidence."

"Thank you, Mohandas. There is one last item. A witness observed a tall man leave Mr. Leak's home, wearing an overcoat and cane, shortly after she heard some soft and muted bangs that sounded like gunshots. She's certain that she will be able to recognize him if required, for she has seen him often at Mr. Leak's house as he appears to be a friend of the deceased."

"This does look good for not only finding the shooter, but also having him charged and found guilty," said Amar.

Frances nodded.

"This is the tall man that we've been searching for. Why he shot and killed his friend is not something I understand yet, unless his friend was going to talk to Scotland Yard. Nevertheless, I am sure if we find him, we'll find the cane and that will be his nail in the coffin."

Mohandas smiled at Frances, and they all got back to eating their food. The mood was lighter and more playful the rest of the evening as they all rested a little easier in the knowledge that Ravi's death would not go unanswered.

Just after Lady Marmalade had finished her first cup to tea and was about to entertain a second cup, a knock on the door indicated that Alfred was here to pick her up.

Twenty Four

It was just before eleven in the morning when Lady Marmalade had received the phone call from Sergeant Pearce of Scotland Yard. He had told her they had some very good news, and that they had just picked up Detective Constable Ryan Webb and were going to interview him if Lady Marmalade would like to attend, and indeed she would. Alfred had driven her to Scotland Yard, leaving Ginny in the house alone as Eric and Declan had gone out to enjoy a game of golf with some clients.

At just after eleven, Frances found herself sitting down in Inspector Davison's office for what seemed like the umpteenth time. Next to her was Alfred, and in front of her sat a happy looking Davison. He smiled at her.

"We're this close, Frances," he said to her, bringing his thumb and forefinger within an inch of each other.

"I have heard, Inspector," she replied, "you chaps have done such a thorough and marvelous job of this case."

And what she wanted to add but didn't say, was that it was only because she had to encourage them in the right direction. Or perhaps even had to lead them really.

To the left of Davison was an envelope that he slid under his arms and opened up. He pulled out a few sheets of paper.

"I got this from my colleague at the Foreign Office first thing this morning."

"That's kind of him for sending it in on a Saturday," she said.

Davison smiled wryly.

"It is a capital murder case, Frances, time doesn't wait on these sorts of things."

Frances smiled at him thinly. He was a difficult, self important and bumptious man at the best of times. Hard to like, but not outside of Lady Marmalade's abilities to appease, though she much preferred his Sergeant. Pearce was a genuinely warm and amiable man, and dare she say, likely as good, if not a better investigator.

Davison looked down at the first sheet of paper.

"This here is the correspondence I received from him related to the whistle. The whistle, as it turns out belongs to the deceased Mr. Leak. Why he was carrying it, we have no idea, but it's his most certainly."

"That's good news," said Frances, "that confirms that he was there, just as the eye witnesses said. It also gives greater credence to the idea that Webb or Hudnall were there too, whoever turns out to be Mr. Leak's co-conspirator."

"It most certainly does. Additionally, as Pearce likely told you, we've picked up Detective Constable Ryan Webb just a little while ago. He's living with his mother in Bromley. It seems he's had some misfortune lately."

Davison looked shuffled the papers around and picked up a different one from the first.

"What's that, Inspector?" asked Frances.

"This is part of Sergeant Webb's personnel file."

"I thought he was a detective constable?"

"Yes, quite. He is a detective constable right now, but that's because he was demoted and sent back here to work in the Foreign Office. Last year, he was a young up and coming sergeant with the British Indian Police, and you can guess where this is going."

Davison looked up at Frances and raised an eyebrow.

"He was in charge of the Dharasana contingent of police officers."

"Quite correct, Frances," said Davison, smiling at her. "He was the sergeant in charge on the 21st of May, 1930 when Chetan Panchal and Ajit Pai died at the Dharasana Salt Works."

Frances nodded. This did not surprise her. Davison looked at the paper in front of him.

"This is the interesting part. All eye witness accounts name and point to Constables Hudnall and Leak as the two men responsible for the deaths of those two Indians I just previously mentioned."

"That is interesting. Tell me Inspector, have you cross referenced Hudnall and Leak with the registry of the Vegetarian Society for Mr. Gandhi's lecture?" asked Frances.

Davison nodded.

"That's a bit of a puzzle you see. Ryan Webb's name is on that list with ticket..."

Davison opened up his drawer and pulled out a copy of the registry for the lecture. Attached to it was a sheet of paper with names and ticket numbers of suspects who had attended. He looked at it for a moment.

"Ah, here it is. Ryan Webb had ticket number 0245, but there are no Hudnalls or Leaks on here at all."

Davison looked up at Frances for her response.

"Interesting indeed, Inspector. But we know these men to have carefully planned this. They used Mr. O'Malley as a red herring, and perhaps the same with Constable Webb. It would not surprise me if they used pseudonyms for themselves."

"You are very astute, Frances, I'll give you that. That is exactly what they have done. Or at least it is exactly what Hudnall has done, and we assume so did Leak."

"What name do you believe Mr. Hudnall is using?" asked Frances.

"Well, that's the thing. We didn't know, and we didn't know how to find him. The only evidence of him being in England comes from the Foreign Office which put him landing ashore on HMS John Huffam on the 12th of September, 1930..."

"A year ago today," said Frances.

Davison looked up at her quizzically before realizing she was right. Then he nodded his head.

"Yes, a year ago today. Both Hudnall and Leak arrived at the same time. As I said, we didn't know how to find him, but Sergeant Pearce here thought we might as well show the photograph around town, and he thought we should start with the Bare Knuckles pub."

Frances turned to look at Pearce and smiled at him while nodding her head in admiration.

"That sounds very logical," she said.

"Well, it was," continued Davison, "because as it turned out, the proprietor of the Bare Knuckles knew Hudnall from the photograph that Pearce showed him."

Davison looked at Pearce to allow him the pride of telling the rest of the story. Pearce took a moment to twirl his mustache before continuing.

"I asked him if he'd seen this man Hudnall. He said he hadn't met anyone with that name, so I described Hudnall to him, and he thought it sounded like someone who was renting a room upstairs. I then showed him the picture and he identified them both."

"Both?" asked Frances.

"Yes," said Pearce nodding. "He noticed both of them, the short fellow, Leak and the tall fellow Hudnall. But he said that Hudnall wasn't his name. I asked him what name did he go by, and he said Hudnall called himself Alfred Jingle."

Frances smiled.

"That's fascinating."

"Interesting, yes. I asked him if he knew who Leak was, if he knew his name, because as you know, Leak wasn't there, at the lecture, as himself, or at least under his own name."

"And what did the publican say?" asked Frances.

"He shrugged, said he didn't know the chap's name. He did however, acknowledge seeing Hudnall and Leak on Thursday evening."

"How did he remember them from that night?" asked Frances.

"He said he remembered them from a fight that they got into. At least he said it was mostly the short one, Leak. Said he had a terrible temper that got himself into trouble that night. The publican said the tall one, Jingle or as we know him, Hudnall, had to intervene and carry his friend out."

"Have you have a chance to pick him up then?"

Pearce shook his head and looked at the floor.

"Not yet. The publican, who's name is..." and he looked at his notes, "Charles Bates, hadn't seen him since Friday morning."

"Are you serious?" asked Frances, trying her best to stifle a giggle. Davison and Pearce both look up at her with raised eyebrows. Sitting next to her, Alfred smiles wryly.

"Why wouldn't I be?" asked Pearce, frowning at her.

"Carry on the, Sergeant," said Frances. "How are you going to catch him?"

Still frowning, Pearce said, "I've left two of my best men in the pub to keep an eye out for him and pick him up as soon as he comes in."

Pearce and Davison looked at each other quizzically.

"So we don't know what name Leak used to buy his ticket, or what name Hudnall gave him to buy his ticket, do we?" asked Frances.

"That's correct," said Davison.

"And I'm assuming that Alfred Jingle is on the registry?"

"He is," said Davison, looking back down at the registry list in front of him. "Ticket number... 0212."

"I just had a thought, Inspector," said Pearce.

Davison looked over at him suspiciously.

"What's that?" he asked.

"Well, if Hudnall is Jingle, and assuming he bought the tickets for both himself and Leak, perhaps Leak's real name is attached to a ticket one after or before his own. What are the names for tickets 0211 and 0213?"

"I like how you're thinking, Pearce," said Davison.

Davison looked back at the list again.

"0211's name is William Sheppard. Hester Abbot has ticket number 0213."

Davison looked up at Pearce.

"It can't be Hester, for we know that Leak was a man," said Pearce.

"Exactly," continued Davison, "so it must be William Sheppard! Good work Sergeant. I think we've found the nom de plume that Leak must have used."

Frances smiled bemusedly at them both. Pearce looked over and saw her.

"You don't agree, Frances?" he asked.

"No, I'm afraid I don't," she said.

"Why?" asked Davison.

"Well, let's exam the logic shall we. If we believe, which I do, that Mr. Hudnall bought the tickets for himself, Leak, Webb - which we'll find out - and O'Malley, then he would have done it carefully. This whole crime seems to me to have been carried out meticulously if you disregard the fact that they missed shooting who they really wanted. And with that in mind, look at the ticket numbers. Jingle, or Hudnall as is his real name, has ticket number 0212. We know that Constable Webb has ticket number 0245, and lastly, Mr. O'Malley was given ticket number 0055.

None of those ticket numbers are sequential, and probably purposefully so."

"That's an interesting idea," said Pearce. "Then how do we know which name Leak actually used."

"I have an idea," said Frances. "May I take a look at the registry please, Inspector?"

Davison slid the papers over to her with a furrowed brow. Frances took her time running her index finger methodically down the column of names for all pages of the registry. She smiled when she had come to the end.

"I think I know what name he used, Inspector," said Frances, smiling and obviously quite chuffed with herself.

"And what name have you decided upon?" he asked.

"The name associated with ticket number 0135."

Davison took a moment to look over the registry until he found ticket number 0135, whereupon he furrowed his brow even further.

"Sam Weller is the name attached to ticket 0135."

He looked up at her, and Frances nodded.

"Quite correct."

Davison looked over at Pearce, and he couldn't help but allow a smirk of satisfaction settle upon his lips.

"And I suppose you chose that from your intuition," he said looking back at her, his grin ever widening.

Frances looked at Alfred and he smiled at her, and nodded.

"It appears that my butler knows better than you, Inspector, why I chose that name. Alfred, would you mind enlightening the Inspector and Sergeant Pearce."

Alfred's smile widened and he nodded is head again.

"With pleasure, my Lady," he said, then he looked over at Davison and his smile fell off his face. "Alfred Jingle and Sam Weller are characters from Charles Dickens' 'The Pickwick

Papers', which was his first novel. Both characters are astute but comical characters, with Jingle being particularly villainous."

"I see," said Davison, his mouth no longer sickled into a smile.

"Additionally, and this is why Lady Marmalade was asking if you were serious earlier, Sergeant," continued Alfred, looking at Pearce, "is because Charles Bates or more specifically Charley Bates is a pickpocket character from Charles Dickens' second novel 'Oliver Twist'. Perhaps that is purely coincidental."

Frances looked over at Alfred and smiled at him.

"Thank you, Alfred," she said, and then looked back at Inspector Davison. "It appears my butler is better read than you are."

Frances smiled tightly at him, and Davison's eyes burned hot for a moment.

"Very clever, Frances, very clever indeed," he said, "but we don't know this for certain."

"No we don't, Inspector," said Frances, "but I'm sure we will know it for certain just as soon as we have the chance to interview Alfred Jingle or Mr. Hudnall about it. Speaking of which, do you have a first name for him?"

Davison sighed like a deflated balloon, and searched through his papers again. He found the one he was looking for, and reviewed it before looking up at Frances.

"Yes, his name is Kian Hudnall. He was a constable along with Trafford Leak in the British Indian Police at Dharasana. As was mentioned before, the two of them were identified as the ones who beat those Indians severely, causing their death."

Frances looked on as the inspector spoke.

"Both he and Leak were dishonorably discharged and dismissed from the police. The only two to have been sanctioned so harshly."

"And not without merit," added Frances.

Davison ignored Lady Marmalade's comment.

"It appears that neither one of them were particularly good at following orders. There are a variety of negative notes in both their files related to both insubordination and the use of excessive force in dealing with suspects and criminals under their care."

Frances nodded.

"Interesting," she said. "I look forward to speaking with Mr. Hudnall when your men bring him in, Sergeant."

"As do we all, I'm sure," said Pearce.

"Well," said Davison, standing up from behind his desk. "I think that's about all the background information we have on him. Perhaps we should go and pay Detective Constable Webb a visit. If that's all right by you?"

Davison looked at Frances but he was quite insincere with his pandering, he had already moved from around the desk and towards the door. Frances stood up, not answering his rhetorical question. Alfred stood up next to her and exited the room after her.

Twenty Five

Frances entered the interrogation room that had last held Godse. This time it held a pale Englishman. He had not been cuffed, and he sat very relaxed, leaning against the back of his chair. He looked at them from bright blue eyes set in a pale and very boyish looking face. His auburn hair was a mop of color that looked out of place against his pale complexion. To Frances it looked, for a split second, as if he might have been wearing a wig.

He didn't smile at them as they all walked in . Davison leading the group with Alfred bringing in the rear, just behind Pearce. Davison offered Frances one of the two chairs that sat opposite the table from Detective Constable Webb. Frances sat down to Davison's left. She was troubled by the lack of security, and perhaps fairness with how Webb was being treated as compared to the three Indians they had interviewed in here previously. Though she chose not to say anything about it.

"It's after noon," said Webb, not wasting any moment to speak up, "and I'm getting quite peckish."

He had the crisp voice of military training, direct and curt. Immediately Frances didn't like him.

"It appears to me, Detective Constable," said Frances, "that as a suspect in the murder of two men, food would the least of your concerns."

Webb looked over at her with a furrowed brow, then he looked over at Davison.

"You didn't say anything about that, Inspector."

Davison looked over at Frances, frustration was plainly painted in a blushing red all over his face. Frances kept his stare.

"Why is he not handcuffed, Inspector?"

"My discretion," said Davison, tight lipped.

Webb looked back at Frances.

"And who are you?" he asked, his manner crisp but not yet hostile.

"I am Lady Marmalade, a servant of His Majesty, and friend to Mahatma Gandhi."

"I see," said Webb, not quite sure what to make of it. "What's this about two murders?"

"I am helping Scotland Yard investigate the murder of Mr. Ravi Meda..."

"I don't know who that is," said Webb.

"And Mr. Trafford Leak."

Frances steadied her eyes on him, but Webb chose to say nothing. He looked away.

"You know both of them, Constable," she said, to him, her voice just as crisp and curt as his had been.

Webb looked back at her.

"I don't know this Mr. Meda you speak of."

And he was being honest, if only because he didn't know the man's name who had been shot at Gandhi's lecture.

"Then I will enlighten you. Mr. Meda was the gentleman who was shot at Mr. Gandhi's lecture you attended."

Webb shrugged.

"I wasn't even there when it happened."

"That's hard to believe, Constable," said Frances. "We have your name attached to ticket number 0245, and we have witnesses who will identify you as having been present at the lecture."

Webb shifted uncomfortably in his chair. He put his forearms onto the table, clasping his hands in front of him, and leaned in.

"Oh bloody hell. All right, I was there, doesn't mean I killed anyone."

"Well, the evidence doesn't look good for you, Constable Webb. We know for instance that you were the sergeant in charge when things went terribly wrong at the Dharasana Salt Works. We've also since found out that you were demoted and transferred back here to work at the Foreign Office as a detective constable."

Webb hung his head dejectedly. He knew where this was going, and he didn't like it. It didn't look good for him. Those two useless police officers were still causing him grief a year later. It was like a bloody shadow that he just couldn't remove. He looked up at her and smiled thinly.

"Alright," he said, "what do you want?"

"I want you to tell me what happened?"

Davison wasn't interested in trying to tear this interrogation out of Frances' grip. The sooner he could finish this investigation the better off he'd be, for he would be finished with this interfering woman.

"Alright. Kian had kept in touch with me when he and Trafford were dishonorably discharged. Listen, you have to understand, I was young, and I lost control of the situation there. The commissioner had told me to use any means necessary to keep those protestors from reaching the salt cisterns. So we had to start beating them off of us, they wouldn't give up. But I never expected anyone to die, things just got out of hand. Especially with Kian and Trafford. They hated it in India, and they hated Indians. I suppose I should have seen it coming, but hindsight always offers perfect vision doesn't it? I got my comeuppance, I've been demoted and tainted, and I'll likely have to finish up my career as a desk constable at the Foreign Office. Look, I have no qualms with the Indians. I liked India, we were just out of our depths, and I've been made to pay, and the commissioner? Nothing happened to him, but I suppose that's the way it goes isn't it?"

Frances kept silent, just looking at him with warm eyes. She nodded slowly.

"It does seem that you were made an example of, Constable Webb. That's unfortunate. I understand it can be difficult to keep those under your command in order. My husband saw the very same sort of thing in the Boer War."

Webb nodded, Frances was building up his confidence in her.

"Exactly. It's not all that easy, especially when you have loose cannons like Leak and Hudnall. In all honesty I'm surprised that Dharasana situation didn't get more out of hand. Look, India was supposed to be a good place to get a leg up on one's career. I mean, I made it to sergeant before my thirtieth birthday. Hudnall and Leak were expecting the same I'm sure. But then this happened. I don't think they understand the power that this Gandhi fellow has over the people. It's not like in Britain where law and order is obeyed and diligently followed. This Mahatma Gandhi has control over the hearts and souls of these people. They'll not let up until they gain independence."

"I can understand that, Ryan," said Frances, trying his first name on to see how it fit. He didn't seem to mind. "So if you weren't involved with Mr. Meda's murder, then why were you there at Mr. Gandhi's lecture?"

Webb leaned back a bit and rested his hands in his lap. He looked down at them, fiddled with them for a bit before looking back up at Frances.

"Like I said before. Kian had kept in touch with me over this past year since he and Trafford were discharged. I had hoped he wouldn't have, but he did. I've tried my best to ignore him, but a few weeks ago, or so, he said he really wanted to meet me at the Bare Knuckles pub. Said he wanted to apologize, buy me a drink and ask for my forgiveness."

"Why would he want to ask you for forgiveness?" asked Pearce, twirling his mustache and looking at Webb from the far wall where he was standing next to Alfred. Webb looked up at him.

"Why?" and his face frowned. "Because he bloody well ruined my career."

"Yes, I can see that, but it cost him his own," said Pearce.

"But if he had been following orders it wouldn't have cost him his career and I might have a chance at making superintendent some time in the future."

Frances nodded at Webb.

"I understand, Ryan, please go on."

"Anyway," said Webb, "I relented, and decided to meet him there."

"Was Mr. Leak with him?" asked Frances.

Webb shook his head.

"No, I met him by myself, and he did exactly what he said he wanted to do. He apologized profusely, wished there was something he could do, and he bought a whole round of drinks. You've got to understand, despite being a bit of a rebel, and having a bit of a temper, Hudnall was a very likable chap."

Frances nodded, and Webb looked back down at his hands again.

"We had a few too many, and at the end of the night he said he wanted to do me a favor."

"What favor?" asked Pearce, who was not jotting down notes in his notebook. Webb looked up at him and then back at Frances.

"He said he wanted to buy me a ticket to Gandhi's lecture. I told him I wasn't really interested in what Gandhi had to say, but he can be pretty convincing when he wants to be."

"How so?" asked Frances.

"Well, he said that it could be a golden opportunity to meet Gandhi and hear what he has to say. He said I should think of it as a reconnaissance. He said I might find out some valuable information that might help me with my career at the Foreign Office."

Webb looked down at his hands again and fiddled with them.

"It sounds silly now, but after a few drinks, I really started to believe it. I thought it was my golden ticket to reinvigorating my career."

"So you accepted?" asked Frances.

Webb looked up at her, and nodded sadly.

"I did," he said. "Turns out there wasn't anything very interesting at the lecture. At least not in so far as what might help me with my career, so I left shortly after I had eaten something."

"Were you around when the Mr. Meda was shot?" asked Frances.

Webb shook his head.

"No, I was just leaving when I saw Hudnall and Leak walk up and join the group gathered around Gandhi afterwards. I was past the hall when I heard the gunshots."

"And you didn't think to come back and investigate?" asked Pearce, looking quite astonished.

Webb looked at him and shook his head slowly.

"No, I didn't. Look, my career is pretty much over as a policeman. I was dejected and despondent, and frankly, I didn't care."

"How do you think your ticket might have gotten left behind at the scene then?" asked Frances.

Webb shrugged as if the whole weight of the world was bearing down on his shoulders.

"I don't know... Wait, I remember putting it down on the table when I sat down to eat. I didn't pick it up again, so I imagine it must have blown off or somehow slipped off the table in the commotion that followed."

Frances nodded.

"How tall are you, Ryan?"

Webb looked up at her and gave her a quizzical look.

"Six two, why do you ask?"

Frances looked at Davison.

"Did you bring that photo?" she asked him.

Davison nodded and reached into his pocket. He took it out and slid it over to Frances. She turned it right side up and then turned it round so that Webb could see it.

"Do you recognize it?" she asked him.

He smiled and nodded.

"Yes, that's me and the lads in Dharasana quite some time before the incident."

"And that chap standing next to you is Kian Hudnall is it not?" asked Frances.

Webb nodded.

"From this picture then, I'd estimate Hudnall to be around six foot five. Would you agree, Ryan?"

Webb looked up from the photograph and nodded.

"Yes, I think that's about right. Why are you asking?"

"Because we believe that Mr. Hudnall is responsible for the murder of both Mr. Meda and Mr. Leak."

"Really?" asked Webb, looking up at Frances.

Frances nodded.

"Do you find it surprising to believe that Hudnall might have killed Leak."

"A little, though those two did have a temperamental relationship. They were both hotheads."

"Do you know where Mr. Leak lives?"

Webb shook his head.

"No idea. Like I said, I didn't really want to keep in touch with them after the Dharasana incident, though Hudnall did. I never heard from Leak, though I did see him at the lecture with Hudnall. Like I said, I left when the two of them walked up to join the group around Gandhi."

"Did you speak with them at all at the lecture?" asked Frances.

Webb shook his head.

"No, I didn't. And that's the thing. Hudnall had become all Jekyll and Hyde with me. He had been so friendly before at the pub, and then when I went to go and talk to them at the lecture he literally turned his back to me and pretended he didn't know me."

Frances looked over at Davison and he looked back at her.

"What is it?"

Frances turned to look back at Webb.

"We have mounting eye witness accounts that noticed a very tall man with a much shorter companion in the group who were gathered around Mr. Gandhi shortly before Mr. Meda was shot."

"Like I said, I saw them there too. They are a difficult couple to miss. But why would either of them want to shoot this Meda fellow?" asked Webb.

"We believe that their real target was Mr. Gandhi," said Frances. "I believe that Mr. Hudnall was carrying a grudge against Mr. Gandhi for what happened at Dharasana, and the loss of his job."

"I see," said Webb, shaking his head. "It's not enough that he's involved in killing two Indians in India, but he wants to kill another one for his own mistakes."

"Irrationality is hard to explain," said Frances.

"I guess he really is like a Dr. Jekyll and Mr. Hyde," said Webb.

"Do you have the whistle?" asked Frances, looking at Davison. He nodded and pulled it out of his pocket and put it on the table next to Frances. Frances picked it up and handed it to Webb.

"Do you recognize this?" she asked.

Webb rolled it around in his fingers, looking at it intently. He nodded his head.

"It looks like the whistles we were issued in India."

"That's because it is?" said Davison. "Do you know whose it is?"

Webb looked at him and shook his head. He placed it back on the table and slid it back to Davison.

"I'd have to have access to the records to find out whose identity number that is."

"We've already done that, Ryan," said Frances, "it belonged to Mr. Leak. We found it at Abbot House. Do you have any idea why he would still be carrying it around?"

Webb shrugged and shook his head.

"No I don't. You're supposed to hand it back in when you leave. Though Leak was always proud to be a policeman, and he was always happy to pull out his whistle and use it at any time."

"I have one more question for you, Ryan, if you don't mind," said Frances.

Webb looked up at her.

"Not at all."

"Do you know a Mr. Alfred Jingle?" she asked.

Webb smiled at her.

"You must be joking. Aren't you?"

He looked at her steadily for a moment.

"Oh no, Ryan, I am definitely not joking. Do you know a Mr. Alfred Jingle?" asked Frances again.

"No, not a real Mr. Jingle," said Webb, shaking his head with a smile still on his face. "But I do know an Alfred Jingle from Charles Dickens' 'The Pickwick Papers'."

"I take it you've read it then," said Frances.

"No, I can't say I have. But Hudnall, he absolutely loved everything that Charles Dickens wrote. His favorite was 'The Pickwick Papers'. He could practically recite whole sections from the book. He loved to talk about Alfred Jingle especially."

"I see," said Frances, looking over at Davison. Davison looked back with a raised eyebrow.

Webb looked back and forth from Davison to Frances with a furrowed brow.

"What?" he asked.

Frances looked at him.

"We couldn't understand why Hudnall's or Leak's name wasn't on the Vegetarian Society's registry for Mr. Gandhi's lecture. But earlier, Sergeant Pearce, found out that Hudnall was going by the name of Alfred Jingle. When I looked at the registry, I found two names that were very intriguing to me. Alfred Jingle and Sam Weller."

Webb was nodding his head.

"Sam Weller from 'The Pickwick Papers' also," he said.

"Exactly," said Frances, "I believe those were the nom de plumes of Mr. Hudnall and Mr. Leak."

"Have you found him then?" asked Webb.

Frances shook his head.

"Not yet. Do you have any idea about where he might be?"

Webb shook his head.

"No idea, though I met him at the Bare Knuckles pub in East London. I would have a look there."

Frances nodded.

"Thank you, Constable Webb. You've been most helpful. I'll put in a good word for you at the Foreign Office."

Webb smiled wearily.

"Thank you, my Lady," he said, "though I'm not sure what good it'll do."

"Well you never know, Ryan. I'll chat with Under-secretary Sir Tomas Lowell."

"Well, you never said you knew the under-secretary," said Webb, unable to control his optimistic and hopeful grin.

Frances turned to Davison, and smiled at him.

"I think Detective Constable Webb has been most helpful," she said. "I see no reason for detaining him any longer, unless you have further questions."

Davison looked over at her and nodded briskly.

"It'll be a matter of a few minutes, Constable Webb, we need to finish up the paperwork and then we'll have you on your way."

"Thank you, Inspector, my Lady."

Frances stood up, and Ryan Webb stood up too. Davison slowly got to his feet, and Frances led them all out of the interrogation room. She turned to Davison.

"Please telephone me as soon as you have Mr. Hudnall in custody. I'd really like to be at the interrogation."

"Certainly," said Davison as he started to lead them towards the main entrance.

"Do you need some help getting out?" asked Pearce as they neared Davison's office. Frances turned to look at him and smiled.

"No thank you, Sergeant, this place has come to feel like home."

Lady Marmalade and Alfred left Davison and Pearce as they entered his office and she and Alfred carried on towards the main area.

"After you've dropped me off home, Alfred," said Frances, "would you be kind enough to call on Mr. and Mrs. Bhandari and invite them over for afternoon tea tomorrow if they could make it. I'd be quite delighted if Mr. Gandhi and Mr. Patel could join to."

"Yes, my Lady," said Alfred.

"I have a feeling that by tomorrow, we'll have Mr. Hudnall securely behind bars and awaiting trial."

Twenty Six

The next telephone call from Pearce came in at just before four in the afternoon. Frances was in the middle of afternoon tea when she spoke with Pearce on the telephone. They had picked up Kian Hudnall and he was just being brought back to the police station for processing. Frances decided that tea would have to wait until tomorrow. Besides, it would be better enjoyed with Mahatma Gandhi and company. She wanted to be sure that Hudnall confessed to his crimes, and the only way to be certain of that, was to actually be there at the time. She told Pearce that she'd be right over.

She took a last bite of scone with clotted cream and strawberry jam, stuffing more of it into her mouth than would otherwise have been polite. But there was no company to be polite in front of, and the scones were still warm from the oven. She called on Alfred and they made their way back down to Scotland Yard.

Lady Marmalade and Alfred stopped into Davison's office which is where Pearce had led them to. Frances and Alfred sat down in chairs that should by now have carried their names.

"He swears he's innocent," said Davison, grinning at Frances.

"And you believe him?" asked Frances, smiling back.

Davison shook his head.

"Of course not, I just wanted to let you know. This might not go as easily as we hope. We might be in for a bit of a battle."

"Oh I don't know, Inspector, we've got a lot of evidence that Mr. Hudnall is the murderer. Did you collect his things from the public house he was staying at?"

Davison looked at Frances and barely nodded.

"You don't miss a thing, do you?"

"I hope not."

"We searched his room when he came back to pick up his items. Looks like he was leaving tomorrow across the Channel to France and from there who knows where he might have ended up."

"Then we got him just in time, Inspector," said Frances.

"It appears so," said Davison.

"So what did you find in his room? Anything that might help us?"

"Everything we need for the crown to convict him of two murders."

"That sounds perfect, Inspector. So you have the weapon then?"

Davison nodded and leaned down to his left. He picked something up and put it lengthwise on his desk. It was a metal cane. The long end had a rubber foot on it and the handle was made of ivory with two triggers and a trigger guard. When not in use, a metal flap slid down from the handle to cover the triggers, and thus making it exceedingly difficult to notice that this cane was in fact a modified rifle.

"That is fascinating," said Frances. "I have never seen anything quite like it."

"Neither have we," said Davison, turning it over. "It fires only two shots, and the casings remain in the barrel, much like a shotgun. You have to unhinge it here," he said, as he unhinged the cane just below the handle, showing the barrel and where the two bullets would be placed. "The triggers as you can see are slightly staggered, so the first shot is fired a split second before the finger finds the second trigger."

Davison showed Frances the trigger mechanism more closely and the triggers were staggered by almost an inch.

"Fascinating," she said. "The lengths some will go to."

Pearce nodded wearily. Davison opened up the drawer in front of him and pulled out a book. He placed it on the desk in front of the cane and facing Frances. It was a paperback copy of 'The Pickwick Papers'. Frances picked it up and thumbed through it. It was heavily used, the pages dog-eared and the edges moth-eaten. Many pages had been underlined in pencil or pen and there were notes scribbled in the margins on just about every page. Frances took some time to look through them at her leisure, smiling. She looked up at Davison and put the book back down on the table.

"This is fascinating, and I'm assuming that the writing in the margins will be Mr. Hudnall's?"

"I imagine so," said Davison.

"Was there anything else of note?" asked Frances.

"Nothing else of note. We found the cane stuffed under the mattress, and under the bed we found a suitcase with this book, his clothes, a few additional bullets as well as some money in the amount of..."

Davison looked over at Pearce, and Pearce brought out his notebook and flipped to the most recent page.

"One hundred and thirty seven pounds, thirteen shillings and seven pence. That includes the money we found on him, as well as the ticket to leave by boat tomorrow at nine a.m."

"That's not a lot of money, but more than I suspected actually," said Frances.

Davison nodded.

"Well, he doesn't have much and he's leaving town. Perhaps he was hoping for a fresh start across the Channel."

Frances didn't say anything. Davison looked at her for a long moment.

"Well, shall we go and get our confession?" he asked.

Frances nodded and stood up.

"I feel similarly confident," she said.

They all exited Davison's office, and he led them to the very same interview room that had held Ryan Webb earlier in the day. Pearce was carrying the cane and Davison had the book. Davison took the chair furthest away from the door, and Frances sat next to him on his left. Pearce walked and stood behind the prisoner, Alfred took up his usual place leaning against the wall in plain sight of Hudnall.

Across from Frances and Davison was Kian Hudnall. He was shackled and hunched over, his head hanging slack, his face looking at the floor or his feet, it was hard to tell which. He was a couple of feet from his side of the table. Even though he was hunched over you could tell he was tall. He was thin and tall and his brown hair had a greasy sheen to it.

He looked up after a while and his face was gaunt and his cheeks sunken. His brown eyes were small and his nose beaked. His lips were as thin as razors, but when he smiled he showed straight teeth and his eyes twinkled mischievously. He smiled when he saw Lady Marmalade.

"And who do we have here, Inspector?" he asked.

Frances looked at him and wanted to smile in turn. He had a charm, an almost boyish charm that Frances could tell would engender kindness from people towards him.

"I'm Lady Frances Marmalade," she said.

"I say, a real Lady. Can't say I've ever had the privilege to be so close to one."

He looked over at Davison.

"Mr. Hudnall," said Frances, "are you by any chance related to a Ms. Florence Hudnall of Puddle's End?"

He looked back at her and cocked an eyebrow at her.

"I am not related to any other Hudnalls that I know of, certainly not her. My father was an only child, as am I. The Hudnall line will die with me. Though I suppose it is not a terribly uncommon surname."

Davison looked over at Frances and knitted his eyebrows together. Frances noticed.

"I'm relieved," she said, looking at him. "I have a very dear friend up in Puddle's End, and she'd be devastated to learn that she was in any way related to a criminal sort."

Davison nodded somberly, and Hudnall shrugged. He didn't care who she thought he might be related to, but certainly nobody from Puddle's End. He'd never even heard of the place.

"So they're allowing women of nobility into Scotland Yard, eh Inspector?"

"No, they're not, Mr. Hudnall, I am here as a consultant to Inspector Davison to ensure that you pay for your crimes."

He looked back at her quickly, and licked his lips. He kept his smile on his face, and Frances could tell that he would be difficult to bring to anger. He seemed quite in control of his emotions.

"Crimes you say. Whatever might you mean. Perhaps I have not dressed appropriately for this visit by your Lady."

He was dripping facetiousness but he said it with the greatest of pomp and sincerity. He was a man who enjoyed the smoke and mirrors of social interactions.

"I believe the inspector has already arrested you for the murder of both Mr. Meda, and your colleague Mr. Leak," said Frances.

"Yes, a pity that. Though I'm innocent I tell you. Innocent. Who would have been foolish to shoot an unknown Indian when you had the chance to shoot the greatest amongst them?"

"You did, Mr. Hudnall."

Hudnall looked at Frances and his eyes smoked and burned like hot coals. He didn't say anything for a while as he gathered his composure.

"You shot Mr. Meda at Mr. Gandhi's lecture," said Frances.

"Quite unlikely," he said, "for I wasn't even there."

"Oh, but I believe you were."

"Nonsense, you'll find no ticket that is associated with my name. I confess to abhorring Indians and India. Certainly not my cup of tea."

"I believe that last part might be the first honest thing you've said so far," said Frances. She looked over at Davison. "Do you have the book?"

Davison pulled it out from his pocket and placed it on the table, and slid it towards Frances facing her. Frances picked it and thumbed through it. Then she put it down and turned it towards Hudnall, though she did not slide it towards him.

"Are you familiar with this book?" she asked.

Hudnall looked at the title and read it.

"'The Posthumous Papers of the Pickwick Club'. Yes, I am familiar with it. In fact, I'd suggest you might even be holding my copy personally signed and addressed to me by Dickens himself."

Hudnall smiled wickedly. Frances hadn't remembered seeing the autographed title page, and so she flipped to the front of it. There was no autograph at all. She looked at him and frowned, annoyed with his deceit.

"I thought so," she said. "Your copy Mr. Hudnall was published several years ago, Mr. Dickens, sadly, has been deceased for quite a bit longer than that."

"Yes, I know. Terribly sad. I do apologize for misleading you, my Lady, but how I do admire the great Boz. Have you read him?"

"I have read everything he wrote, though I confess that 'The Pickwick Papers' are amongst my least favorite."

"That is a tragedy, for there is much gold to be mined from the undercurrents of that stream," said Hudnall.

Frances smiled, Hudnall was having his way with her, which is not a situation she got herself into often. He was a deft conversationalist and had found his way to steering this ship of theirs off course. It was time for Lady Marmalade to retake the helm.

"You are a clever young man," said Frances, "you joust well with words and your rapier wit. But let's bring the conversation back to Mr. Gandhi's lecture. I was there, and I saw you, Mr. Hudnall."

It was a lie, for as much as Frances hated to admit it, she did not remember seeing him at all, not that she had been paying much attention. She was not, after all, expecting a murder to be committed right before her eyes.

"I doubt that, my Lady, for I did not see you..."

Hudnall bit his tongue, but it was too late. The cat had been let out of the bag. Frances smiled at him.

"I have caught you out, Mr. Hudnall, you have just admitted being there."

"I did not, you treacherous and contemptible woman, I merely suggested that you would not have seen me for I was not there."

Hudnall was still smiling, but he was clearly unbalanced by Frances' deftly parried blow.

"That which has been said cannot be unsaid, Mr. Hudnall, or would you rather be called Mr. Alfred Jingle."

Frances put her index finger on the middle of the book in front of her.

"Where is this proof, this man you speak of, Mr. Jingle, he is but a dream of Charles Dickens. You will find no ticket on me to suggest that I was ever there."

"No, I suppose we won't," said Frances. "I believe you are a clever man, nay scoundrel, and you would have destroyed the evidence."

"I do protest to your barbed tongue, my Lady, I might not be a gentleman but I am certainly no scoundrel."

Hudnall's eyes still twinkled and his mouth still carried a smile as light and ethereal as a feather.

"Be that as it may, Mr. Hudnall, we have other evidence more damning."

"Like what?" he asked.

"The registry from the Vegetarian Society for all tickets sold that night, as well as eyewitness accounts from several people who noticed you there."

Hudnall hung his head in shame, and then looked up, his boyish grin still stuck to his face.

"Sergeant Pearce, would you be so kind as to inform us to the ticket number that Mr. Jingle had?" asked Frances.

Pearce hooked the cane behind him, attaching it to his belt. Then he took out his notebook and flipped the pages until he came upon the information he needed.

"Mr. Alfred Jingle bore ticket number 0212."

"Well fancy that," said Hudnall, "a character born into reality to attend a lecture by an Indian. Such a tale reminds me of Dickens' 'The Signal-Man'."

"I'm not sure how, Mr. Hudnall, that is a ghost story, and we're not speaking of ghosts," said Frances.

"Well yes, perhaps, though it appears that this Mr. Jingle is a ghost come to hound me to an early grave. I fear he gives presage about my coming doom. It appears that you are using him to drum up a case against an innocent man."

Davison raised his eyebrows.

"An innocent man, my left foot."

"Why, Inspector, do not draw conclusions before all the evidence has been weighed," said Hudnall.

"This is not a court, Mr. Hudnall, all we need is enough evidence of your guilt, which we have by the bushelful," said Frances, then she looked back at Pearce. "What other tickets did Mr. Hudnall purchase?"

Pearce looked down at his notes.

"He bought ticket number 0135 for Mr. Leak under the name of Mr. Sam Weller. He also brought ticket 0245 for Detective Constable Ryan Webb as well as ticket number 0055 for Mr. Patrick O'Malley."

"Absurd!" shouted Hudnall. "I won't sit around and listen to this slander."

"Not slander, Mr. Hudnall, but evidence."

"You have not proved that I am Mr. Jingle. Can't you see, someone is having you on. Mr. Sam Weller, Mr. Alfred Jingle, they are both characters from 'The Pickwick Papers'."

"Yes, Mr. Hudnall," said Frances. "I am well aware of who they are, and if anyone is having us on, that would be you. You see, the publican at the Bare Knuckles recognized you, and he said you used the name Alfred Jingle. In fact, he showed Sergeant Pearce your signature in his rooming book under that name. A signature that resembles the writing in the margins of this book, Mr. Hudnall. Does it not, Sergeant Pearce?"

Pearce leaned in, and he couldn't say for certain. It did look quite similar but he was sure that looking at the rooming book would likely show them to be by the same hand.

"Most certainly," he replied.

"Inspector, do you have that photograph to show Mr. Hudnall."

"I will get it," he said.

Davison got up and left.

"Mr. Hudnall, I am tiring of your theatrics and misdirections. It would help you if you came clean and confessed. That is the only way you will find any compassion from the courts or from any recommendation I might make to the crown."

"I thought Britain was a country where a man was deemed innocent unless he was proven guilty. It appears you are proving me guilty without taking into consideration my innocence."

Davison walked back into the interview room and sat down next to Frances. He gave her the photograph. Frances placed it on the table in front of Hudnall, facing him.

"This is a picture of you, and at the time, Sergeant Webb as well as Trafford Leak, is it not?" asked Frances.

Hudnall glanced down at it.

"Why, it most certainly looks like it, doesn't it? So what?"

"Well, it proves that you knew both of them."

"Indeed it does. Is that a crime? Am I guilty for knowing two men?"

"That's not the crime, but what this tells me, is that you were at the Dharasana incident where two innocent men were beaten to death. Furthermore, Sergeant Webb attests to the fact that you were there, that you've been hounding him ever since you were dishonorably discharged from the British Indian Police, and that you and Mr. Leak were in fact responsible for the deaths of those two Indian men at Dharasana."

Hudnall's cheeks flushed, and he lowered his eyes for a moment. He took a deep breath.

"Yes, that was most unfortunate what happened in Dharasana. But that was not deemed murder. You can't know what it's like to have hundreds, no, thousands of people walk towards you, intent on breaking the barriers you've erected. It was chaos and things got out of control. I was punished, unfairly I might add, and now I find myself here, already found guilty for something else I didn't do."

"I hardly think you were punished unfairly, Mr. Hudnall, you killed two men," said Frances, exasperated.

"Hardly, I killed one man, and not on purpose. These people are savage animals. This docility of theirs would drive anyone to madness."

"It's called pacifism and non-violent action, Mr. Hudnall."

"Regardless, we should have given them a greater thrashing than they got, look at the continued ongoing problems."

Hudnall's tone was becoming sharper.

"And now you have offered your motive. You do not like Indians, Mr. Hudnall, do you? You do not understand them, and because you were punished, and rightly so, for your egregious behavior in Dharasana, you have carried a grudge in particular against Mr. Gandhi ever since."

"If that is so, then why is it that Mr. Gandhi is still alive? Why was this Mr. Meda chap shot instead?"

"Because you are a poor shot, or perhaps you were jostled just as you were ready to fire."

"And pray tell, my Lady, you who know so much about me. How did I shoot him?"

Frances looked over at Pearce, and nodded. Pearce took the cane from behind him and put it on the side of the desk out of reach of Hudnall. He put his hand into his pocket and took out one of the bullets that he had found at the public house's room where Hudnall had been staying.

"You shot him with this, Mr. Hudnall. Quite inventive, both Davison and I have not seen anything quite like it before."

"You're having me on now," said Hudnall, "somebody must have planted that in my room."

"We didn't say where we found it, Mr. Hudnall, how do you know we found it in your room?"

"Well...I, I just assumed," stuttered Hudnall.

"Unlikely, Mr. Hudnall, that someone would stick this cane under your mattress to frame you. And the interesting thing is that this same weapon will likely have your fingerprints all over it. Additionally, it is the very same weapon that shot both Mr. Meda and Mr. Leak. We also have an eye witness who saw you leave Mr. Leak's home at the time of his murder."

"Impossible!" exclaimed Hudnall, "I made sure no one saw me."

He shut up quickly then, he was being outwitted by Frances. Like the fox who had met a more cunning wolf.

"That's as good as a confession," said Frances, smiling at him. Pearce was at his notebook again, taking furious notes.

"Yes, I suppose you'd like that, wouldn't you?" said Hudnall, his tone now cold and hard. "A dirty curry eating lover like yourself. Well, you shan't have it. I won't give you the satisfaction. To my dying breath I'll not admit to what you've suggested I did. I hate them, to be sure. They're nothing but a blight upon this planet and why we're even over there is beyond me. It's a filthy, stench filled hellish dump of feces. My only regret is that whoever killed Gandhi's friend, didn't finish the job and end Gandhi's life."

"You, Mr. Hudnall, are full of bile and hatred. And it has eaten you up from the inside, left you a shell of a man and human being. You are a walking canker, a sickness that must be excised from the otherwise decent facade of Great Britain. And you will meet the hangman's noose, whether you confess or not. Your only hope at any sort of redemption is a sincere and contrite confession..."

"Which you'll never get," he sneered.

"And so your name will be reviled in infamy for many years to come. A hatred like yours, Mr. Hudnall can only be extinguished by the just man's scythe."

Frances got up, and looked over at Davison.

"I wish to have nothing further to do with this crippled and spiteful example of humanity."

Frances led herself out as Alfred followed.

"I am not the only one!" yelled Hudnall. "There are others. Even within his own kind, there are others who'll finish the job."

Frances closed the door to the interview room, and turned around and looked at Alfred. Her eyes were damp with sadness.

"Never in my forty nine years, Alfred, have I come across such hatred based on such small and mean spirited thinking."

Alfred looked at her with kind eyes and nodded slowly.

"I know, my Lady. It boggles my mind to even try and comprehend the depth of depravity required to stoop that low that one can carry a hatred so thick in one's soul for another man based solely on him being from a different nation. Humanity will never find peace, I fear, until we can embrace each other as brothers and sisters, whatever our creed or color."

Frances nodded sadly, and started walking down the hall.

"Will it ever be?" she asked, not really to Alfred, but rather giving voice to her own worry and concern.

"I hope it will," said Alfred. "I believe it will, or humanity will enter a darkness that has no light."

Twenty Seven

As the grandfather clock in the living room chimed four p.m., there was a knock on the front door. Frances got up from the settee and went to see who it was. She caught up with Alfred in the hallway. He looked at her and smiled.

"It must be your guests," he said, warmly.

Frances nodded. Alfred opened up the door to see the friendly faces of Mr. and Mrs. Bhandari, Sujay Patel and Mohandas Gandhi.

"So nice of you to come," said Frances, giving each of them a hug and inviting them into the foyer.

It was a warm summer afternoon and nobody had any sweaters, so Frances led them down the hall and into the living room where her husband and son were sitting down in arm chairs. They both stood.

"Amar, this is my husband Eric, and my son Declan," she said.

Frances introduced everyone to each other, and offered them their seats. Amar and Gita sat down on the one couch. Declan offered his armchair to Patel who graciously accepted it. Eric took his armchair and Declan sat down with his mother on the settee she had been in. Gandhi took the remaining chair. They were all gathered around the table.

"Do any of you mind if I smoke?" asked Eric, picking up his Liverpool pipe, and looking around.

Nobody objected so he filled it with tobacco and went to lighting it.

"We were all at your lecture, Mr. Gandhi," said Declan, trying to start the conversation going. "What very erudite arguments you made for both vegetarianism and non-violence. My friend, who's a vegetarian got us the tickets."

Gandhi looked over at Declan and smiled at him, nodding slowly.

"That is very kind of you to say. Please call me Mohandas, or perhaps even Mohan if that is easier. I speak from an area of great interest. I have long held that vegetarianism is a cornerstone to living a non-violent life. One cannot be a true believer in non-violence if one still partakes in the violence that is so apparent upon our plates three times a day. And perhaps more worrisome is that in this day and age, when we are now finished with war, the greatest violence that we partake in, is the violence of food and eating."

Declan listened intently.

"You know, I'm quite convinced, I'm just not sure I can do it right away."

Gandhi smiled.

"Perhaps in time, Declan. A long journey begins with the first step. The way I see it is like this. The life of a lamb, in my mind, is just as precious to me as the life of a human, and as such, I am unwilling to take that lamb's life just for my human body's want."

Ginny came into the living room carrying a large tray full of teacups, a teapot and assorted sandwiches. Many had salmon, some had egg and others were filled with butter and cucumber. Ginny placed the tray down and put an empty plate as well as teacup and saucer in front of each guest.

"Thank you, Ginny," said Frances, when she was finished.

Ginny headed out of the living room and back into the kitchen where scones and cake were being baked.

"Those sandwiches over there," said Frances, pointing to the sandwiches containing eggs, and the ones containing cucumber, "are filled with egg, and the others are cucumber alone."

Gandhi smiled at her.

"You are very kind, Frances, you have thought about our diets."

"Of course," she said, smiling. "I would be horrified if you did not eat even just the smallest morsel."

Taking that as a hint, Gandhi put a triangle of cucumber sandwich on his plate. Amar, Gita and Sujay all did the same. Frances poured them each some tea. Amar, Gita and Sujay sweetened theirs and added milk to it. Gandhi left his black.

"Frances was telling me that the conference is not going as well as planned," said Eric, blowing smoke up towards the ceiling, and cradling his pipe in his right hand which he rested on top of his right leg which was crossed over his left. Gandhi looked over at him.

"Yes, I'm afraid that is correct. On our side, we're having difficulty offering a unified approach, and it appears there seems to be some reticence on your side, for reasons which we can't quite determine."

Eric nodded.

"I can understand. You know," he said, "I was speaking with Lord Winston of the House the other day, and this very same issue came up. From what he tells me, Britain is concerned about too quickly and easily allowing for independent rule of India. There are a variety of reasons for this. Lord Winston cited the current lackluster economy and the need for cheap and available resources that India provides. Though I think that with India gaining independence, I think a subconscious concern of theirs is all the other territories that might wish to secede."

Gandhi nodded at Eric.

"I can imagine that to be true," he said. "Though of course, that has no bearing on our belief in independence. India is an independent nation, not part of Britain, as much as some in your government would like to see it that way, as such, India should be ruled by Indians. It's really as simple as that. Where we're getting into trouble is amongst the many associations and religions in India who wish for special consideration, an approach I do not agree with. I believe all Indians should be governed under one India and be treated equally."

Eric nodded, pulling out the pipe as smoke streamed from his mouth.

"I quite agree, and I am sure that before this decade is out, India will have self rule."

Gandhi nodded slowly, chewing on a bit of cucumber sandwich.

"I hope it happens before that, but these things will take their natural course, as they must."

"I was hoping to have you all over this afternoon so that I might bring closure for you regarding the murderer of Mr. Meda," said Frances.

Everyone looked over at Lady Marmalade.

"She's a wonderful sleuth, you know," said Eric.

Gandhi looked over at him and smiled.

"I had the feeling she was. I was immediately put at ease when we met this past Monday, and you have shown much kindness and consideration," said Gandhi, looking back over at Frances.

"Sadly, I am not able to offer the closure I was hoping to give you today, though I give you my word that justice will be meted out, the case is strong against the man responsible for this heinous act."

Gandhi looked at her and sipped some of his hot tea.

"What do you mean?" asked Patel.

Frances looked down at her teacup and squeezed some lemon into it.

"I'm afraid," she said looking back up at him, "that I was unable to get a full confession out him."

"I see," said Amar.

Frances took a sip of tea, then she looked back up at them and smiled thinly.

"Yes, I'm afraid so. It very seldom happens, especially when I know I've got him with all the evidence presented. And believe me, this case has strong evidence, more than enough to send him to the gallows. Yet he wouldn't relent. It was quite upsetting really."

"Who did it?" asked Gita.

Frances looked over at her.

"It was a man by the name of Kian Hudnall," she said.

She looked around at all of them, but the name did not ring a bell for any of them.

"Related to Flo?" asked Eric.

Frances looked over at him, and shook her head.

"Thankfully not."

Then she looked back at Gandhi and the others.

"Florence Hudnall is a friend of mine," she said. "Thankfully, no relation to Kian Hudnall."

Gandhi nodded.

"It would be no matter if she was," he said. "One cannot hold innocent members of the same family accountable for the crimes of their relations."

"Kind of you to say."

Gandhi nodded and sipped more tea.

"This Kian chap, almost let the cat out of the bag a couple of times. In fact, I'm certain that will be brought into evidence. For example, I told him that we found the weapon he used, a cane modified to shoot bullets as it happens, and he said that someone must have planted it in his room, though I made no mention of where we found the weapon."

"Very clever, Frances," said Amar, "you tripped him up then?"

"A few times," she said, smiling, "but sadly, he would not come straight out and admit to it. But we have the weapon, we have additional bullets found in his room. I'm sure we'll find his prints on the weapon, and we have his name on the Vegetarian Society's registry along with a handful of witnesses. And I am certain that by the time it gets to the court there will be many more witnesses. I want to assure you that Mr. Hudnall will bear the fullest brunt of British justice. I will make sure of it."

Gandhi smiled at her.

"You continue to inspire with your confidence, Frances, of that I have no doubt. But were you able to find out why he did this terrible act?"

"He was one of two policemen involved in the death of Mr. Pai and Mr. Panchal. He was dishonorably discharged from the British Indian Police, and I believe he continues to hold a grudge against Indians generally, but you specifically, Mohandas. I'm afraid he's just a man twisted and filled with terrible bile and hatred."

Gandhi nodded and placed his teacup on his saucer. He smiled at her.

"I have met such men before, and I have noticed that you sometimes cannot turn all hearts with love and kindness."

"I fear you are right, Mohandas. Some are so blackened that no light can get through their hatred," said Frances.

"Thankfully they are few and far between," said Gandhi.

Frances nodded at him, and smiled weakly, as weak as the tea she had not allowed to steep long enough for her liking.

"Is the evidence good that he was responsible for killing his colleague?" asked Amar.

Frances looked up at him.

"It appears to be just as solid. I did not question him on why he killed Mr. Trafford Leak, as he was so disagreeable, and I finally couldn't stand his vitriol anymore, so I left. But the coroner confirms the same weapon fired all bullets that killed both men. I'm sure that confirmation will be strengthened when he has a chance to test the weapon. As to why he killed his friend, if indeed they were friends, is beyond me. Perhaps they had a falling out. Perhaps Mr. Hudnall wanted to finish the job but Mr. Leak protested. There could be a myriad number of reasons."

Amar nodded.

"I suppose that if a man can kill one, he can go on to kill many," said Patel.

"I believe so," said Frances. "After all, is that not what war is all about? The sanctioned development and cultivation of mass murderers."

Eric looked over at his wife but he didn't say anything. There wasn't much to say. She was right, as she often was, but that was only one slice of the whole pie. War was a much more complicated matter, out of which nothing good really ever came.

"Non-violence might be the harder path in the short run, as it requires great patience and belief in humanity, but in the long run, the results are sound," said Gandhi, "it isn't stained with the blood of lost souls, and the guilt that comes with it."

"You're quite right, Mohandas," said Eric, "I have had the displeasure of serving in war, the Boer War, and I've never seen any good come of it. But sadly, your non-violent approach is something new and strange, at least to the eyes of Europeans. I fear it may yet take several years for us to get a handle on how to best deal with it."

Mohandas nodded. Frances saw Ginny as she came round the corner from the hallway and into the living room. She was carrying another silver tray. This one was covered with scones, biscuits, lemon curd tarts and two different cakes. The cakes that Ginny had baked were an Angle cake and a Battenberg cake. Clotted cream and jam were also on offer.

Ginny lay the tray down on the table, and then looked at Frances.

"Will that be all my Lady?" she asked.

Frances nodded, and smiled at her.

"That will be plenty, Ginny. Thank you my dear, you have outdone yourself."

Gandhi looked at Ginny and smiled kindly at her as she left.

"After the savories must come the sweets," said Frances. "I hope you have all saved some room. More tea?"

Frances went around and filled the teacups of those present, and the conversation turned to the baked goods on offer as Amar, Gita and Sujay helped themselves. Gandhi did not take anything. The rest of the afternoon was spent talking about a variety of topics from Indian and British relations, the parts of India that the Marmalades had visited as well as an optimistic future where the economy of Britain recovered.

Twenty Eight

Lady Marmalade had come down to join her husband and son for breakfast. It was just after eight in the morning. Eric as usual was reading the paper. He folded it over and put it to the side when Frances came up and kissed him on the lips.

"There's some good news in here," he said, stabbing at the paper with his finger, "that I'm sure you'll want to read."

Frances walked over to her chair and sat down, having kissed her son on the cheek.

"Really, how wonderful. I hope it has to do with the economy. I can't fathom why unemployment still remains above twenty percent. And those poor souls searching the coal slag heaps to keep warm. I can't believe in this great country we have allowed such a disenfranchised group to form amongst our midst."

Eric smiled at her.

"I know, my love, but this has nothing to do with any of that. In time, hopefully we will learn to take care of the less fortunate amongst us. No, this is more personal. Here, have a look."

Eric handed the paper to Declan who handed it over to his mother.

"Can I tell Ginny what you'd like to eat, my Lady?" asked Alfred.

Frances put the paper next to her and looked up at Alfred.

"Just a poached egg and some sausage. Thank you, Alfred."

Alfred bowed and left the dining room. Frances poured herself a cup of tea and added some lemon to it. She then picked up the paper, it was The Manchester Guardian. The front page was another story about how poorly the economy was doing. The paper was Thursday's, the 8th of September, 1932. Frances looked up at Eric and frowned.

"The inside pages. Go to the city section," he said.

Frances leafed through several pages until she got to the section Eric had mentioned. The headline read, "Former Indian Police Officer Guilty of Two Murders". Frances read the story with interest. Kian Hudnall had been found guilty of murdering both Trafford Leak and Ravi Meda. The article went on to say how damning the evidence had been. Mr. Hudnall was sentenced to death by hanging. Frances looked up and smiled at Eric.

"Isn't it good news?" he asked.

She smiled and nodded at him.

"It is. I knew he couldn't get away with it. Justice has been served, though I've been thinking ever since we last spoke to Mr. Gandhi, whether capital punishment is the answer."

"Well, it is the answer we have at the moment. And we can rest assured that this Hudnall chap will no longer be a threat to anyone else."

Frances smiled wistfully and looked down at the paper again, and nodded.

"It is good to see justice served," she said. "I must mail this to Mr. Gandhi, I am sure he will be interested in the outcome."

"That's a terrific idea," said Eric.

"Maybe if Mr. Hudnall had only confessed. Shown just the smallest bit of contrition, perhaps the court would have been lenient and he might have dodged the death penalty. An eye for an eye will leave the whole world blind. I think Mr. Gandhi might have spoken truthfully when he said that."

"I agree, Mum," said Declan. "But until the time when the law changes, Hudnall will no longer be poking out anymore eyes."

About Jason Blacker

Jason Blacker was born in Cape Town but spent most of his first 18 years in Johannesburg. When not grinding his fingers down to stubs at the keyboard he enjoys drinking tea, calisthenics and running. Currently he lives in Canada.

Under his own name he writes hard boiled as well as cozy mysteries, action adventure, thrillers, literary fiction and anything else that tickles his muse. Jason Blacker also writes poetry and daily haikus at his haiku blog.

You can find his haikus and other poetry at his website **www.haiqueue.com**.

To stay up to date and learn about new releases be sure to visit **www.jasonblacker.com** where you can find more information about his writing and upcoming projects.

If you enjoy space opera in the tradition of Star Trek then take a look at Jason Blacker's pen name "Sylynt Storme". It is under the name Sylynt Storme where you can find both sci-fi and vampire fiction written by Jason Blacker.

"Star Sails" is the space opera series and "The Misgivings of the Vampire Lucius Lafayette" is his vampire series.

www.ingramcontent.com/pod-product-compliance
Lightning Source LLC
Chambersburg PA
CBHW030935260626
47169CB00002B/483